ZOMBIEWOOD

RAYMOND LEE

ISBN: 9798630755131

ACKNOWLEDGMENTS

Thanks to all my readers who gave me a try and came back for more!

1

"Wait here. Mr. Justain will be with you shortly." The slender woman with the heavy Spanish accent gestured toward the black leather L-shaped sectional taking up the entire front wall of the producer's waiting room as her eyes roamed over Misty's body.

Misty didn't fail to notice the barely suppressed smirk or the slight shake of the woman's head before she turned away to go back to her desk. Having made the cover of Playboy recently, it was no secret she had a great body and knew how to use it, but this was not a modeling job she sought. She was going to become a serious actress. Looking down at her wardrobe, Misty reassured herself she'd chosen smartly. She wore black slacks and a hot pink silk button-down blouse with only the top two buttons undone. Paired with black stiletto heels and dangling pink diamond earrings, her attire was sexy, yet completely appropriate for business. Let the woman smirk at her, thinking the ditzy model needed to let her boobs hang out in order to get an acting job. She'd show her.

The phone rang, prompting the secretary to sigh before reaching over to pick up the handset. "Harry Justain's office."

Harry Justain's office. A frisson of nervous excitement coursed through Misty's blood. Born and raised in Palmyra, Indiana, the daughter of a diner waitress and a deadbeat truck driver, the very idea of being in such a highly sought-after producer's waiting room was unimaginable. People from Palmyra didn't make it to Hollywood. They were lucky to make it out of the Kentuckiana area at all.

Realizing her heartbeat had increased and her palms had grown wet, Misty took a deep breath. She couldn't blow this opportunity. She wiped her hands on her slacks and looked for something to focus on. The artwork in the office consisted of posters of movies produced by Justain, movies featuring movie stars way out of her league. If she focused on those, her nervousness would give way to a full-blown anxiety attack. She looked at the flat-screen TV she'd ignored up to that point and saw the president of Russia's long, narrow face looking back at her. Ah, the news would be a good distraction to tamp down her nerves. Nothing bored her like the news. She picked up the remote control on the black marble coffee table before her and turned the volume up a notch just as the president's face disappeared, replaced by an attractive brunette news anchor.

"That was the video released to American news stations just this morning," the news anchor stated. "There have already been twenty confirmed cases of the outbreak in the local area, over one thousand nationwide. As the president stated in the video, the Z-1219 virus was injected into the Russian mail-order brides' systems before they were given their K-1 visas. The virus, described as working similarly to a bomb, was detonated today. From what we currently know, all mail-order brides directly injected with the virus would now have that virus activated in their bodies. The Russian president states the disease is highly contagious through blood and sexual contact, so the exact numbers we may face are unclear."

"Misty Waters?"

Misty jumped a bit, the deep baritone voice drawing her away from the news story. She turned her head to see Harry Justain standing outside his office door, a warm, inviting smile showing perfectly white capped teeth.

"Yes!" She quickly stood and smoothed her hands over her clothes in case she'd wrinkled the material, the news story instantly forgotten.

"Please come in." He stepped aside and calmly gestured toward what lie beyond his door, as if what happened in that room wouldn't determine the outcome of Misty's entire life.

Trying to project the same sense of casualness so as not to appear as nervous and amateur as she felt, Misty took a deep breath, squared her shoulders and breezed past the tall, heavyset man.

"Hold my calls and see that we are not disturbed," Justain instructed the secretary before stepping into the office behind Misty and pulling the door closed.

The office was large, with a huge mahogany executive desk and at least a dozen bookshelves filled to the brim with framed pictures of Justain with various celebrities, POP figures of the characters from his movies, and other movie memorabilia. A large glass case held awards he'd won.

"I hope I didn't keep you waiting long," he said, sandwiching her left hand between both of his larger ones.

Glad she'd wiped the sweat from her palms, Misty smiled at him. "Not at all. I'm sure you stay busy. I'm honored you gave me this appointment time."

Whoa, Misty. Ease up a bit. Don't look too desperate.

Justain smiled down at her wolfishly, her hand still trapped between his. "The pleasure is mine."

He stared at her a moment longer, his eyes roving

down her form before he released her hand so he could gesture toward the black leather chairs before his desk. "Please make yourself comfortable."

Misty settled into one of the offered seats, expecting Justain to take a seat in the larger chair behind his desk, but instead, he sat on the edge of the desk, placing himself directly in front of her.

"Your recent spread impressed me very much," he said, his voice husky. His eyes seemed to be fixated on her breasts.

Misty gripped the armrests as her back stiffened. She fought the urge to squirm away from the heavy weight of his gaze. She was a Playboy centerfold, she reminded herself. He'd seen and liked the spread. That spread was what had increased her Twitter and Instagram followers by the thousands and got her this meeting. If she hadn't wanted her breasts to be admired, she wouldn't have paid good money for them.

"Thank you." She smiled, hoping it looked natural and didn't reveal just how afraid she was that she was going to blow this. "I'm a huge fan of your work."

He shrugged his shoulders and made a humble face. "I am only as good as my stars. My talent is finding the right projects and the right people, then combining the two to create a masterpiece, which is why you are here today."

Misty's smile widened. "I loved the script. I read it faster than I've ever read anything in my life."

Justain chuckled. "Enthusiasm is good. I instantly thought of you for the role of Amber, but I'm a little confused now."

Misty's smile faltered. "You don't think I'm right for the part?"

"Amber is a very sexy character. Her every word, action, her very breath has to ooze sex." He angled his head to the side as he studied her once more. "This outfit doesn't say sex kitten to me. It says office professional. I need the woman from the centerfold, the woman from the Rage Pistols video. That woman belongs in Hollywood. Show me that woman."

A cold clamminess washed over Misty as his meaning sank in. The secretary's smirk flashed through her mind as she started undoing buttons, allowing her cleavage to spill out of her blouse. She'd arrived at the producer's office dressed for a job interview, but this wasn't a regular job. This was the chance to be a star. Harry Justain didn't give a damn how professionally she presented herself. He'd chosen her for the role because he'd seen her naked. Her body had gotten her inside his office and if she needed to use her body to get on the screen in theaters throughout the country, she would. She would be the woman she needed to be to stay in Hollywood because she could never go back to being the girl stuck in Palmyra.

"What do you mean they passed on me?" Mike Rha's hand wrapped tighter around his cell phone as he sat in the dressing room chair, waiting for the makeup artist. "You said the role was in the bag."

"Sorry, Mike," his agent apologized insincerely. "I thought you had it, but relax. You're coming off a huge series run. Offers are pouring in."

"Offers for guest spots on sitcoms and minor roles."

"You were offered the lead in The Corpse Killer."

"The lead in an indie movie from a production company no one has ever heard of," he snapped. "I need better than that. I was perfect for that role. Who did they offer it to?"

"It's between Brad Pitt and Cruz Thomas."

"Brad Pitt and Cruz Thomas?" Mike realized his voice had raised several decibels and attracted the attention of people outside the dressing room. He took a calming breath before continuing. "So they're passing on me, a

Korean man, so a white guy can play the role of a Korean man?"

"Well, Cruz Thomas is actually—"

"Hispanic, I know. He might not be pure white, but he's a long fucking way from being Asian."

"I know," his agent said, and this time the empathy in his tone was genuine. "It sucks, man. I know it does. That's Hollywood for you though. You're going to get something great soon. Trust me."

"Yeah," Mike said as a slim black guy in skin-tight jeans and a black Selena T-shirt entered the dressing room.

"Ooh, you're early," the man said as he opened a makeup case on the counter and started pulling out items.

"The makeup artist is here," Mike told his agent. "Find me something."

He disconnected the call and tossed the cell phone onto the counter, not giving a crap if it broke. He didn't expect any good job offers to come through soon anyway. Brad Fucking Pitt. Cruz Thomas wasn't much better, but at least if he got the role it would be a win for one minority community. Then again, Cruz Thomas was one of those lucky bastards who could play white or Hispanic, so he wasn't exactly hurting for roles.

"Rough day, honey?" the makeup artist asked as he placed a black drape around his shoulders and caught his eye in the mirror before them.

"Just lost an Asian role to a white guy," Mike muttered. "Typical Hollywood whitewashing."

The makeup artist shook his head. "Damn, dude. I feel your pain."

Mike raised an eyebrow.

"Don't be raising that eyebrow at me, honey. You think straight white dudes haven't been taking roles from black brothers and gay men for decades? Hell, even Will Smith's black ass took a gay role and refused to do the kissing scene, but he still got the role."

"Fair enough." Mike smiled. "I'm usually not so irritable."

"It's cool. Hell, I'm impressed you're on time. I usually have to wait around for most actors." He held two different shades of base up to Mike's face and narrowed his eyes while determining which one to start with, then grabbed a brush. "My name is Damian Quincy Jones and I am about to make you so fabulous every studio will want your Asian ass in everything."

Mike laughed, his mood lifted. "I'll hold you to that. I could use the help."

"Shoo, you just came off a pretty hot show and this movie should do well. Jennifer Lawrence is crazy in demand right now."

"Yeah, and I get one scene with her in this movie."

"One scene that millions will be watching," Damian said as he starting applying base. "Use the opportunity and make it count. Sell yourself like a two-dollar hooker, sugar, and steal all J-Law's thunder right out of that scene. She's actually really nice, but this is war. You gotta take care of you."

"Damian, did you see the news?" A young mocha-skinned woman with bright pink dreads and a silver hoop through her left nostril barged into the dressing room and turned on the television set on the wall behind them.

Blake Lowell, the blond news anchor for the local news station, appeared on the screen. "The military is sending soldiers to all known addresses of mail-order brides brought over in the past five years, which is when the Russian president claims the virus injections began. At this time, we ask all citizens to stay inside. If you have been in contact with any Russian mail-order bride, please call the number flashing at the bottom of the screen. A military unit will be dispatched."

"Tonya, girl, don't you see I'm busy turning this man into a monument of sexy?"

The pink-haired woman eyed Mike up and down. "Looks like his mama and daddy did a good enough job of that already. You hear what that man just said? This shit is serious!"

"All I heard was some Russian hookers are sick."

"Mail-order brides," Tonya corrected him.

"Like I said, hookers."

"Not all mail-order brides are green card scammers," Mike interjected, knowing there were plenty of Asian women who used the internet to find husbands in other countries. "Did he say they're sending out the military? What kind of virus do they have?"

"Hell if I know, but it's not just the flu," Tonya said. "I've been checking Twitter and there's some people saying some woman in Utah tried to eat her husband."

Mike barely restrained himself from rolling his eyes. "Oh man. Is this another one of those stupid stunts to hype some movie?" Or maybe the next season of The Walking Dead, he thought, trying to keep a lid on his envy. Damn, his life would be set if Steven Yeun hadn't beaten him out for the role of Glenn Rhee.

"This is national news. I don't think they'd be part of some scam."

"They would if they didn't know," Damian advised. "People go too far on the internet sometimes and they believe every damn thing." He looked at Tonya pointedly.

"I don't know why you're looking at me like that, Damian. This is the news, not some website."

"No, but the story about the woman eating her husband was from Twitter and here you are spreading it. This is how shit gets started. This is why I thought Bill Cosby was dead last year."

Tonya rolled her eyes and started for the door. "Don't say I didn't warn you if some Russian woman tries to eat your ass."

"Where am I going to run into a Russian mail-order

bride in Hollywood? These men marry supermodels and actresses."

"Yeah, but they screw anything," she reminded him before leaving.

"You'll have to excuse her," Damian said, laughing as he muted the television. "That girl loves to gossip, and she believes everything."

"No problem," Mike said, continuing to watch the television through its reflection in the mirror before him. With the sound muted, the closed captioning kicked in, but it was backward, making it more difficult to read.

"Are you actually worried about this?"

He looked up to see Damian looking down at him, amused. "I'm not terrified or anything, but it looks like they might be talking about some kind of epidemic."

"Well, don't go shopping for any mail-order brides from Russia and you should be fine, and honey, you are fine." Damian used a wedge-shaped sponge to blend the makeup around Mike's nose and stood back to study his work. "Mmhmm. Fine. You're welcome."

Mike laughed. "Thanks."

"Knock 'em dead, honey."

"Reports of violent attacks are coming in from coast to coast and many hospitals are already full of sick people."

"Whether this influx of sick patients has a direct link to the Z-1219 virus or not has not yet been confirmed," the Hispanic news anchor interjected, cutting off her male counterpart, Brad Finn. "While there is no cause for alarm, the CDC strongly urges people to stay inside their homes and contact the military if they have been in contact with any Russian mail-order brides within the past five years and show signs of illness. Do not go to the local hospitals. Contact the military."

"We are receiving an update." Finn placed his finger

over the monitor in his ear. "The CDC is stressing anyone who has had any contact with any Russian party within the past five years or has received blood to call the military number flashing on the screen, and to report anyone acting suspiciously immediately. If you feel as if you are a danger to yourself or your family, or that someone near you is a danger, call the number."

"This is getting serious, Brad."

"I agree, Christen." Finn shuffled the papers in front of him, then wiped the back of his hand along his forehead and coughed into his hand.

"Pick up the damn phone," Ladeja said as she listened to it ring. She'd dialed her son's number ten times since the start of the news program and each time it went to voicemail.

"You've reached C-Dawg. Leave a mess—"

"Damn it!" Ladeja thumbed the button to disconnect the line and stopped herself just short of throwing the cell phone across the room. Of all the times for her ex to have their son. Then again, he had Cory the most nowadays. Cory had changed drastically over the last year. He idolized his father and if he had the choice, he would spend every moment of his life with the man, or with his money. She hated to admit it, but her son had grown extremely shallow despite her efforts to keep him grounded. None of that mattered now though. She just wanted to make sure he was safe.

"Ladeja, what are you doing?" Aubrey entered the dressing room, adjusting the spaghetti straps on her long black gown. "You know Georgios doesn't like it when we stay off the floor too long. Hey, somebody do something to you?"

Ladeja looked into her redheaded friend's concerned eyes and shook her head. "I was trying to get hold of Cory. He's not answering. I need to know he's fine."

"Of course he's fine. He's with his dad, right?"

"With him or his people," Ladeja answered, not bothering to hide her bitterness. "I've called him over a dozen times and left three voicemails and ten texts."

"He's a kid. They aren't exactly known for their prompt response to their parents' messages." Aubrey smiled. "Relax. This virus they're talking about seems to affect Russian mail-order brides or something. Cory is safe somewhere on gated property with bodyguards making sure no one gets near him."

"Yeah." Ladeja nodded. "That's right. He'd have his bodyguard with him."

"Exactly. Now get out there before you lose your job. You can punish him for not returning your calls later."

"I know, I know." Ladeja hugged her friend and checked her reflection in the long vanity mirror that ran the entire length of the wall. She touched up her wine-colored lip gloss and tugged on the hem of her short burgundy dress before stepping out of the dressing area to join the other girls on the floor.

She traveled down the brightly lit hall and took a breath before pushing open the door that led out to the balcony floor of the club. It took a moment for her eyes to adjust to the darkened club, illuminated only by strobe lights and the bright red words identifying the emergency exits.

She'd come to Hollywood to make it big, but other than a few commercials and some music videos, she'd never really made it. Her ex had, though. He'd started by selling CDs out the trunk of his car back home and had ended up signing with a major label. Now he was doing movies while she worked as a club companion.

No one approached her, so she turned right and slowly made her way around the upper floor. Her job was simple. All she had to do was look beautiful and be approachable. Once someone approached her, she provided company, but nothing sexual. They tried sometimes. Actually, they tried a lot of times, but Manny was good about keeping the girls safe and although he might not be the perfect boss, Georgios didn't play when it came to his girls' safety. If a girl said no and you kept pushing, being banned from the club was the least of your problems. Anything short of a hospital stay would be extremely lucky. Georgios also didn't want the law interfering with his business, so if you were caught being too friendly with the clubbers, you were out.

As Ladeja neared the far right end of the building, she caught sight of the television set in the small lounge area. She couldn't hear what was being said, but she could tell by the video clips that it was more news about the virus going around.

"Crazy what's happening out there, isn't it?"

She turned to see the large multiracial security guard hovering behind her. "You're not on the doors tonight?"

Manny shook his head. "The boss wants me deep inside in case of trouble."

"What kind of trouble?"

He nodded toward the television. "They're trying not to cause a panic, but our hospitals are filling up. This thing is all over."

"You don't think the hospitals filling up could be caused by people imagining the worst? You know how some people are. A minor case of the sniffles and they're online checking WebMD and diagnosing themselves with cancer."

"Are you trying to convince me of that or yourself?" He smiled at her, or what passed for a smile on Manny. Just a slight upward turn of the lips. Very rare, and according to the other girls, few got to witness it.

"My son is with his father and he isn't answering his phone."

"I'm sure he's fine. His father has security. He wouldn't be hanging around anyone sick."

"Are you trying to convince me of that or yourself?"

She turned his words back on him.

"Touché."

Ladeja chuckled.

"What?"

"I never imagined your big, beefy ass saying touché."

Manny made a show of looking over his own physique, including his ass. "It's not beefy. It's well-crafted and sturdy."

Ladeja laughed again, her worries momentarily forgotten.

A blood-curdling scream seemed to echo off the walls, shattering the moment.

"Shit," Manny muttered as they looked around, searching for the origin of the noise.

They both zeroed in on a disruption on the first floor of the club. People ran screaming from a darkly lit corner, high-pitched screams coming from both men and women as they fled. The last time Ladeja had seen a similar scene, it had been a different club, and the people had been fleeing a shooter, but she hadn't heard any gunshots and men generally didn't scream in such terror. "What the hell is happening down there?"

"Hell if I know, but I have a bad feeling. Get in the dressing room and stay there until—" His eyes widened as he leaned over the balcony. "Holy shit!"

Ladeja leaned over and a scream escaped her as a woman stumbled onto the dance floor, her white dress covered in the unmistakable splotches of blood. The woman looked up with milky eyes perfectly illuminated by the strobe light above her, and Ladeja saw blood dripping down her pale chin as she opened her mouth and snapped it shut.

"Lock yourselves in the dressing room!" Manny yelled to her and the other club companions on the balcony level, already running toward the stairs that would take him to the first floor, right into the heart of danger.

"Manny!"

"That's an order, Ladeja! Get your ass in that dressing room and lock the door!"

"Come on!" Hannah, a thin, willowy blonde, grabbed her arm and pulled her in the direction of the door she'd entered through not even a full five minutes before. They were almost run over by clubbers who'd caught on to the fact that something beyond a normal security incident was happening and were now either trying to clear the building or get a better view of the action.

They made it through the door and ran toward the dressing area as quickly as they could in stiletto heels. By the time they were safely inside with the other club companions who'd obeyed Manny's instruction and had locked the door behind them, they were both breathing heavy, more from fear than from the cardio.

"What happened?" Gena, a curvy Hispanic woman, asked. "Did anybody see anything?"

"I did," Ladeja answered, pointing to the television. "It was that. There was a woman down on the dance floor with blood dripping down her chin. It's the virus."

"Oh, come on," Gena said, clearly not buying it. "I saw that shit on Twitter about someone biting someone or something like that. That's bullshit."

"I know what I saw."

"You saw a woman with a bloody chin. She probably fell and busted it."

"Possible, but why were her eyes milky white?" Ladeja asked, recalling what had frightened her more than the bloody chin and snapping mouth when the woman had looked up at her.

"Uh… contacts?" Gena suggested before rolling her eyes.

"All I know is Manny has never looked that spooked," Hannah interjected, "and I've been working here for a couple of years. I've seen some stuff."

"People were screaming and running away," Aubrey added, visibly shivering as she wrapped her arms around her middle. "Something pretty scary happened on the first floor."

Gunshots rang out and the girls automatically crouched down as low as their tight attire would allow.

"Shit just got real," Kim, the newest club companion, cried out before standing again and crossing over to her locker. "I'm out of here."

"The shots came from the first floor," Gena advised as the rest of them straightened back up. "Security will handle it. Just stay cool. We're safe."

Ladeja shook her head and turned up the television, already dialing her son's number. She chewed her bottom lip while listening to the phone ring, warring with herself over what to do. She needed this job, but her son's safety came first. He wasn't answering the phone and the fear clawing at her insides would slowly kill her. "Call me, damn it!" she yelled as the call went to voicemail.

"This just in. A massive pile up has completely stopped traffic on US Route 95 in Nevada," Christen Guerrero, the news anchor appeared to be reading off a teleprompter. "Eyewitness accounts report that a woman emerged from the wreckage moments after two cars collided and cut across lanes, causing another collision before attacking someone in a stopped vehicle."

"We have just received footage from the scene," the co-anchor announced. "This footage is extremely graphic and not suitable for children or anyone with a heart condition."

"Anyone with a heart condition?" Ladeja murmured as two more gunshots rang out. She turned toward the door, distracted by the sound, but a nearby gasp redirected her to the television where she saw the as-promised extremely graphic footage of a woman ripping a chunk of flesh out of a man's neck with nothing but her teeth.

"Holy shit," Gena said, her shocked voice nearly a whisper.

"Still think this virus scare is bullshit?" Ladeja asked.

"I can't believe they actually showed that on television," Hannah said, her pale skin taking on a green tint.

"I can. If this thing is as bad as they've been saying it is, no one is safe and we're going to see shit like that everywhere, up close and personal. Showing that probably just saved a lot of lives, namely from people who refused to believe any of it until they saw with their own eyes." Ladeja looked pointedly at Gena as she crossed over to her locker and entered her combination.

"Where are you going?" Hannah's voice raised several octaves. "We have to stay here until security tells us it's safe."

"We don't even know if security is going to survive whatever the hell is happening out there," Ladeja advised, pulling clothes out of her locker. The image of Manny dead on the club floor popped up in her mind, and she quickly pushed it away. She couldn't afford more fear than she already felt for her son's safety or she'd be a basket case. "Whatever's happening, I'd rather face it in jeans and Nikes instead of this tight-ass dress and hooker heels. Besides, I can't wait in here. My son is out there somewhere, and he's not answering his phone."

"She's right about the clothes," Aubrey said, opening her own locker. "Whether that was an infected woman downstairs or just some drunk starting shit, I'm not going back out on the floor to work. We all need to put on something we can run in and get out of here."

"We could lose our jobs," Gena argued. "You know how Georgios is."

"Fuck Georgios!" Ladeja snapped. "I don't see his ass in here with us. They advised people to stay at home and he went home early, yet didn't give us the same courtesy. I can lose this job. I can't lose my life or my son's."

She quickly kicked off her heels and peeled off her dress, letting it drop to the floor before pulling on the jeans and Oakland A's T-shirt she'd worn in to work. The girls followed suit, discarding their slinky dresses and pulling on more practical clothing as fast as they could move, despite shaking hands. Even Gena showed signs of panic setting in.

Ladeja finished tying her shoes, slid her arms through her drawstring backpack, and scooped up her cell phone and keys. Beyond worried about her son, she thumbed through her contacts and dialed the number of the man she only talked to when absolutely necessary. The phone rang in her ear as she unlocked the dressing room door and opened it to see a bloody man running toward her.

She screamed in response before realizing the man barreling toward her was Manny.

"Club's closed," he said, reaching the door. "Ladies, go home and lock your doors."

"What up? You reached Thunda Carter—"

Ladeja disconnected the line as her ex's voicemail message started and shoved the phone into her back pocket. "What the hell happened down there, Manny?" She checked him over, looking for the source of his injuries. "Were you bit?"

The club companions moved backward as one, eying the security guard warily.

"No, but some of the other guys weren't so lucky." He swiped his free hand across his forehead, rubbing blood from a scratch above his eyebrow. He held a gun in his other hand. "I bashed my head on the bar after getting mowed over by a group of people trying to get out. It was complete fucking chaos down there. Half the security team split. They just fucking bailed, the pussies."

"You stayed."

"Someone had to remember there were women in here

who needed to be protected and advised when they could leave safely." He looked down at her with a gentle warmth in his eyes that should have looked out-of-place given his menacing size and tough guy looks, but oddly seemed to fit. "It appears you were on your way out though."

"My son still hasn't answered his phone, and I just got voicemail when trying his father," Ladeja explained, her voice apologetic. "I have to get to him."

Manny nodded. "You got everything?"

"Yeah."

"Let's go get your son." He turned and started walking toward the stairs.

"Let's?" Ladeja followed him, the other women close on her heels. They let out a collective gasp as they looked over the balcony rail to see multiple bodies lying on the dance floor and blood splattered everywhere. Realizing she'd stopped moving, Ladeja shook off her shock and ran after Manny. "You mean let's as in us?"

He turned and looked down at her. "Well, I'm certainly not letting you go out into this shitfest by yourself."

A scream pierced the studio, causing Mike and the actor opposite him to jump.

"Cut!" the director yelled. "What the hell was that? What moron doesn't understand what 'Quiet on the set' means?"

Another scream rang out, followed by a loud crash.

"The hell?" Mike murmured.

"Does this type of thing usually happen on set?" John, the newbie actor in the scene with him, asked in a hushed whisper.

Mike shook his head.

"For fuck's sake, is no one professional around here?" The director stood from his chair and tossed his script onto the seat he'd just vacated. "Take five, everyone, while

I find out who is making all that commotion… and fire them!"

"Oh great, just what I need to calm my nerves. A pissed-off director."

"You're doing good. Besides, directors are generally irritable, so you might as well get used to it now." Mike smiled at the anxious young actor before walking off set, figuring he might as well check his messages while given the opportunity.

Various crew members and studio staff ran around him, searching for the source of the disturbance that had halted production, as he made his way to his small dressing room. He grabbed a mini ham sandwich from the craft service table and shoved it into his mouth before finding the room.

His cell phone was on the glass coffee table where he'd left it. He glanced up at the television set as he retrieved it and thumbed the text icon. A video flashed on the screen of a disheveled woman walking around a group of wrecked cars.

His phone beeped, drawing his attention back to it and the text that had just come through.

"Whoa." He showed over thirty messages from his parents, and a quick glance was all he needed to sum up that they desperately wanted him to notify them that he was all right.

Are you safe?

Call us!

Have you seen the news?!?!?!?!?! Are you safe at home?

The virus is in California!

The virus is everywhere! Are you safe?

ARE YOU SAFE?!?!??!??!?!?!??!?!?!

Michael this is your mother. I demand you call me NOW!

"What the hell?" Mike muttered as he scrolled through

and saw the rest of the messages were along the same lines. He sent a quick reply that he was safe but busy filming and couldn't call at the moment, knowing that if he called, he would never get off the phone with his mother. The director was already pissed. He didn't want to add any fuel to the fire.

After getting through his parents' texts, he saw a text from his agent advising he'd gotten a meeting with Harry Justain for an action movie and sent a quick reply asking for details on the role, hoping it wasn't some typical Asian stereotype.

He glanced back up at the television mounted on the wall as he sent the text through and caught sight of the disheveled woman eating a man.

"What the actual fuck?" He reached up to unmute the television, stopping at the sound of something bumping into something behind him. He turned to see a portly man leaning against the doorframe, his hand covering the center of a gaping wound in his belly as blood seeped through his fingers. Another wound in his neck bled profusely, the deep red color stark against the man's pale skin.

"Shit!" Mike jumped back, the television forgotten.

"Help… me," the man said before falling face-forward onto the carpeted floor.

Mike stood still, staring at the man for a moment as a blood stain grew in the light carpet under his body. His heart pumped fiercely, his legs twitched as his body all but screamed for him to run. His head attempted to wrap itself around what he was seeing.

"It's a prank." He laughed, the sound coming out much too loud and unnatural, and he looked around the room for cameras. He didn't see any cameras, but he did see the replay of the footage showing the woman taking a huge bite out of a man on the highway.

His cell phone buzzed. Startled by the sound, Mike

yelped and the phone sailed out of his hand to bounce off the glass table, cracking the tabletop in the process.

"Shit." He bent down and retrieved the vibrating phone, not surprised to see his parents' number show on the screen. He suspected his mother would not quit calling him until she actually connected with him.

A scream from within the studio nearly sent his phone flying again. He turned it off and shoved it into his pocket before snatching his keys and shoving them in another pocket. Roles for Asian actors were extremely hard to come by, but they weren't worth his life. He didn't know what the hell was going on, but a man was bleeding out on his dressing room floor. He wasn't going back on set.

He carefully stepped over the man's body, nearly pissing himself in fear at the thought the man might rise up and grab him, but he passed him without incident to nearly be mowed down by three people running past him, yelling for him to get out while he could.

He looked in the direction they'd come from and saw a herd of people racing toward him.

"What happened?' he called out.

"The virus!" a woman yelled as she sped past him. "It's real!"

Mike looked back at the dead man on his dressing room floor and decided it was time to leave before he ended up the same way. He merged in with the crowd and ran with them until they poured out onto the studio back lot.

"Yeah?"

"Cory?!" Ladeja nearly shrieked her son's name when he finally answered the phone.

"My name's C-Dawg," he corrected her.

Too worried about his safety to acknowledge the attitude coming from him, Ladeja didn't address it. "Baby, are you all right? I've been calling and texting! Didn't you get my messages?"

"I'm fine."

"Why didn't you answer the phone?"

"I was busy. We're having a party and I was shooting hoops with Lamontez Jones!"

Ladeja blinked, the NBA star's name not impressing her much. She didn't give a damn if Cory had been shooting hoops with Michael Jordan. Her only concern was keeping her son safe, and it didn't seem safe for him to be surrounded by people who could be infected.

"You're having a party?! Cory, there is a virus spreading like crazy. Anyone around you could be infected."

"Relax, Ma." His tone reeked of eye roll. "Cynda doesn't let just anybody roll up in her crib. No dirty people are going to get in here."

Ladeja sputtered, unsure where to begin with her child. The fact he'd mentioned the demon whore's name didn't help calm her nerves either. "They're not dirty people, Cory, they're sick. The virus can spread to anyone. Lock yourself in your room. I'm coming to get you."

"My name is C-Dawg!" he snapped. "Get it right, it isn't that hard! And I don't need you to come get me. I'm safer here than in your little-bitty house."

"Cory James Carter!" Ladeja's hand tightened around the phone. She wished she could replace it with Thunda's neck. "Put your father on the phone."

"He's not here. He's shooting a movie."

Ladeja suppressed a growl. "You're there all alone?"

"Cynda and her sisters are here. I told you there was a party."

Ladeja closed her eyes and took a deep breath to keep from screaming. She knew what a party at the Camilleri's was like. Her young son was probably surrounded by drunk and high people during the middle of a dangerous viral outbreak. Sure, the family had security, but they would protect the Camilleri family before they'd even think about her son. Cory was supposed to be with his father, not the whore who'd inherited her riches and gained fame by leaking a sex tape and showing her fake body on Instagram every other day. "Cory, lock yourself in your room like I said."

"You don't need to come here—"

"Do as I said! That's an order!" She hung up, afraid the tears she willed back would spill over if she continued to hear such disrespect from her son's mouth.

"Everything all right?" Manny asked. He muttered a curse and floored the gas as they turned a corner and saw a small blockade of infected people in the alley.

Ladeja cringed and covered her mouth as the truck plowed right over the people, splashing blood and viscera as it crushed them under the tires.

"Sorry. It's easier to take them out that way than to get out and fight them off one by one. Plus, I only have so many bullets. I'd rather not waste them."

"I hope we aren't going straight to hell for killing these people."

"I think they're already dead," Manny advised. "They sure as fuck aren't people anymore. Your son all right?"

"Yeah." She sighed. "His father isn't there with him. He's shooting a movie and apparently left my child with that fake-ass wife of his. Cynda Camilleri. They're throwing a party. The entire city has gone mad, and that stupid bitch has my son in a house full of potentially dangerous people."

Manny swerved around a dog that ran out in front of them, side-swiping the infected pair chasing after it. "The Camilleris are loaded. They have good security and the property is gated. That's good."

"You know the Camilleri property layout?" Ladeja raised an eyebrow.

"I do some freelance security sometimes. I've worked

some of their parties, which is a good thing."

"Why?"

"Because… if the current security gives us any shit when we get there, I know how to get inside. I could hear your son on the phone. He didn't sound very, uh, obedient."

"You mean respectful?" Ladeja looked away, her face growing warm. "He's really not a bad kid. He's been spending a lot of time with his father and that uppity-ass family. They give him whatever he wants."

"Hmmm. All I know is if I'd used that tone with my mother, she'd have whooped my ass until I didn't have an ass left."

They turned another corner, and a man leaped out of the shadows to throw himself at the truck. His face smashed against Deja's window, startling her. He left a trail of red drool as he slid down the side of the vehicle.

"I just want my baby safe."

"We're almost there."

"Crazy-ass bitch," C-Dawg muttered, scrolling through the multitude of messages his mother had left. He hadn't received any texts from his father. He should have returned home by now. He was shooting in the city this week.

"You shouldn't talk about your mother like that."

He looked over at Mateo, the maid's ten-year-old son, lying in the lounge chair next to his. One year younger than him, but he acted like a baby. C-Dawg was a man and didn't have time for whiny brats trying to tell him how he should or shouldn't treat anybody.

"Did I ask for your opinion? Why are you even out here?" C-Dawg waved his arm in an arc, showing the massive pool they lounged by. It had mostly been abandoned an hour ago, except for the hideaway area under the waterfall. That was the one place he wasn't allowed to go because people did things there they didn't want him to see. They thought he didn't know what happened there, but he wasn't a baby. He knew a lot of things.

"I thought you might want to play."

"Play?" C-Dawg laughed at the kid. "Does this look like preschool? My family is having a party. I'm not bailing on more important people to play with some kid."

Mateo scrunched his brow. "You're eleven years old and your dad isn't even here. All the people here came for the Camilleri family."

"My dad married Cynda Camilleri. I'm family."

"If this is a family party and you're family, how come the only other kid here is me, the maid's son?"

"A better question is why is the maid's son talking to me like he doesn't know who I am? I could have your mother fired."

Mateo's eyes widened. "You would not do such a thing. I have done nothing to you."

"You're breathing my air, peasant. I don't want to talk to you. I don't want to play with you. Go run along and hide wherever the help hides."

"I just saw that you were alone a lot and thought you might want a friend," Mateo mumbled.

"Alone a lot?" C-Dawg laughed to himself. He wasn't alone a lot. He had friends. Just that night he'd played ball with not one, not two, but three different NBA stars. He knew a ton of rappers and had mingled with countless stars at the party. A swimsuit model had even kissed him on the cheek. Just because there wasn't anyone else his age at the party didn't mean he was alone. People his age were juvenile or jealous. He preferred this crowd.

He looked around again. He'd come outside because the pool had cleared when the entertainment started inside. Tonight some woman was singing. He forgot who, but she was pretty famous, just not his style of music. His stomach growled, reminding him he hadn't had dinner, or lunch for that matter. Everyone had been busy taking care of the guests and he didn't really like the caviar and fancy stuff the help had been passing out.

"Whatever, man. I'm about to grab something to eat and hang out with some stars. Have fun playing, kid." C-Dawg stood from the lounge chair and stepped toward the house.

A group of people poured out of the sliding glass doors, several of them screaming, before another group crashed through the glass, sending shards everywhere.

"What is happening?" Mateo asked, his voice shrill.

C-Dawg shook his head as he took in the scene before him. He didn't see his father or the Camilleri family in the melee, but he did see a lot of bloody people running like the devil himself was on their heels.

"Yo, Mateo. Where exactly does the help hide?"

"My mother told me to stay in the guesthouse. Why?"

A heavy round of gunfire came from inside the Camilleri house. "Because of that!""

2

"No!" Ladeja gripped the dashboard as they neared the Camilleri mansion and saw the front gate wide open.

"Stay calm," Manny told her. "If anything has happened, it's best we go in with cool heads."

"If anything has happened? That gate is off its hinge and there's no security at the entrance."

"The way that gate is opened, it looks like a large vehicle took it out on its way out, which means someone got out of here fast."

"How is that good?"

Manny shrugged. "It's better than it being crushed under the weight of a herd of infected people wanting in. I don't see any signs of any sick people walking around."

They sped right up to the front of the mansion, and Manny brought the truck to a screeching stop, attracting the attention of the security team. Four armed men came pouring out of the house, guns pointed at them.

"See. Told you they'd have security. Come out on my side." Manny opened his door and slid out of the truck, his hands raised up.

"Mancuso?" one of the men questioned, recognizing him.

"It's me," Manny said as Ladeja slid out of the truck behind him. "I got Cory Carter's mother with me. We came to get her son."

"Who?"

"C-Dawg," Ladeja said. "Thunda Carter's son."

"Oh." The dark-haired, pale man frowned. "He's here?"

Ladeja gasped, unable to actually form words, and ran past Manny.

The other security guards aimed their weapons at her, but the guard Manny had been speaking with ordered them to stand down as Ladeja ran past them and entered the foyer. The first thing she noticed was the busted sliding glass door at the end of the foyer and blood splatter on the floor being mopped up by a guard.

"Where is my son?" she screamed as she searched the downstairs rooms, eventually finding the Camilleri sisters in a large sitting room. The room which was wall-to-wall white didn't show any signs of violence, but the abundant amount of cigarettes and roaches in the ash trays covering the top of the white grand piano and the shot glasses on the bar showed evidence of the party Cory had told her about. "Where's Cory?!"

Cheyanne, Chelle, Cara, and the she-devil herself, Cynda Camilleri, nearly jumped off the sectional sofa they were huddled on together.

"Where is he?"

"I'd tell her right now if I were you," Manny advised, entering the room behind her. "It's not smart to piss off a mama bear."

Cynda looked at her sisters for help. Not finding any — in fact, they all averted their eyes — she slowly stood. "I…"

"Where is he?!" Ladeja screamed, tightening her fists. Her entire body shook as horrible nightmare images flashed through her mind. She'd just spoken to him an hour ago. It shouldn't have taken that long to get to him, but there had been so many sick people in their way. Still, she'd just spoken to him. He was alive. What had happened in that hour?

"I don't know. Someone went nuts at the party and everyone was running all over to get out. I haven't seen him."

Ladeja's nails cut into her palms. "Have you even looked for him?"

Cynda, the fake woman Thunda had made his wife, despite not finding *her* worthy of that title after all she'd done for him, looked away. "We've been busy."

Ladeja launched herself at the woman, but Manny grabbed her around the waist, stopping her from doing something that would get her shot by the Camilleri security team.

"Calm down, Ladeja. We need to find Cory." He looked over at the tense security team who had placed themselves between her and the Camilleri women. "Her eleven-year-old son was here and perfectly safe about an hour ago. She spoke with him on the phone. He's just a kid. We have to find him now."

"All right. I'll go with you," the man who'd recognized Manny outside said before addressing his team. "Reyes, Martin, check the upstairs again. We're going to check out the grounds. You other two, stay on the Camilleri sisters."

The man tilted his head, gesturing for them to follow him as he stepped past them to leave the sitting room.

"What the hell happened in here, O'Donnell?"

"Hell broke loose," the man answered as he led them through the foyer and out the sliding doors that had been destroyed. They stepped outside to a long, spacious pool and a large amount of lounge chairs that had been scattered all over the lawn by the partygoers desperately escaping. "You know how the Camilleri family likes to party. They were having one of their bashes when this swimsuit model got sick and asked to lie down. Cynda left her in a guest room and about an hour later, she came out with milky white eyes and a hard-on for human flesh. It was that virus that's been all over the news."

"Why the fuck did you allow them to throw a party?"

"You know the Camilleri family doesn't take advice from the hired help," O'Donnell answered him.

A small anguished sound escaped Ladeja as she thought about her baby in this mess. A party full of stampeding people was dangerous all by itself, but there'd been an infected person on the property and she'd seen enough of them roaming the streets of Hollywood to know the degree of damage they could inflict on a young boy.

"Ma'am, I assure you we put that model down pretty damn quick, and the four others she bit, none of which were your son. I haven't seen C-Dawg in hours. He probably got scared when he saw all the people freaking out and ran away to hide somewhere."

"This had to have happened right after I got off the phone with him. You've had time to kill the infected model and I assume dispose of the body somewhere since I haven't seen it, and the victims you said she got to before you stopped her, but you never thought to look for the eleven-year-old boy that you knew was here?"

"They hired my team to work security for the party," O'Donnell advised. "Regular security was out at the gate, but they abandoned their post when shit went nuts. I think the only people who didn't take the virus seriously were the rich and famous dumbasses in the mansion."

"Doesn't Thunda have security specifically for Cory?" Ladeja asked, refusing to call her son by that stupid C-Dawg name.

O'Donnell shrugged. "I work for the Camilleri family. I've never worked directly for Mr. Carter. You said you spoke with your son an hour ago. Is he not answering his phone now?"

Ladeja slapped herself in the forehead and muttered a curse. "I'm so fucking stupid."

"Fuck," Manny muttered himself. "That makes two of us."

Ladeja pulled her cell phone out of her jeans pocket and speed-dialed her son, silently cursing herself for not thinking to do so the moment she'd arrived at the mansion.

"Mom?" Cory's shaky voice whispered before the phone could complete its first ring.

"Baby! Baby, where are you?"

"Guesthouse," he whispered. "It's in the back by the tennis court."

"We're on our way," Ladeja promised, unease gnawing at her gut. She heard sniffling. "Why are you whispering? Who's crying?"

"Mateo. The maid's kid," Cory whispered. "We're not alone."

"Honey, what's happening?"

"There's a man in the other room. He killed Mateo's mom, and now he's eating her."

"Hold on, baby, Mama's coming!" Ladeja looked over at O'Donnell. "My son and another boy are hiding in a guest house by the tennis court and there's an infected man in there with him. Move!"

O'Donnell took off at a fast clip, Manny and Ladeja following close on his heels as he removed his gun from his shoulder holster and gripped it tight in his hand.

They reached the tennis court, and Ladeja saw the guest house just beyond it. The front door stood open, but she couldn't see any movement inside. She pushed herself harder and quickened her pace, soon passing Manny.

"No!" He grabbed her and held her tight as they slowed to a stop four feet away from the guesthouse. "We're going to get your boy, I promise you, but we're going to do this the safe way. That way we all get to survive, all right?"

"I want my boy!" Tears streamed down Ladeja's cheeks.

"You're going to have him in just a moment. Now, stay right here."

"No."

"Fine." Manny shoved her behind his body. "Stay behind us."

O'Donnell led the way, Manny at his back, and Ladeja close behind. As they entered the guest house, she looked around frantically for the source of the sickening crunching, slurping sounds coming from deep in the room and the foul smell of rot.

"Behind the bar," O'Donnell said.

He moved left. Manny and Ladeja moved right. They rounded the bar and saw the infected man face down in a woman's stomach. Realizing fresh meat had arrived, the man raised his head, still slurping up the woman's intestines like pasta.

Bile rose in Ladeja's throat. She clapped a hand over her mouth and willed it back down as the men shot the infected monster. A pang of guilt hit her, but she shoved it aside. He could have been a perfectly nice man before the virus, but after he'd attacked, actually eaten a woman, there was no other name for him but monster.

"You all right?" Manny asked, looking down at her.

She turned, noting he'd positioned his body to block the majority of the gruesome scene while O'Donnell covered as much as he could with a throw he'd grabbed from a nearby sofa. Ladeja nodded and took one more deep breath through her mouth to calm her stomach before calling out for her son.

"Cory?! It's all right now. The man is dead!"

They heard movement behind a closed door, the click of a lock, and the door opened. Cory ran out and looked around. "Where's Dad?"

"I don't know." Ladeja rushed toward him, pulling him

close to her as she checked him over. "Are you all right, honey? Were you hurt?"

"I'm fine." Cory maneuvered out of his mother's arms and pulled his cell phone out of one of the pockets in his baggy jeans. "I've been calling Dad. I'm worried about him."

"Hey Ladeja," Manny called from the doorway to the room Cory had emerged from. "I think we could use a woman's touch here."

Ladeja squashed down the knee-jerk pain she felt from knowing her son had been so concerned about his father he called him but hadn't called her, and met Manny in the doorway.

"It was his mom," Manny said softly.

Ladeja looked past him into the room. She saw a young Hispanic boy around Cory's age sitting on a bed with his back against the headboard, his knees to his chin and his small hands clenched together around his shins. Tears streamed freely down his cheeks from red, puffy eyes, but he made so sound. The bedsheets were dark blue silk, and the dresser set looked expensive, not the type of stuff you'd find in a kid's room. Three landscape paintings adorned the walls, typical guestroom décor, she assumed, but the toys on the dresser and the Captain America pillow told a different story.

"Hey there." Ladeja sat next to him on the bed. "I'm Cory's mother. He said you were Mateo? Do you live in the guesthouse, Mateo?"

"My mom moved us in here last week. She told the Camilleris she would take less pay if we could stay here." He turned his head so that he looked up at her. "She had a dream that the monsters would come."

Ladeja's blood ran cold. She searched the boy's eyes and found only complete sincerity. "Your mother told you she knew the virus would happen?"

"She saw it a week ago. She saw them in our apartment with me. She brought us here to keep me safe." He looked out the door to the room he knew his mother had died in. "She's dead now instead of me. I did what she told me to do. I hid here just like she told me to do if there was trouble, but she came in her to make sure and that's when the man came in behind her. Now she's dead."

Ladeja wiped her eyes and took a deep, controlled breath, willing herself to stay strong for the boy. "A mother's job is to protect her child. Never take any blame for what happened. Any mother would do what she did."

"To save me?"

"Yes."

"She's all I had. I'm alone now." His thin body trembled. "The Camilleris told her I had to stay out of sight. They won't take care of me."

"I will, sweetheart." Ladeja wrapped her arms around him. "I will."

"Can we go now?" Cory asked as he entered the room, his cell phone up to his ear. "Damn," he said, as he disconnected the line, apparently still not getting his father to answer.

"Language, Cory."

He rolled his eyes, then looked at Mateo and curled his lip. "He gonna stay in the main house now that his mama's dead?"

"Cory!"

"I told you my name is C-Dawg! It's not that hard to—" he quit talking as Manny gripped his shoulder and gave him a warning look.

"Manny, I can deal with my own child," Ladeja informed him as she stood from the bed and looked around for something to pack Mateo's things in. "Mateo is staying with us, and we are not staying here. You're coming with me."

She opened a closet and retrieved a backpack. "Here, honey. Pack a couple changes of clothes and if there's something of your mother's that's important, take it with you."

"Take him if you want, but I'm not going anywhere with you," Cory said. "Dad has me now."

Ladeja whirled around on the boy, her jaw clenched in response to his tone. "Your father is not here. Your visitation was supposed to be with him, not his skank and her skank family. I said you're coming with me and that is final."

"Make me!" Cory turned and ran off.

"I'll get him!" O'Donnell yelled from the next room, having heard everything.

"It might not be my place to say this," Manny said, "but that boy needs a serious ass whoopin' before he gets too far out of control."

Ladeja glared at Manny, more angry because she knew he was right than because he'd said it, but she couldn't deal with Cory's attitude right then and there. She needed to get her son somewhere safe before she could even think of straightening him out, and now she'd taken in another child, another small, helpless person in need of protection.

"You have everything, Mateo?" she asked, noticing the boy had stopped shoving clothes into the backpack.

"My mom has a locket with a picture of her and my dad in it."

"Okay, that sounds like something beautiful to remember her by."

"She never takes it off."

Ladeja's heart sank into the pit of her stomach. She opened her mouth but couldn't find words. What was she supposed to say? Sorry, kid, choose something else?

Manny groaned. "You are so going to owe me for this," he said before leaving the room.

She smiled over at Mateo. "Manny's going to get it for you. Is there anything else you need? Do you take any medicine?"

"I'm not sick." Mateo zipped the backpack and slid his arms through the shoulder straps. "I'm sorry Cory is so rude. I just met you and I can tell you are nicer than his father."

"There's a lot going on right now and he's worried about his father. He's just upset and not thinking." The words spilled out of her mouth as fast as she could form them and even to her own ears, they sounded like part of a weak cover-up. At some point, her son had stopped respecting her. Even the young boy in front of her could see it.

"Son of a motherfuckin' bitch," Manny grumbled from the next room.

"You all right, Manny?"

"I'm just great," he answered, his tone full of disgust. "You have no idea how much you owe me."

She heard him running water from the kitchen sink and knew he'd gotten the locket.

"Thank you for letting me come with you," Mateo said, "and for getting the locket."

"I owe it to your mother," Ladeja said. "She kept that man away from you and Cory. She protected my son. I'll protect hers."

He looked up at her with wet eyes and his bottom lip trembled. "Please don't die too."

The sound of gunshots outside saved her from having to think of a response to the heartbreaking request. Without even thinking, she grabbed Mateo's hand and ran toward the gunfire.

"Ladeja!" Manny ran across the room and blocked her before she could reach the front door.

"Move! Cory's out there!"

"So is O'Donnell, and it sounds like he found trouble. If you go running out there, you could distract him and somebody could die."

"If you don't get the hell out of my way, you could die," she growled.

Manny raised an eyebrow but did not move. He folded

his beefy arms and stared her down, a giant wall of muscle blocking her path.

"Out of the way!" she heard O'Donnell yell as his footsteps drew close.

Manny moved aside and the pale man ran through the door with a gun in one hand and Cory sideways under his other arm, being carried like a fussy sack of potatoes. He dropped Cory to the floor and slammed the door closed, quickly sliding the lock in place.

"Cory!" Ladeja dropped to her knees and checked him over. "Are you OK?"

"I'm fine, I'm fine! Everybody trippin' over nothing." He batted her hands away and stood.

"You're welcome," O'Donnell said sarcastically. "If I hadn't been trippin', you'd be dead right now. There were some infected people loose in the yard. I took care of them."

"How many?" Ladeja asked.

"Three. I didn't see any more, but the property is pretty big. We need to get back to the main house. Are you ready?"

"Just a sec." Manny walked over to the sink and turned it off. He took the locket out of the water and wiped it dry with some paper towels before bringing it over to Mateo.

The kid hung it around his neck and tucked it under his Hulk T-shirt. His jaw clenched tight as he fought to stay strong. It was then that Ladeja noticed he'd kept his eyes down the whole time he'd been in the room, avoiding seeing where his dead mother lay.

Ladeja pulled him to her and hugged him tight. "It's going to be all right, sweetheart. You're going to be fine."

"Can we go to the mansion now?" Cory groaned. "I want to see if my dad is home yet."

Gritting her teeth, Ladeja stood and turned toward the door. "Mateo has everything he needs. Is it safe for us to leave now?"

O'Donnell peeked out the front window through the

blinds and nodded. "Everybody stay together and if we run into any trouble, let Manny and me handle it. If anyone runs off, shit's gonna go south real fast, understand?"

They all nodded their understanding.

O'Donnell placed a finger to his lips, commanding quiet, and slid the bolt to unlock the door. He slowly pulled the door open and peeked outside, scanning left to right. He swiveled his head back to look at them and nodded before leading the way out the door.

Manny ushered the kids and Ladeja ahead of him so he could bring up the rear. Ladeja didn't mind her and the kids being sandwiched between the two muscular men. Just the thought of being out in the open while infected people could be prowling the grounds made her feel she could wet herself at any moment. She'd seen some horrible stuff on the way to the mansion, but she'd felt much safer in the truck, and much safer without two kids unprotected by some sort of shelter.

"With that big hole in the foyer, how do you know nothing has gotten into the mansion?" she asked softly, not wanting to draw any unwanted attention by any sick people who might be hidden from view.

"I called ahead." O'Donnell tapped the radio holstered at his hip. "There's five men inside the mansion and two are on that busted door."

As they neared the mansion, hurrying to get to safety, Ladeja saw the busted door, and the two armed men standing just inside scanning the grounds. She saw a large smear of blood on the ground just beyond that she hadn't seen before and knew they'd had an encounter with an infected person. The smear seemed to run right into the pool.

"You're discarding bodies in the pool now?"

"It looks like they did. Quick thinking."

"You said you killed some after Cory ran out of the

guesthouse."

"C-Dawg," Cory muttered.

Manny growled low in his throat, and the blood drained from Cory's face. Ladeja gave Manny a warning look. Cory might be being a brat, but he was her brat to reprimand, not Manny's.

"Yeah, I grabbed Cory and walked off with him, made them follow a safe distance from the guesthouse before I fired. If there were any others nearby, I didn't want to draw them to where you all were. These infected have weird, smoky eyes, but they appear to see well enough and they can definitely hear. They move slow so one on one I don't think they're much trouble but you get a bunch of them together you might as well kiss your ass goodbye."

"Anyone bitten or scratched?" one of the guards asked as they reached them.

"All good," O'Donnell advised, ushering them through.

"Is my dad back yet?" Cory asked the guard hopefully, his face falling as the guard shook his head. "Did he call?"

The guard shrugged.

"Let's get somewhere safer than this foyer," O'Donnell recommended and guided them into the sitting room where they'd originally found the Camilleri sisters.

Cynda cursed under her breath, texting on her phone while walking a circle over the plush white carpet in stilettos. Cheyanne also paced while checking her phone, but her black leather ankle boots were a bit more practical in case they needed to run. Chelle and Cara, the younger sisters, sat together on the sectional watching the news. Chelle leaned forward, completely engrossed, while Cara applied a fresh coat of nail polish.

Ladeja rolled her eyes. "You know there are infected people all over the place and they are eating people, right?"

Cara and Chelle were the only sisters to acknowledge she'd spoken by looking at her.

"Yeah?" Cara said, her gaze already returned to her

nails.

"Don't you think you should trade the heels and dresses for something better for running or fending them off?"

"We have security," Cara advised, punctuating the statement with an exaggerated eye roll only a teenager could pull off, or in this case a twenty-year-old who still acted like a bratty fifteen-year-old because she was loaded and got by with everything because of her family name.

"They're ridiculous," Ladeja muttered, turning toward Manny. "I just came for my son and I have him."

"We can go then." Manny reached into his pocket for the truck keys.

"I'm not leaving without my dad!" Cory yelled, his face blossoming with red. "You can't make me go anywhere. I'm staying right here!"

This caught Cynda's attention, and she finally looked up from her phone. "Oh, C-Dawg, have you heard from Thunda?"

"No." He turned toward her. "He hasn't called?"

"No." She pouted and went back to her phone. "Stupid cell phones. Calls keep dropping so I've sent texts, but they're taking forever to go through."

"The grid is overworked," O'Donnell said. "With everything going on, everyone's on their cells trying to get hold of loved ones and the cell towers can't handle it."

"People need to stop and let us get our calls through!" Cynda snapped. "Do they know who we are?"

"Are you fucking serious?" Ladeja blurted, already miffed by Cory's attitude. "You're just a bitch with money, Cynda. Your call to Thunda or your hairdresser or whoever else you're trying to reach isn't any more important than some random person's call to their spouse or child. Get over yourself, snap into reality for a moment and see what is actually going on!"

"I don't recall inviting you into my house," Cynda

responded, scrunching her nose as if she smelled something while she looked her over from head to foot. "I don't care whose mother you are. When you bring your ghetto ass into my home, you better know your place."

Ladeja lunged for the woman and managed to grab a fistful of hair before Manny grabbed her. He pulled her in one direction while O'Donnell pulled Cynda in the other. Ladeja yanked on Cynda's hair, trying to pull her in closer to deliver a solid punch while Cynda screamed and swatted her hands like she was trying to take out a fly. Cory yelled at her to stop, taking Cynda's side, while everyone else enjoyed the show.

"Hey, everybody!" Chelle yelled. "They're saying something about the studio Thunda was filming at!"

Ladeja let go of Cynda's hair and straightened herself up so Manny would let her go. He loosened his grip but still kept his hand on her back as they turned toward the giant flat screen television nearly taking up the far wall.

"What did they say?" Cory asked, joining Chelle on the couch. He leaned forward, elbows on knees, watching the news with more enthusiasm than he'd watched any of the Marvel movies.

Chelle used the remote to go back to the beginning of the clip.

"The North Hollywood Studios was overrun yesterday as the infected attacked, spreading the disease. We do not know how the incident started, but we do know the entire studio was cleared as chaos erupted. The footage you see now was taken from the air and shows the sheer panic as the uninfected desperately ran for their lives."

They held their breath, watching as a video of people running out of the studio played. They saw a large group run out onto the back lot, screaming and trampling over anything in their way as they moved in a giant wave of panic.

"That's Dad!" Cory yelled, pointing to the screen. "That's him with Rex Miller right there with the cameras!"

"He's right," Ladeja said, peering closer. "They must have been in the middle of shooting on the back lot when this happened."

She gasped along with the others in the room as they saw Thunda and Rex Miller turn toward the crowd and get plowed down by them immediately after. No one said a word as they watched the enormous sea of people roll right over the spot they'd seen Thunda standing in. Ladeja looked at her son and saw his eyes grow wet. He shook his head silently, his jaw clenched.

Manny gripped her shoulder and looked down at her. She met his gaze, and they shared a look, both knowing how thin the chance was that Thunda had gotten swept up in the crowd and not just plain mowed over. They turned back to the television and held their breath as the last of the sizeable crowd poured out of the building. As they ran off screen, the camera panned away toward the studio where a smaller group of people stumbled out, their jerky motions identifying them as infected. They were just barely able to see a pair of legs lying at an awkward angle on the ground where Thunda and Rex Miller had been. Both had been wearing all black, so it wasn't definite which person they'd seen laying there, trampled to death by the crowd, but there was no doubt in her mind that the man who'd given her the best gift in the world before crushing her heart and leaving her alone to raise that gift had left the world.

"That wasn't him," Cory said adamantly, shaking his head as Cynda wailed, falling to her knees behind the sectional. "He's tough. He ran with them. Twice that many people couldn't have knocked him over. He's Thunda Carter!"

Ladeja sat beside him on the sectional and reached out to hug him. "Baby—"

"No!" Cory shoved her off of him and stood, stepping over to where the television hung on the wall before turning to address her. "You want him dead. You want him dead because he has fame and money and all the things you don't have. You want him dead because you're jealous! My daddy ain't dead! He's coming here and I'm gonna be right here when he makes it. I ain't going any damn where with you!"

Manny made a move toward him.

"Manny, stop! He's my child!"

"Does he know that?" Manny asked, nostrils flaring. "You better do something with this boy. He keeps talking like he thinks he's a grown man, I'm gonna show him something."

"My father will show you something, you ghetto loser," Cory yelled. "Do you know who I am? You a grown man and can't get on my level!"

"Ghetto loser?" Manny laughed. "C-Dawg? What the hell is that but a fake-ass thug name for a fake-ass thug wannabe? You're soft, little boy. Don't start shit you can't finish and you better start respecting your mom because she's all you got. Your daddy—" Manny snapped his mouth shut, growling instead of finishing what he wanted to say.

"My daddy what?"

His daddy got squished. Ladeja knew what Manny wanted to say. She wanted to say it too. Hell, maybe a small part of her was happy Thunda was gone after all he'd put her through, but she couldn't say something like that to her son and purposely hurt him, no matter how badly his words had stabbed her right in her heart.

"Your father is gone, Cory," she said instead, calmly, and with sympathy. "Even if he survived getting trampled over, he wouldn't have gotten away from the infected afterward. He's gone, and it's awful and I'm sorry you have to feel this loss so young. I'm sorrier you saw that, but I can't make it not true. Your father is gone, and this is not your home. You're my son and you belong with me."

"I don't want to go with you. I like it here. I have my

own basketball court."

Ladeja laughed in disbelief, amazed at the level of his selfishness. "Cory, do you not understand what has happened? A virus has been unleashed on the whole country. Infected people are everywhere and they are eating people, Cory, *eating people*! If they catch you and you're not lucky enough to die, you get sick too, and then you try to kill everyone around you. There are sick people all over just trying to eat you alive and you're worried about leaving a basketball court? If we're lucky enough to survive this mess, you're not going to play basketball for a long damn time."

"If it's that bad out there, why would you take me out into it?" he asked. "You can't tell me this house isn't safer than yours. You can fit your whole apartment in less than a wing of this one, and there's security. What are you and this dude you just picked up from somewhere going to do to protect me that's better than professional security?"

Gunshots sounded from the front of the property and a voice came through O'Donnell's radio. "We got incoming! A couple dozen infected moving onto the property and it looks like a second wave coming in after!"

"They're on the property," O'Donnell announced. "It sounds like it's a lot. You're not safe down here with that foyer door busted open. Women and children upstairs. Men, we hold them off down here. You got enough ammo, Manny?"

"I could use some more."

"I got ya. Chelle, get everybody to the library upstairs. Move, now!"

Ladeja grabbed Mateo's hand and reached out for Cory. He sidestepped her, but she was thankful he at least followed Chelle. As long as she could keep him safe now, she'd take all the attitude he could throw her way until she actually had time to straighten him out, and she was afraid it was going to take a great deal of that.

They climbed a tall spiral staircase to the second floor and hurried down the hallway to a set of mahogany double doors. Chelle threw them open and stepped aside as everyone entered. Cynda delivered serious side eye as she walked past Ladeja, completely ignoring Cory. Her eyes were red from her crying fit, but her dislike of Ladeja seemed to have stopped the flow of her tears.

The room was immense, with mahogany paneled walls which were lined with shelves of books. White and gold sofas and chaises were spaced throughout the room to provide comfortable places for reading, and a white and gold bar took up a corner. The floor was white and gold tile that looked incredibly real to Ladeja, as did the gold-leaf design in the frame holding the floor to ceiling painting of the family taking up the center of the wall in between two bay windows parallel to the doors. All the gold accents in the room looked real, and she would be more surprised if they were not.

The Camilleri family was loaded. Giovanni Camilleri had been a prominent attorney who regularly represented very high-profile sports stars and others in the entertainment industry. A Hollywood sex scandal case had thrown the whole family into the spotlight and, as the girls aged, their own scandalous behavior ensured they never fell out of the public eye. Cynda held the most star power thanks to her beautiful face and body (which included a nose job, lip injections, and butt implants she denied having along with who-knew-what-else) and a sex tape that had been "leaked" to the media. Cheyanne had been mostly ignored by the media because they did not deem her as beautiful and she had weight issues, but she'd dropped the pounds and was the brains behind the family's fashion and fragrance lines. Cara was a very thin, snotty supermodel and then there was Chelle, the baby of the bunch who'd had so much plastic surgery in her teens in order to compete with her plastic-enhanced sisters that a before and after photo of her no longer even looked like the same person. They all went through celebrity men pretty quickly, mostly rappers and athletes, and didn't appear to have a non-selfish thought in their overly made up heads. And Thunda had made one of them his wife instead of her, the mother of his child, the woman who'd had his back when he didn't have a damn thing but talent and a dream.

Chelle closed the doors after everyone had entered and turned the lock before pattering across the floor in her pink velour tracksuit and fuzzy slippers to take a post by one of the windows. Cynda and Cheyanne had already taken seats in the other one. Cara had plopped down on one of the sofas and grabbed a fashion magazine off the gold accented mahogany table in front of it, leaving Ladeja and the boys to themselves.

Ladeja turned to assure the boys everything would be all right, but Cory left her to sit in the bay window with Chelle. The teen looked his way but said nothing, quickly going back to watching out the window as she chewed on her plump bottom lip. Of all the sisters, she seemed to be the only one scared. Cynda switched between pouting and shooting darts with her eyes as Cheyanne comforted her and Cara seemed completely oblivious to reality.

"Do you want to take a look at the books?" Ladeja asked Mateo, thinking it best to get the child's mind off of the situation or at least offer him some sort of outlet from thinking about all that he had just lost.

He shook his head. "How long do you think we will be in here?"

"I don't know." She guided him to a sofa and sat next to him. "There's what, five security guards out there, plus Manny?"

Mateo nodded.

"That's a lot of bullets between them. They should be able to take care of the infected pretty quickly and after that, we can leave. Manny has a really big truck parked right out in front of the front doors. All we have to do is jump in it."

"Do you think they'll make it?"

Ladeja swallowed, taking the moment to gather herself. She'd be lying if she said she wasn't afraid the infected would be too much and they'd lose Manny and the security guards, and get stuck inside the mansion with four twits she could not imagine being any more useless in the current situation, but she was not about to share that fear with a kid who hadn't even had time to truly come to grips with his mother's death yet.

The sound of gunfire erupted from outside and Ladeja pulled the boy in to her side as she scanned the room for anything she could use as a weapon in case the infected made it past the guards, soon realizing she would have to be extremely creative, not to mention lucky, if they did.

"They'll make it," she said. "They have to."

3

Misty pulled her knees to her chin and cried, her tears mixing with the water raining down all over her from the showerhead. She didn't feel the cold tile under her at all, nor did the hot water fogging up the surrounding glass do anything to thaw out her body. She considered getting out of the shower and using the large corner bathtub instead. It was deep, deep enough for her to slide down beneath the surface and see if it could warm her. If not, she only had her miserable life to lose.

How could she have been so stupid? So desperate? Had it even been rape?

She replayed the events of the night through her mind, as much as she could remember of it, anyway. She'd met Justain in his office and not even five minutes in to the meeting she'd unbuttoned the top four buttons of her shirt, providing him a clear view of her abundant cleavage. He'd smiled appreciatively, maybe a bit wickedly, before starting up his spiel about how far he could take her, dropping names of actresses he'd launched into superstardom left and right. Then he'd told her about the women he'd tried to help but they'd shot themselves in the foot thinking they were good enough on their own. He told her he could see it in her eyes that she was hungry for the fame and fortune and as long as she trusted him he would take her places she'd never dreamed of.

She hadn't thought twice about it when he'd suggested they continue their meeting over dinner, not even when that dinner turned out to be in his hotel room. It was an executive suite, after all. She thought it a bit odd the man would have a hotel room in the same city he had an office and apparently lived in, but what did she know about the rich and famous? She was still trying to become one.

They'd dined at a small table lit by candlelight, but he'd made no overt advances toward her as they discussed the script. As they continued the meal, he'd repeatedly topped off her wineglass.

"I'm really not a big drinker," she'd said, covering the glass with her hand as he'd started to top it off the fourth time.

"This is a very expensive bottle," he'd advised her. "I will be offended if you do not share it with me."

She'd started to point out that he was still on his first glass and it seemed she was going far beyond sharing. She was being forced to hog it all, but she hadn't wanted to offend him. She continued to drink and restrained herself from saying anything as her glass kept refilling. Eventually, all the wine made its presence known in her bladder and she'd had to excuse herself.

"Stupid idiot," Misty chastised herself as she recalled coming out of the bathroom to a freshly topped off glass from their second bottle of wine. Justain had all but shoved the glass into her hand and watched her intensely as she drank. It had tasted a little different, and seemed to go straight to her head, but she'd thought it was just because of all she'd had previously.

"You look tired," Justain had said. "I've kept you up too late."

"No, it's not…" She'd raised her wrist to look at her watch, but the numbers had seemed to duplicate.

"You should stay the night."

Alarm bells had finally rung in her inebriated head. "No, no. Thank you for the dinner. I should leave now."

She'd stood to leave but found her legs wobbled. She'd gripped the edge of the table to keep from falling as her head grew incredibly light.

"Nonsense."

Justain had left the table. Misty turned her head to see he'd opened the double doors that separated the bedroom area from the rest of the suite. She saw a king-sized bed covered in red rose petals.

"No," she'd whispered as her uncle's face flashed through her mind. She saw him over her, panting breathlessly as his sweat dripped onto her and bile threatened to rise in her throat. She'd swallowed hard past her growing panic as the memory cleared and Justain closed in on her. "No!" she'd yelled, louder.

The next thing she remembered was waking up in the hotel room bed, completely naked and aching between her legs. Her vision swam for several minutes as she struggled to figure out where she was and why she had no clothes on. She never slept naked.

The alarm clock on the nightstand told her it was afternoon. The nausea in her stomach and the pain in her head told her she was hungover.

The naked man sleeping next to her in the bed was a damn good indicator something horrible had happened.

She'd grabbed her clothes and purse, and ran for the bathroom, locking herself in before running the shower as hot as she could get it without boiling her skin off. Even that was stupid. She should have left while he was asleep. What was she supposed to do now? How could she face him? No one would believe her if she accused him of rape, and even worse, she'd never work in Hollywood again. All she had was her face and body, and the nude layout had been a stepping stone to something great, not a place she planned on being stuck at. She could act. Hell, if Kristen Stewart could become rich and famous, so could she. But not if she blackballed herself by accusing one of the top producers of a crime.

"It happened. It's over now. I'm alive. It's no big deal," she told herself as she rocked back and forth under the shower spray. "If I lose everything, he wins. I won't lose. I refuse to lose. I'm stronger than this."

Misty turned off the water and stepped out of the shower. She quickly toweled dry and pulled on her clothing from the previous night. She glanced at the hairdryer but nixed it. There was a chance the pig who'd assaulted her could still be sleeping and if so, she didn't want to do anything that might wake him. She roughly towel-dried her hair and ran her fingers through the damp locks. She applied deodorant and lipstick, both found within her purse, and took a deep breath. All she had to do was make it out of the hotel.

With her hand wrapped around the doorknob, she closed her eyes, squared her shoulders, and summoned all the strength she could muster.

"I'm strong," she told herself as she opened her eyes and twisted the knob.

The swine was still sleeping, flat on his back with his jelly-like belly hanging out, snoring loud enough to wake the dead. The urge to grab the pen on the nearby nightstand and stab him through the heart seized Misty. She'd taken three steps toward it before shaking herself out of the wicked fantasy. No, the damage had already been done. It was over and she was alive. She nodded to herself. She was fine. She was a survivor. No one, not even the all-powerful Harry Justain, could break her.

She left the bedroom, leaving behind the sickening smell of scattered rose petals cloying in her throat. She cringed, realizing she'd never be able to see a rose again without also seeing horrible images of Harry Justain violating her. Since she couldn't actually remember the incident, her imagination would more than likely make it a hundred times worse.

"I'll survive," she promised herself as she opened the door and escaped the suite without having to face Justain. Thankful for small miracles, she breathed a sigh of relief and quickened her step. All she had to do was make it to the elevator around the corner, take it down twelve floors, and she was free. If she didn't have any trouble hailing a cab and traffic wasn't bad, she'd be back at her tiny little apartment within the hour and then she'd call her agent. Pam would know what to do.

Misty turned the corner and froze, her brain working overtime to comprehend what she was seeing. Once she comprehended there was a man on the floor surrounded by a group of people currently eating his innards from a massive cavity in his chest and the feet of another stuck out from an open door, she screamed. She realized her mistake as the cannibal-like people, men and women, all pale with milky white eyes, looked up at her.

"Oh shit." She turned and ran, but there was nowhere to run except back into the lair of the devil. There were only two suites on the thirteenth floor and it appeared the occupants of the second one were dead in the hallway, the door to the suite blocked by them and their murderers, who also blocked the elevator.

The sick people rounded the corner, shambling toward her. One opened its mouth and bloody chunks of she-didn't-want-to-know-what fell out, hitting the floor with a sickening thud.

With nowhere else to run, she pounded on Justain's door, screaming as they closed in. "Justain!!! Let me in! Let me in!"

The door finally opened as one of the pale people

reached for her and she leaped inside, knocking Justain on his ass as she turned and slammed the door, or tried to. The people who'd killed the other occupants on the floor pushed against the door.

"What the hell is going on?" Justain asked, surly.

"Help me lock this door or we're going to die," Misty yelled at him.

He opened his mouth to say something but stopped, blinking as he looked at her. As quickly as the large man could, he got to his feet and slammed into the door with his shoulder.

Misty slid the extra security latch despite the hotel door's automatic locking feature and backed away until she reached the middle of the room, desperate to space herself from the thuds opposite the door and the wicked man she'd chosen to lock herself inside with.

"What's going on?" Justain asked, tightening the sash on his silk robe.

"Walking Dead, Resident Evil, take your pick," Misty answered as she searched the television remote.

"What?"

"Zombies!" she clarified, shoving her hand between the sofa cushions and retrieving the remote. She turned the television on to see an emergency news broadcast. A video of sick people ripping other people apart in the street played as a voiceover advised everyone listening to seek shelter away from people and wait for help.

"That's happening outside?" Justain's eyes widened as he looked at the bloody images on the screen.

"It's happening out there." Misty tilted her head toward the door just as a particularly large thud made it shake. "It isn't safe here."

Justain picked up the hotel phone and held the receiver to his ear.

"What are you doing?"

"Calling for security."

Misty rolled her eyes as he stood there, waiting for someone to pick up, muttering under his breath when they didn't. Not only was she stuck in the suite with a rapist, but he was a moron too. A rich, overly entitled moron who expected to be able to pick up a phone and boss the right worker bees around to save his ass.

"The entire hotel staff is probably dead," she advised him, looking around the room for a way out.

He cursed, slamming down the phone. "Then we're stuck here until help comes."

"What if it doesn't?"

"Do you know how important I am? Heads will roll if I'm not out of here soon."

"Yeah, ours." She walked over to the balcony and pulled open the doors before stepping outside. The streets were barren of vehicles except for those parked along the curb, which made sense given the news footage clearly showed people were fleeing the city.

Another loud thud cracked the door.

"Fuck, they're going to get in," Justain cried, his voice elevating with fear.

"Let them," Misty said. "I don't know about you, but I won't be here."

"Where are you going to go?"

"Down there," she said, looking at the ground thirteen floors below them as another thud widened the crack and popped a hinge off the door.

Mike expelled every curse word he knew as he ran down the alley, doing his best to press on despite the sharp stitch in his side. He had no idea how long he'd been running since all hell had broken loose at the studio. Taking a second to glance at his watch could be all the time the infected needed to finally get him.

He yanked on every backdoor he passed, finding them

all locked. He'd taken the metro to the studio, which had left him without transportation, not that he even thought he could have made it to his car had he driven. Once he'd reached the studio back lot, he'd been forced to follow the flow of the crowd. He'd seen those who'd tried to move against it get trampled over by people too terrified to care who they had to stomp on to get away.

He tried another door, growled out an epithet when it didn't give, and glanced over his shoulder. What had started as five infected people had grown to a crowd of twenty or more, as others had stumbled out of alleys and side streets to join those already following him. They didn't run, so he'd been able to keep a good distance between them and himself, only running into real trouble when one stumbled out of a hiding place close to him. His side was hurting like a bitch now and he was slowing down, tired, so the gap between him and them was lessening.

He just wanted to get inside somewhere, but all the doors he passed were locked up. He rethought his idea of sticking to the back alleys and veered left when a side alley came up, hoping he'd have better luck with a front door. Surely not all the businesses had been locked up. Even if everyone had closed up shop when shit started hitting the fan, surely someone somewhere had run out in a panic, leaving a building unlocked. He just had to get into someplace where he could rest safely and figure out his next move.

He jogged up the side alley, too damn tired to run, and his heart plummeted as he looked ahead to the main street and didn't see a single car driving by. Catching a ride could have really helped him out. At the rate he was going, he'd be happy to come across an unlocked bike. He didn't give a crap if it had ribbons on the handles and Barbie stickers as long as he could move faster than a walk without pain stabbing his side.

Something lunged at him as he passed a Dumpster. He twisted in time to register that it was an infected man who appeared to be about in his forties with thinning hair and a spray-on tan so dark he wasn't nearly as pale as the other infected people Mike had seen. If not for the cloudy eyes, Mike might have taken too long to recognize he was sick. Fortunately, he had recognized it in time to grab the man's arms as the two of them fell to the ground.

He twisted so he landed on his back and stretched his neck forward to keep the back of his head from connecting with the concrete hard enough to seriously injure him. He didn't have time to see stars with the groaning man snapping his teeth right above his face in an attempt to take a bite out of him.

The man smelled like piss and half a bajillion buckets of body odor and that wasn't half as bad as the stench coming out of his mouth, but Mike was more concerned with the sharpness of the teeth trying to clamp onto him than the smell threatening to overpower and kill his olfactory senses.

"How the fuck is this taking so much effort, you undead son-of-a-bitch?" Mike asked between clenched teeth as he pushed his biceps to the max, growling as he finally shoved the man off of him. He quickly rolled away to gain some distance and found a long piece of thin metal. He had no idea what it had once been part of, but it was solid and the broken end was jagged enough to work like a knife.

He snatched up the metal and turned just in time to see the infected man had gotten to his feet again and was almost on him. Working purely on reflex, he rammed the piece of metal through the man's neck, angling it upward before kicking the guy in the gut hard enough to send him falling backward.

He turned and ran before the guy could get back up, pretty sure the damned bastard was still moving, and before the infected pouring into the end of the alley could get to him. The stitch in his side immediately made itself known, but he ran through the pain until he came out on the main street.

He didn't see a single car traveling on the street, but he saw some parked along the curb. None of them included drivers, so unless he could find someone who knew how to hotwire, they didn't do him any good.

He turned to make his way down the street and start trying front doors when he caught sight of a shapely blonde dangling from the end of what looked like multiple sheets tied together. She appeared to have tied them together before tying one end around the bottom of a balcony rail on the fifth floor and then climbed down the makeshift rope until she reached the bottom, which had ended around the second floor. The drop would be survivable, but with the heels she wore, she'd definitely break an ankle. Above her, a familiar-looking man in a bathrobe was just reaching the balcony where the sheet-rope started, having climbed down from a higher floor.

Mike glanced back down the alley and felt his balls draw up inside his body as he saw how much ground the infected had gained, including the one with the broken piece of metal lodged in its throat. He could run now and escape.

He looked back at the woman dangling from the sheet like a perfect snack for the monsters that would be on her soon enough. The blood he saw dripping from her arm, staining her blouse, would probably make them even more frenzied with hunger. He remembered the people he'd seen trampled at the studio and the guilt of not being able to stop and help them punched him in the gut.

"Damn it to hell," he muttered before running over to the woman. "Hey!"

She twisted, her eyes widening in surprise as she saw him approach.

"Don't let go! You'll break an ankle, if not worse than that. I'll help you!" He stopped under her and reached for her as he looked up, immediately regretting it. Looking up at her meant he was also looking up at the man now climbing down the sheet-rope in his bathrobe, nothing but his bathrobe, which from that angle did nothing to cover parts of him Mike was afraid he'd never be able to scrub the visual of out of his brain.

He placed his hands on her lower legs, as far as he could reach, and braced himself. "Let go."

She released her grip and fell. Mike managed to catch her about her hips, her stomach in his face, before stumbling back, but he righted himself and was able to stand her on the sidewalk without incident.

"Oh, thank you. I thought I could jump, but it was so scary once I got to the bottom," she exclaimed. "Oh! Hey! You're Steven Yeun! I love you!"

"I wish I was Steven Yeun," he grumbled, turning to see the first of the infected exit the side alley. He grabbed the woman's hand and started running. "We gotta go!"

"Hey!" the man in the bathrobe yelled.

"Climb back up to the balcony!" Mike yelled over his shoulder as he kept running. "There's no time!"

"Where are we going?" the blonde asked, struggling to run in the damn heels.

"Hell if I know. I've been running and hiding since last night, and haven't come across one unlocked door so I can get inside." He scanned the street, checking his options. Obviously, the hotel the woman had to climb out of wasn't a good prospect, and he didn't know if the others along the street would be. Lots of rooms with lots of tourists probably meant lots of infected people. The other buildings were restaurants, souvenir shops, and a car museum across the street. With mostly hotels on the side of the street they were on and an entry point to the metro that he didn't want to go near, Mike decided to cross the street.

"There's so many!" the blonde cried as he tugged her across the street.

"Yeah, I know." He yanked on doors as he zipped past buildings as fast as he could. Most of the infected had stopped under the sheet-rope the robed man was struggling to climb back up, but some were spilling onto the street, crossing it to chase them. Finally, a door opened. Mike pumped his fist in celebration and pulled the woman through before closing the door and locking it. It was glass which didn't give him the most secure feeling, but he was finally inside somewhere.

That somewhere was the car museum and from first glance it appeared empty with no one at the front desk, not that Mike expected to find an employee there charging admission. Not sure whether the infected people were smart enough to actually think or were just going after anything they could see or hear, he decided it best to get out of sight of the street before they reached the museum front and the wide expanse of glass that they could possibly shatter in effort to get to him.

"Keep your eyes open," he told the woman quietly as he walked beyond the lobby and into the exhibit area.

The museum housed several cars used in movies or owned by the rich and famous. The lighting was done in a way that highlighted the vehicles and, unfortunately, created a lot of dark corners anything could hide in. The red carpet beneath their feet softened their steps, as it would the steps of any infected people if they were inside.

"Do you think we're alone in here?" the blonde whispered.

"Maybe. Hopefully." Mike glanced sideways at her. She looked familiar, but then again, she did have the classic Hollywood look. Blonde hair, big breasts, tiny waist, long legs. She didn't wear a ton of makeup, but she also didn't look like she'd spent much time putting herself together that morning. Since he'd found her dangling from bedsheets tied around a hotel balcony rail, it made sense she'd had to get out before preparing herself for the day. She wasn't an actress he recognized, but he'd seen her somewhere. He thought about models and it clicked. "Misty Waters?"

Her eyes widened. "You know who I am."

He nodded. "Saw you on Entertainment Tonight."

Her cheeks reddened. "And you're not Steven Yeun?"

"Wrong Asian," he said, grinning.

"I'm sorry."

"It happens a lot." He shrugged. "At least you confused me with another Korean. I'm Mike Rha. I was in that less popular show about the walking dead, *Horror High*."

"I knew it!" She smiled. "I knew who you were. I just got the name wrong."

They turned a corner and Mike bumped into a menacing-looking man in shades and a dark suit. He yelped and jumped back. Misty gasped, too scared to scream, as her nails dug into his shoulders from behind.

A whole group of similarly dressed men stood around a Lincoln Continental, and every one of them was made of wax. Mike bent over, laughing.

"They're fake?"

"Yeah. They're supposed to be the secret service," he said, reading the nearby placard. "They used this in Reagan's inauguration."

"That nearly scared me to death."

"Yeah, me too." He straightened and swiveled his head, seeing nothing but vehicles. He eyed a small tour bus that had belonged to a rapper who'd been killed in a drive-by. "I think we're safe in here. We need to find an employee or manager area and see if there's a first aid kit for your arm. What happened to it?"

"I was on the thirteenth floor and so were they. I

couldn't get to the elevator or a stairwell because they blocked the way and I couldn't hide in the room because they were breaking through the door. My only option was to climb down the balconies. When I reached the fifth floor balcony, there was no balcony below because of the hotel design. The balconies to the side were spaced too far for me to risk a jump over, so I broke the glass on that balcony door to get in to the room and cut my arm in the process. Before you ask, I'm pretty sure there were infected people on the fifth floor as well. I heard screaming in the hall and chose not to risk trying to get out that way. I pulled the sheets off the beds and made a rope to climb the rest of the way down to the street, or as far as the rope would get me."

Mike eyed her shoes as they took a turn back in the direction of the entrance, keeping a lookout for any doors that looked like they could lead to employee only areas. "You climbed down seven floors in heels?"

"A girl's gotta do what a girl's gotta do." She shrugged. "Had I expected the zombie apocalypse, I would have worn my gym shoes. I'd seen something on the news about it right before going into a meeting, but didn't think too much of it. I should have."

"Yeah. I was getting makeup done for a scene and saw a news clip. I was too concerned with knocking my scene out of the park and lining up the next gig." He remembered all the messages on his cell phone from his worried parents. "I lost my phone while rushing out of the studio. I really need to let my parents know I'm fine. They're probably going nuts right now wondering where I'm at, especially if news got out about the studio. I saw news helicopters flying over."

"I left everything in the hotel, including my keys, so even if I can manage to get back to my apartment alive, I can't get into it."

"Same here. Everything happened so fast. We were just

running for our lives."

"You said you've been running since yesterday?"

"Yeah. The studio was invaded, for lack of a better word, right before nightfall. Everyone was running for their lives. I don't even know how I split away from the crowd or where everyone else went. I just heard so much screaming and knew not everyone was going to make it, so I cut off from them the soonest I could and I just ran, looking for a place to hide. When I absolutely had to take a breather I'd find a deserted alley, climb on top of a Dumpster or a car, but I don't think I ever got more than twenty minutes of rest before I'd see another infected stumble out of somewhere and I was off again."

"You have to be exhausted."

"You have no idea. I'm running on pure adrenaline right now. I can't move faster than a walk anymore without pain stabbing my side and I think I could eat a sewer rat if it were offered to me. Don't even get me started on what I'd do for water."

"Do you think we'll find food or water in here?"

"Maybe in an employee break room, or in that gift shop that was across from the front desk when we came in. Right now, we need to get you patched up and then rest. We can look for food in the restaurants, bust out windows if we have to, but I have to give my body a breather before I try to go back out there. I'm not going to be any good if I can't even run. One of those bastards almost got me right before I saw you. I had the damnedest time fighting him off."

"Look!" Misty pointed as they rounded a corner and saw a door with a STAFF ONLY sign.

"Eureka!" Mike quickened his step and pushed through the door, elated to see a refrigerator, sink, and microwave. The break room also included a snack machine, drink machine, and a telephone hanging on the wall with a sign advising a five-minute talk time limit.

Before he could eat or drink anything, he had to take care of his new partner. He led her to the sink area and checked the cabinets there until he found a first aid kit. "I knew there'd be one."

"Maybe you should get a quick drink of water first."

"You're bleeding. You're top priority," he said, surprised by her suggestion. Most women he'd met in Hollywood would see a man dying of thirst and instead of offering him a drink, they would order him to get their car or, worse yet, bring them a beverage.

Blood had seeped through most of the torn blouse sleeve, so Mike used the scissors he found in the kit to cut the sleeve off. "Sorry."

"It was already ruined."

"A lot of women in this city would scream their heads off if someone cut their clothes, even if they were already torn and stained."

"I've only had a few guest spots on sitcoms and one really huge layout. Give me some time and some bigger paychecks and I'll try my best to wear that diva crown."

Mike laughed with her, but they both quickly sobered.

"Do you think we're going to be okay?"

"I want to say yes," he answered. "I don't really know what exactly is going on though. I don't understand how this virus has spread so fast here or how far it's reached. I haven't seen a single police car or ambulance since the studio incident yesterday. That seems really fucked up."

"Do you think that still works?" Misty nodded toward the TV mounted to the wall on the opposite side of the breakroom.

"Rinse the blood off," Mike instructed, turning on the water faucet, relieved to see the water still ran before he turned and crossed the room. He picked the TV remote up from one of the three tables in the center of the room and hit the power button.

The TV came on and he saw clips of infected people

attacking people stranded in their cars in traffic jams. A red message ran along the bottom of the screen urging people to stay inside, stay quiet, and wait for further instruction.

"That clip you just saw is from the expressway leading to a rescue site set up by the military to take in healthy people trying to escape the clutches of this deadly virus," the news anchor, a brunette woman with dark bags under her eyes said. "At this time, the military has released a statement urging people to not travel to the site in Modesto. The routes leading to the base are not clear. The rescue site set up at Fort Huachuca in Arizona is still operating, as are the sites which you can see at the bottom of the screen."

Mike checked the sites, his heart sinking as he realized the closest one was Fort Huachuca. Without a vehicle, he'd be damned lucky to survive even a three-block walk in all the madness.

"How's that arm looking?" he asked, walking back over to Misty to inspect the damage.

"Not as bad without the blood."

He washed his hands before turning the faucet off and dried them on a paper towel before dabbing her wound dry. She was right. Without all the blood, it wasn't as severe as he'd thought. It was mostly just a scratch, but the glass had gone in deep in the center of the cut and that was where most of the blood had gushed from. It definitely wasn't a bite mark, which he'd been worried about in the back of his mind. Hell, he wouldn't blame someone for lying about getting bitten if they thought their other option was to face this shit alone, but he would have had to have left her on her own if there was even the slightest imprint of teeth marks on her. The thought of facing what was out there alone reminded him of the man.

"Did you know that man climbing down the balcony?" he asked as he wiped the cut with an alcohol pad. "He looked familiar, but I can't place him. Granted, I think I got a better look at his ass than his face."

Misty winced as the alcohol hit her wound. "I was too worried about making it out safe to care about who was up above me. Honestly, I was terrified to look up and see one of them climbing down to me."

"I don't think they can." He applied ointment to the cut and started wrapping the bandage around tight. "They don't really run. It's more of a shuffle that quickens a bit when they see prey."

"Prey?"

"Us." He shrugged. "It's what we are to them. I found that out pretty quick. The virus does something to their eyes, makes them really cloudy. Cataracts or something. They can see, but I'm not sure how well. I think they can hear."

"Why wouldn't they be able to see and hear? They're still people, aren't they?"

"I don't think so." Mike finished bandaging her injury and removed a couple packets of Tylenol before closing the kit. "I hate to say it, but I think those things out there really are zombies."

"Zombies? Like… *The Walking Dead*? I mean, I called them as much myself, but… is it possible?"

"Well, this all started with a virus and those infected are dying and getting back up and eating people, so yeah, I'd say very much the same thing." He walked over to the refrigerator and opened the door.

"Is there food?"

"Looks like some leftover pizza, macaroni, some sandwiches, and cupcakes. There's also this apple juice." He pulled out the half gallon bottle and grabbed a couple of paper cups by the coffeemaker. "We both should take some Tylenol, get a quick bite, and get some rest. Maybe after we're rested up, that group of infected will be gone. Thankfully, they don't seem smart enough to wait outside the door for us. If they were really smart, we'd have heard glass breaking out front not long after we got inside."

"Thank goodness for dumb zombies," Misty muttered before ripping open a packet of Tylenol and handing the other one to Mike. She thanked him for the glass of apple juice and downed the two pain-reliever tabs before grabbing a cupcake from the refrigerator.

Mike swallowed down the Tylenol and grinned. "That's your idea of fuel?"

"It's my idea of comfort food. I definitely need to be comforted now." She sat at one of the tables and settled in to view the television, which was now just nonstop news programming, largely playing videos of different massacres with no new information.

Mike grabbed a sandwich out of the refrigerator, a plain ham and cheese on wheat bread, and set it next to her on the table before crossing over to the telephone. He read the sign and scoffed at the posted time limit. He was pretty sure nobody was going to say anything if he went over and, knowing his mother, it would take ten minutes just to calm her down after she heard his voice.

He picked up the receiver and dialed the number, thankful he'd memorized it. He couldn't begin to think of any of his friends' numbers since he'd just programmed them into his iPhone and had been spoiled by the ease of simply tapping their name to dial.

He braced himself for the inevitable shrieks of surprise and relief followed by worried tears that would assault his ears when his mother answered, but nothing happened. The phone didn't ring. He hung up and tried again with the same result. Nothing. Not even a dial tone.

"Damn it." He hung the phone up. "This phone doesn't work."

"I just saw something on the bottom of the screen about phone and internet outages in some areas."

"Too many people using them must have overpowered the grid." He sank down into the chair next to hers and took a bite out of the sandwich. It was bland and fell to his stomach like a block of lead, but he was so hungry he finished it in two more bites before letting out a huge yawn.

"You really need to sleep," Misty commented.

"Yeah, I was thinking of that tour bus."

Her eyes widened. "We can lock ourselves in too, in case something does get in here."

He nodded. "I can't imagine you're tired though. It's still pretty early in the day. I'll go nap. You should be fine, but just run to the tour bus if anything happens. I'll keep it unlocked just in case."

"No." She wolfed down the last bit of her cupcake before tossing the wrapper into the garbage can and snatched up a stack of magazines from a nearby counter. "I'll come with you. It's a tour bus, so there might be things to do while you're sleeping."

"I really think we're safe in the museum."

"I'd feel safer locked inside somewhere and I don't want to be alone." She held the magazines protectively to her chest.

"Okay." Mike turned the TV off. "Grab some food if you think you'll need it, or the juice. I'm going to try to take just a little nap."

"Get as much rest as you need." She grabbed the remaining cupcakes and the juice out of the fridge. "If we have to leave here soon, who knows where we'll wind up next and how long it will be? That news footage didn't give me much confidence."

Nodding his agreement, Mike walked to the door and poked his head out, scanning for any danger before he led her out onto the floor. Mike's conscience niggled at him as they started toward the tour bus and he stopped.

"What is it?" Misty asked, nearly running into him. She'd been following so close behind. The fact that her hands were full with cupcakes and magazines was probably the only thing keeping her from digging her nails into his shoulders to feel secure.

"That guy." Mike turned toward the entrance. "Stay right here. I'm just going to look out there and see if he made it."

"You can't leave me!"

He looked between her and the lobby he knew was just around the corner up ahead. "Stay with me then and be very quiet. If there's any of those things hanging around outside, we don't want to attract their attention. We were lucky enough that they didn't break in here after us."

"Exactly, which is why we should stay as far away from that lobby as we can, at least a couple more hours."

"What if it was you stranded out there?"

"What if he's an awful person? What if he deserves to be out there alone?"

Mike frowned, studying her. Her eyes had suddenly developed a sheen and her voice had gone up an octave. "Why would you think that? Did you talk to the man or see something?"

"I just, I mean…" She shrugged. "I'm just saying don't risk your life helping someone who might turn out to be a really bad person."

"Misty… You'd probably be dead right now if I thought like that." He turned and headed for the lobby, knowing she'd follow behind. She was too scared to do otherwise.

When he reached the corner he'd have to turn to enter the lobby, he held his breath and peeked around to the front door, knowing it was all glass and if any infected were out there looking in at that moment they could lose their safe spot. To his relief, he didn't see anyone at the door.

He quietly tiptoed into the lobby, crouched down, and crawled toward the door. Once he'd assured himself there was no one dangerous close enough to see him, he put his face to the glass and looked out at the hotel.

A small group of infected, or zombies, as he'd started to think of them, were still outside the hotel entrance, just under the bedsheets still hanging from the balcony. The man wasn't on it or on any of the balconies. To his relief, Mike didn't see any broken, bloody bodies on the ground either. To his dismay, he saw a balcony door open and a young girl step out to check the street, going back in after spotting the group of killers on the sidewalk beneath her.

"Hang in there, kid," he whispered. "Hold on until I figure out how to get to you."

He heard something to his right and turned to see Misty had wandered over to the gift shop and was stuffing candy into a tote bag bearing the museum logo. He looked back out onto the street, studying the hotel, and wondered how many survivors could remain behind all those windows. He remembered Misty telling him she'd heard screaming on the floor after she'd broken into one of the rooms and wondered how many infected people were in there with the survivors. The thought sent a cold chill down his spine, which grew downright icy as he recognized the balcony door she'd broken the glass out of and realized it was on the same floor as the room the young girl had stepped out of.

The man in the bathrobe stepped out of the room with the busted door, carefully stepping around broken glass and leaned over the railing. He must have made a sound because the zombies beneath grew agitated and starting reaching up for him.

Mike shook his head. Hopefully, the man wouldn't keep coming out and the infected bunch would leave. Then again, maybe he'd step out the same time as the young girl and then help her. That thought made Mike feel a little better about waiting to attempt a rescue. He was just too exhausted to be much help to them now. He hoped the pain in his side would be completely gone after a good rest and the zombies would move along while he slept.

"Do you see anything?" Misty asked, stepping out of the gift shop. She'd replaced her torn blouse with a black T-shirt featuring Elvis and one of his cars and had traded in her heels for fuzzy slippers that looked like Herbie the Love Bug. The tote appeared to be filled to capacity.

"The man survived. There's also a young girl in the hotel."

"With him?" Her eyes widened in shock. She almost looked scared.

"No, another room. If they can just be quiet, they should be fine until I can figure out a way to get them out. I need to rest up before I try plotting any escape routes." He nodded toward her fuzzy slippers as he stood and started across the lobby. "Nice duds."

"I figured I could probably run faster in these than heels," she explained as she followed him out of the lobby.

"Until a shard of glass goes through the bottom and slices your foot wide open. We definitely need to find you some good shoes as soon as possible." He led the way back to where they'd found the tour bus, thankful his wardrobe for the scene he'd been working on had consisted of jeans, a black T-shirt, and black LeBrons. He'd seen a lot of women in heels stumble on their way out of the studio and would be surprised if they'd made it off the back lot.

The tour bus door was open. It looked as if it had been set up so people could actually go inside and look around as part of their museum tour. Mike went in first, checking for any hidden dangers before giving Misty the okay. A living slash kitchen area sat behind the driver's seat. He saw an entertainment center fully set up with an Xbox and a TV set. Past that was a small bathroom followed by a section with bunk beds, two on each side of the bus, and the very back was a master bedroom with private bath. It took every ounce of willpower and shred of human decency he had to go back to the front and tell Misty it was all right for her to come in before just falling onto the master bed.

"Does the TV work?" she asked, setting her tote on the sofa in front of the entertainment center before plopping down and picking up the remote from the small table in front of her. She pressed a button, and the TV came to life, greeting them with more violent images of what was happening to people not lucky enough to be hidden away somewhere secure. "Awesome. It works. I'll keep it down so you can sleep."

Mike locked the door, tugging on it to make sure they were safe. "There are bunk beds and there's a big bed in the master bedroom. If —"

"Take the master bed." She waved him away as she kicked off the slippers and settled onto the sofa before pulling a candy bar out of the tote. "If I get tired, I'll take one of the bunks."

Too tired to argue with someone being generous, he nodded his head and left her to the TV and her tote of goodies. Once inside the master bedroom, he paused only long enough to close the sliding door, and fell face first onto the bed. He didn't bother taking his shoes off in case he was awakened by an intruder or some other danger and needed to run.

A hundred thoughts flooded his mind as he lay there. How bad was this thing going to get? Were his parents all right? Where was he going to go? What was the military doing? Why hadn't he seen any law enforcement? How many people had survived the incident at the studio? How long would it be before he could work again? Where did he know the man in the hotel from? Why did Misty seem adamant they shouldn't help him? Was the little girl still alive? How was he going to help them?

He drifted off on that thought and continued to dream

about the people in the hotel, horrible dreams where he saved them, only to watch them die right in front of him as he stood helpless to do anything to stop the monsters from eating them alive.

4

"I can't believe this shit," Justain muttered as he paced the hotel room floor. He'd tried to get someone on the phone for hours, but every time he tried to call from his cell, the call would drop immediately before it even rang. Every so often he looked out the balcony door to see if he could find anyone, but all he found were infected people down there making awful noise. He couldn't tell if it was a moan or more of a growl, maybe a groan. Whatever it was they were doing, it was awful. "Where's my assistant? Where's security? I'm firing everybody. Everybody's fucking fired!"

He was Harry Fucking Justain. How was it possible for him to be stuck in a hotel overrun by the diseased with nothing but his cell phone and a bathrobe with all the people he had at his disposal? Why had no one sent help for him? This was unacceptable and heads would roll once he was back in his office, starting with that piece of ass who'd just run off with the Asian, leaving him.

Did she really think she had any shot at making it in Hollywood now? Once he got through with her, she'd be lucky to get a commercial for herpes medication.

"Maybe they'll come back." He shook his head. It didn't matter. She'd left him. Him! Harry Justain! The audacity!

He sat down on the foot of the bed and watched the silent television. He'd heard screaming on the floor earlier and feared turning up the volume to hear what was being said. From what he could see, the infected savages were causing a lot of damage. The message running along the bottom of the screen kept repeating over and over to stay inside and wait for help. He had yet to see any of that. All he knew was that if he was stuck having to get himself out of the hotel and back to safety, there were a lot of people who were going to need help, starting with the blonde who'd ran out on him and the man who'd helped her.

"Is it over?" Mateo asked, his voice a shaky whisper after the gunfire stopped.

"I don't know," Ladeja answered, her arms wrapped protectively around the boy like she longed to wrap her arms around her son, but Cory didn't want her protection. He'd barely looked at her during the time they'd been locked inside the library, waiting for the security team to handle the threat outside. She couldn't help thinking this could be the last day of their lives and they were going to die with her son hating her, and for what reason? She wasn't as rich and famous as his father?

"Open the door!"

She jumped at the sound of O'Donnell's voice, but it was Cory who ran across the room to unlock and open the door just as O'Donnell reached it.

"Ladies, it's not safe here. I need you to hurry and dress in something sensible in case we lose the vehicles and have to run on foot."

"Where's Manny?" Ladeja asked, panic making her voice come out much higher-pitched than she intended, just as gunfire started up again.

"He's holding them back, but he can't do it for long." O'Donnell looked at the Camilleri women who'd had yet to make any effort to move. "I said get your shit! Jeans, sneakers, boots, put something normal on now!"

"Are you serious?" Cynda folded her arms. "There's a gaping hole in the foyer, the gate is down because the incompetent security team left their posts and you expect us to just leave our home open for invasion? Do you know how many creepy weirdos try to get on our property daily to swipe things? Do you know how much money is sitting here?"

"Fuck it." O'Donnell threw his hands in the air. "There's dead people getting up and walking and *eating* people. I'm not going to argue with you. Ladeja, get the kids and let's go. You crazy-ass celebrity bitches can try your luck with the foggy-eyed demons that'll be up here in a few. Screw you and this job."

Ladeja quickly gathered Mateo up and walked over to the door while the Camilleris stood slack-jawed and below them, gunfire continued to erupt.

"Hurry them up, O'Donnell!" Manny yelled from below. "They're coming up the stairs!"

"I'm going with them," Chelle said, rushing across the room and through the door.

"Whatever." Cara walked across the room, her face the same mask of boredom she'd been wearing since Ladeja had first arrived.

"Come on." Cheyanne pulled Cynda across the room by her arm. "You can't buy more stuff if you're dead. You can totally wear that cute pink camo outfit with the pink diamond-accented camo boots."

"Unfuckingbelievable," O'Donnell muttered as they passed him to enter their bedrooms down the hall. "You got two minutes, if that! Change quickly and don't be grabbing unnecessary shit!"

Cory ducked out the door and ran down the hall.

"Cory!" Ladeja started to run after him, but O'Donnell stopped her with an arm stretched out at chest level. "He's dressed all right for the trip. He's probably just grabbing something. Kids are sentimental about stuff."

"I could use some help!" Manny yelled, reaching the second floor.

O'Donnell removed his gun and leaned over the banister to shoot the infected people progressing up the staircase as Manny reloaded.

Ladeja eyed a set of swords hanging on the wall and reached up to remove one. "Are these real?" She pulled one free and nearly cut her foot off as the heavy blade immediately arced down to the floor, her arms not strong enough to support it. "Shit!"

"What the hell are you doing?" O'Donnell asked, glancing her way. "Can't wait for these bastards to kill you, you gotta do it yourself?"

"I thought I could help if I had a weapon." She let go of the hilt and let it clank to the floor. "How do they swing these so easily in movies?"

"For one, the ones in movies generally aren't real, and for two, neither are those. Pure decoration."

"Are they ready yet?" Manny yelled, backing completely onto the second floor. "We have to do this now!"

"Get your asses out here now!" O'Donnell yelled down the hall. "We got no time!"

"Stay here, Mateo!" Ladeja ordered as she saw Cory leave the room he'd disappeared into and cross over to the room across the hall. She ran into the room and found him rooting through a jewelry box, shoving bulky rings and chains into his pockets. He'd added a jacket to the baggy jeans and Nike T-shirt he'd already had on and was carrying a Nike backpack.

"What are you doing?"

"I'm taking Dad's jewelry." He glanced at her sideways

before taking another ring and crossing over to the bed to pick up the Grammy sitting on a shelf above the headboard.

"What do you need that for?" Ladeja asked, talking through the bile that rose in her throat, realizing she was in Thunda and Cynda's bedroom. The last thought she needed running through her mind was the two of them together.

"I'm not leaving his Grammy," Cory said, shoving the award into his backpack.

Cynda and Cheyanne stepped out of a room and stopped when they saw her, their eyes turning into narrow slits. Cynda wore skin-tight pink camo pants with pink diamond-accented combat style boots and a pink tank top that barely stretched across her ample chest. Cheyanne had traded in her clothes for tight jeans, a diamond studded T-shirt that spelled SEXY and blindingly white hi-tops Ladeja knew would be from some basketball star or rapper's line. Beyond them, she could see rows and rows of clothes and shoes and realized they had an entire room they used as a closet between their bedrooms.

"Why are you in my bedroom?"

"I'm getting my son," Ladeja answered, refusing to cower under the woman's snippy tone. "The infected are coming up the stairs. O'Donnell said we need to get out now."

Cynda pierced her with a dark look for another moment, then grabbed a Louis Vuitton purse off a dresser and started pouring jewelry into it.

"Seriously?" Ladeja rolled her eyes. If the woman wanted to risk her life over some jewels, let her. She grabbed Cory and turned for the door, tightening her grip around his arm when he tried to shrug her off. "Bring your ass on, boy. I don't have time to play with you right now. We're all going to die over some stupid shit if you don't come on!"

She pulled him into the hall and was surprised to see Chelle and Cara had emerged from their rooms, ready to go. Cara still looked as if she couldn't be bothered to care that they were all in a dangerous situation, but at least she'd changed into designer jeans and a black tank top. Her ankle boots weren't the best option in case they had to run on foot at some point, but at least they were a wedge heel. Chelle had changed into leggings and a fitted T-shirt with gym shoes. Even the gym attire the women in the family wore looked like it cost hundreds of dollars.

"Time's up!" Manny yelled.

"You led all of them up this way?" O'Donnell asked, quickly moving to his side.

"I think so. A few may have branched off, but we'll just have to deal with it if they did."

"Okay. Let's do this."

They worked together to pick up a large bust displayed on a pedestal near the top of the staircase and on the count of three, tossed it down the stairs sideways where it hit the first row of infected people coming up the stairs and caused them to fall into the others, creating a domino effect all the way down.

"Let's go now!" O'Donnell bellowed as they ran toward the end of the hall. "Cynda! Cheyanne! We will leave your asses here!"

The women stepped out of the bedroom just as the rest had reached it. Ladeja was confused why they had run to a dead end until O'Donnell opened a panel in the wall. "Manny, go first and provide cover if needed."

"Only if Ladeja and the boys go next," Manny said, his tone brooking no room for negotiation.

"That's fine. Hurry up before shit starts coming up those stairs again or our exit gets blocked."

"Hold on," Cynda said, incredulous, as Manny climbed into the wall and disappeared. "You want us to go down the laundry chute? Are you crazy?"

"Stay if you want," O'Donnell answered. "Those of us who want to live are going down the chute before this floor is crawling with infected. Boys, you're up. Ladeja, you go after them."

Cory started to climb in just as they heard a groan waft up from the stairs. Reacting to the threat, Cynda grabbed Cory's arm and pulled him back. "This is our house. We're going first!"

Ladeja's fist connected with Cynda's face before she could think about what she was doing. She regained her composure as Cynda's body hit the wall and the woman looked back at her bug-eyed while blood dripped out of her nose and her sisters stood by her side in shocked silence. "Touch my boy again, and I won't stop at one punch. Cory, get your ass down that chute."

"Shit," O'Donnell whispered in awe before shifting back to business, helping Mateo climb in after Cory. "Go, Ladeja."

She climbed in the wall as Cynda broke out into an ugly cry, and slid down the chute, landing softly in a bin full of clothes in the laundry room.

"What the hell is that?" Manny asked, looking up the chute as he helped her out of the bin.

"Ladeja punched Cynda in the face and now she's having a tantrum," Mateo explained the wailing sound, which grew louder as Cynda made her way down the chute.

Manny arched an eyebrow as he gave her a sideways glance.

"She deserved it," Ladeja defended herself.

"I'm sure she did. I'm actually surprised you were able to refrain from clocking her this long." He frowned, looking up the chute as her wail amplified, but she didn't pop out. "Where is she?"

They heard another scream, a cry of pain, and Cynda's legs came into view. It appeared she'd slid down sideways.

Manny grabbed the radio at his hip and pressed a button. "Don't send anyone else down, O'Donnell, until I give you the all-clear. This bimbo done got her fake ass wedged in there. I'm going to have to yank her out."

"Do we have time for this?" Ladeja asked. "O'Donnell acted like we had a very small window of time. What the hell happened down here?"

"I'll explain later," he said as he moved the bin out of the way and grabbed Cynda's ankles, squeezing tight when she tried to kick him away. "Quit kicking! I have to pull you out!"

He yanked, and she screamed bloody murder. "Stupid bitch is going to get us killed," he growled as he took a breath and yanked harder, the veins in his muscles bulging under the pressure. There was a loud pop, and she came free of the chute, quickly followed by Chelle, who'd been the unfortunate person to slide down after her and crash into the blockage her butt implants had caused.

They both fell onto the floor, but Chelle's fall was cushioned by Cynda, who grunted in pain and rolled over before lashing out, starting a slap fight with her sister.

"Clear," Manny said into the radio before placing the bin back under the chute and yanking Chelle up by her arm to place behind his body. He pointed at Cynda. "Stop or I'll tell Ladeja to knock your ass out."

Cynda opened her mouth to say something but looked at Ladeja and thought better of it, opting instead to walk to the corner of the room and pout.

Cheyanne came down the chute, moving a bit slower than the rest due to her thickness, followed by Cara and finally O'Donnell.

"Sound like anything came around this side?" O'Donnell asked as he climbed out of the bin.

"If they did, I couldn't hear over the sound of crying and screaming," Manny complained.

O'Donnell nodded his understanding, his eyes speaking

volumes about how he felt about his current employers. "I'll take lead. You cover the rear. Once we clear the house, get your girl and those kids to your truck and be ready to follow me out. If we don't make it, God be with ya, my friend."

"What do you mean if we don't make it?" Cheyanne asked loudly. "We're paying you to protect—"

"I just lost all my men because you stupid bitches wanted to throw a party, despite knowing a deadly virus was going around. These boys lost parents. I swear if you keep bitching, I'll leave your ass here. Do you spoiled princesses understand?"

"I lost my husband," Cynda reminded him, puffing her chest out indignantly.

"My daddy ain't dead," Cory said. "We didn't see him for sure."

"We don't have time for this," O'Donnell snapped. "Just stay alert and follow me. For chrissakes, keep your mouths shut."

He opened the door and peeked out, gun in hand, finger poised over the trigger. He stepped out and surveyed the room, his gun pointed out in front of him. After scanning left to right, he used one hand to place a finger to his lips, reminding them to stay silent, and then motioned them out.

The Camilleris exited the room first, huddled together, followed by Ladeja and the boys, with Manny bringing up the rear as instructed. O'Donnell led them through a large kitchen so shiny and spotless Ladeja wondered if it were there purely for looks, and out a door leading to the back lawn.

He waited until everyone exited the house, then started carefully walking the length of the house, toward the pool they'd passed earlier. He continued to scan the perimeter, as did Manny, but he seemed particularly focused on the busted glass door in the foyer they'd used for entering and exiting earlier.

His shoulders tensed as they neared it and he paused long enough to once again raise his finger to his lips, but this time he delivered the same warning with his eyes too. After fixing them all with the stern look of warning, he turned and continued to lead them.

Cynda gasped as she passed the foyer, her sisters following suit. They turned their faces away from whatever had startled them and Cara covered her mouth as if holding back bile. It was the first time Ladeja had seen any type of reaction out of the young woman.

Manny moved from the back to the side as they reached the foyer, angling his body so the boys couldn't see whatever it was in there that had startled the Camilleri family. Ladeja considered falling back to get a look, but the message Manny sent her with his eyes told her she really didn't want to know what it was.

He fell back behind them after they passed the foyer, and they continued on wordlessly. The bodies they'd previously discarded in the pool had floated to the top of the murky, blood-stained water. Cory looked at the pool in fascination while Mateo suddenly shifted his interest to his shoes, most likely the only place he felt he could safely look without seeing something that would haunt his nightmares. Ladeja reached over, placing her arm around his shoulders, and he moved in closer to her. The action warmed her heart and at the same time broke it. She wanted to hold her son close, but he shrugged her off every time she tried.

Ahead of them, O'Donnell rounded the corner of the mansion and cursed. "We're going to have to run for it. Camilleris, you're running with me to the SUV. Manny, wait for the infected to go after us and then get your people to your truck."

"Wait." Cynda held her hands up, palms out. "Why are they waiting for the infected to go after us? I know you're not using us as bait so they can get away safe."

"We can't go at the same time," O'Donnell said, his tone showing his frustration. "The SUV is farther away from the infected group on the lawn, so we're going first."

"Why can't they run for the SUV and we run for the truck once the infected are following them? I'm not sure you comprehend who's important here. We have like a hundred million Twitter and Instagram followers. Nobody even knows who this woman is."

"I'm the woman who punched you dead in your face about ten minutes ago and I'm about to again if you don't shut the hell up," Ladeja advised. "Listen to the man trying to save our lives. Nobody gives a shit about your social media stats!"

"Mom." Cory looked at her, disappointment etched into every inch of his face.

"What?"

"Do you have to act so ghetto?"

"Ghetto?" Ladeja looked back at him sideways, knowing damn well the child who wanted to be called C-Dawg wasn't complaining about her acting ghetto.

"They're headed this way," O'Donnell said. "I'm running to the SUV and whatever Camilleris aren't with me are going to be stuck here with them." He nodded his head in the direction the infected were coming from and ran, making a mad dash for the SUV.

"Come on!" Chelle cried as she took off after him, making her running shoes earn their expensive price tag. The remaining sisters looked at each other, expressions alternating between fear and stubbornness.

"Screw it. I'm not letting those nasty people near me." Cara shrugged and started running after Chelle and O'Donnell.

After a shared look of defeat, Cheyanne and Cynda followed O'Donnell's plan.

"About time," Manny muttered, stepping up to the

edge of the mansion and peeking around. He held his arm out when Ladeja tried to step up next to him and see what exactly they were running from. The corner of the house had been blocking her view.

A moment later she saw a group of people quickly walking, or shuffling to be more accurate, in the direction O'Donnell and the women had run, chasing them as they made their way to the SUV parked in the section of the driveway that looped past the main house and curved around a basketball court. The infected people might not run, but they could shuffle along pretty well and when there were multiple ones together, it was pretty scary.

"Once the entire group passes my truck and we have enough of a gap, we're going to make a run for it," Manny whispered. "They're focused on the others, so as long as we stay quiet, they won't even notice us."

It sounded like a good plan, but Ladeja instinctively pulled the boys in front of her anyway, placing a protective hand on each one's shoulder. She pushed down the pain when Cory squirmed beneath her hand, trying to break free, and gripped his shoulder tight. He stopped squirming after she dug her fingers in firm enough for him to know she'd grown tired of his behavior. She could feel Manny's judging eyes on her and refused to look his way. Cory was her son, and she'd deal with him her way in her own time. He'd just lost his father and couldn't bring himself to admit it. She could take a little acting out if it helped him deal with the loss. That was what she told herself as she took a deep breath and pushed her own emotions down.

"Where did they all come from?" Mateo asked, pulling her out of her thoughts.

"They came through the gate and up the driveway," Manny answered quietly. "We shot down the first group, but more kept coming from who knows where. I think the gunfire attracted them. Their eyes are all white and cloudy, but they seem to see close-up. They definitely hear."

"All this started with Russian mail-order brides?" Ladeja watched the group shuffle along, counting at least thirty people of different ethnicities, ages, and both genders. "How many men have married those women?"

"Apparently a lot." Manny shook his head as if to say he didn't understand why. "The virus is transmitted through blood and body fluids though, and the news said they injected it in every mail-order bride who came over from there in the last five years, so that's a shitload right there. Now factor in every man they've slept with and every person those men have slept with in that five years, how many times they've donated blood, and it adds up."

"How is the government going to stop this?"

Manny didn't answer, and the look in his eyes didn't leave Ladeja feeling very hopeful.

"Shit," he muttered, looking toward O'Donnell's SUV. The Camilleris were still running toward it except for Chelle, who'd taken a tumble. Her sisters ran right past her, yelling back at her to get up, but as she grabbed her ankle and rocked back and forth, it became clear she was hurt.

"They're not even stopping for her!" Ladeja pointed out, incredulous. "That's their own flesh and blood."

"Bad time to bring up flesh and blood." Manny nodded, indicating the infected group gaining on Chelle now that she was on the ground.

Ladeja instinctively started to yell to Chelle that she needed to move her ass, but realizing what she was about to do, Manny clamped a hand over her mouth just in time. "I don't particularly want to watch that girl get eaten either, but you can't draw the attention of those things to us."

"Too late," Mateo squeaked, pointing behind them.

They turned their heads to see an infected man step out of the broken foyer door. He immediately saw them and started moving in their direction.

Ladeja pulled the boys against her and looked back at the truck. The majority of the infected group that had swarmed the lawn had passed the truck, but there were still stragglers. O'Donnell was almost to the SUV, three Camilleri sisters behind him, and Chelle had finally gotten up but was limping across the lawn, desperately trying to get to the SUV while the shuffling infected closed in on her.

"We can't go for the truck until they're all a decent distance past it." Manny said. "It's just one bastard here. I can handle him quietly."

"We need to draw attention away from Chelle."

"And die ourselves?" Manny shook his head as he stepped toward the infected man creeping up on them. "O'Donnell is almost to the SUV. He might be able to get to her first. We can't risk our lives for hers."

The infected man made a horrible sound as Manny neared it, an undead man's version of a battle cry, and Ladeja checked to see if the other infected people had been drawn to the sound, her heart in her throat, but they didn't appear to be. Their attention was one hundred percent on the teenager limping as quickly as she could but unfortunately not moving much faster than them.

Afraid to take her eyes off Manny too long, she turned back to him to see the infected man on the ground and Manny's large boot stepping back out of his smooshed head. She gagged, quickly looking away before she lost the contents of her stomach.

"All right. We're good here," she heard Manny say. "Easy peasy, lemon *motherfucker*!"

Ladeja looked up at him, noting the sudden alarm in his voice, and saw him backing away from the foyer as three more infected people poured out.

"Shoot them," she suggested, knowing taking on all three hand-to-hand would not be nearly as easy as it had been for him to take the first one out.

"And draw every infected person on this property right to us while we're standing out here with our asses hanging out?" He looked over his shoulder as he neared her, judging the situation. "They kind of shuffle along, so I want you three to walk really fast, but stay really quiet. We're going to try walking fast to the truck, but if those others that are still near the truck move toward us, we're going to have to run like hell, so be ready."

Ladeja nodded even though he'd already turned his head around to keep watch on the new group still spilling out of the house, and started walking toward the truck, a hand tightly clamped onto each boy's shoulder. She moved quickly but quietly as instructed, half scared the infected would hear her heartbeat as it thumped away at what felt like a billion beats a minute. Mateo panted so heavily she feared the boy might go into an asthma attack. Cory seemed to be handling the situation fine. If she couldn't see how wide his eyes had grown since they'd stepped past the mansion wall, she'd not even suspect he was afraid. Behind her, Manny had turned around so he no longer walked backward, but he kept his head on a swivel, constantly scanning the threats behind and in front of them.

Ladeja glanced in Chelle's direction. The gap between her and most of the infected was tiny, and she'd slowed down since she'd first started limping away from them. Ahead of her, O'Donnell had just reached the SUV and started the engine.

The truck loomed about ten feet ahead of them and all the infected had now passed it, intent on getting to Chelle, who was providing what looked like a very easy target for them. Manny had driven them right up to the front door instead of parking in an area actually reserved for parking when they'd arrived earlier, so they now had to walk the length of the front of the house to get back to it. Ladeja tried to keep her eye on the front doors in case anything spilled out of it, but also had to keep watch of the group following the Camilleris in case any of them randomly turned their heads and noticed them.

Four feet away from the truck, she breathed a little easier. They were going to make it without incident. O'Donnell's SUV was already moving. They were all going to make it.

The SUV lurched forward, then screeched to a stop. The driver's side door opened and O'Donnell emerged, a larger gun than she'd seen him carry in the house now in hand. He shot off a few rounds and she watched as blood splattered out of the infected bodies that had been closing in on Chelle.

"Yes! He's saving her!" Ladeja blurted. She slapped her hand over her mouth as soon as she realized she'd spoken out loud, but it was too late. Multiple infected people near the back of the group turned their heads in her direction and let out that awful sound the infected man Manny had just taken out had made before starting toward her.

"Run!" Manny ordered.

"Fuck, I'm sorry!" she cried as they immediately ran for the truck, trying to reach it before the predators, now aware of their presence, reached them.

"Just get in the truck! The keys are still in the ignition and doors are unlocked. We just have to get our asses in there!"

Ladeja ran faster than she'd ever ran in her life, tugging Cory along when he started to fall back. Mateo kept up pretty well, pumping his arms and legs like a track star. Behind them, Manny fired off a few shots as some of the infected people got dangerously close to the truck. Ladeja instinctively cringed as the bullets whizzed past the side of her head, but stayed on course.

She went straight for the back door of the extended cab when they finally reached the truck and practically shoved the boys inside before slamming their door closed.

With his back to her, Manny yanked open the front passenger side door with his free hand, his other hand wrapped tight around the gun he held before him as he acted as a wall of defense between her and the infected gaining on them. "Get in!"

Ladeja climbed into the truck, slid across to the driver's seat, and turned the key in the ignition. "Get in!" she yelled as the truck roared to life.

Manny looked at her, mouth agape, then looked over at the infected closing in on the front of the truck and the ones approaching him from the side before muttering a curse and jumped into the truck, slamming the door after him. "I've never let anyone drive my truck before."

"Oh, I'm sorry," Ladeja apologized with a wallop of sarcasm as she arced her palm out to bring his attention to the mob of infected people he'd have had to go through to get around to the driver's side. "Would you like to walk on around? I'm not trying to climb over your super-sized ass to switch up, or of course we can just sit here."

"Just drive, woman. Damn."

"Where am I going?" She put the truck in Drive and turned the wheel to avoid the majority of infected coming at them from the front.

"We're supposed to follow O'Donnell, but he looks busy shooting down the front wave of that group. Damn, that girl needs to pick up the pace."

Ladeja drove toward the front gate, placing them along the edge of the infected group, then made a sharp turn toward where she estimated Chelle to be.

"What are you doing?" Manny asked as she accelerated, side-swiping any diseased people who got too close to the moving vehicle.

"What's it look like? Get ready to help her if she needs it." Ladeja barreled down until she reached the front of the group and cut right, stopping in front of Chelle.

"Fuck, Ladeja! You know O'Donnell was shooting this

way, right?"

"He saw us. Help her out."

Manny cursed under his breath but jumped out of the truck, quickly scooped up a crawling Chelle into his muscle-bound arms and unceremoniously dumped her into the back before popping back into his seat. "Go!"

O'Donnell had already disappeared back into the SUV and was maneuvering it toward the front gate, so Ladeja cut the wheel to the left and switched her foot from the brake to the gas pedal, quickly catching up to him. "I know you said we're following him, but following him where?"

"We didn't get that far in the planning. Once it got down to just me and him left, we made the quick decision to get you all out of the library and make a run for it. We're pretty much making it up as we go now. All I know is if this uppity, rich neighborhood where every house has a yard with this much acreage spacing it from the next has this many infected people roaming around, the neighborhoods we live in are going to be twice as infested with them."

"Yeah." Ladeja nodded, thinking about her apartment. There were at least forty units in her apartment building, and it wasn't the only apartment building on her street. She couldn't take Cory and Mateo there. They needed to find someplace distanced from highly residential or popular retail areas, but she couldn't think of such a place in Los Angeles. Just the sheer amount of tourists visiting on any given day alone was enough to cause concern.

As they reached the front gate, four more infected people shambled onto the property. Two were men in what she'd consider normal people's clothes, maybe a couple of tourists as nothing they wore really looked expensive and they didn't look as if they focused that much on their appearance before they'd succumbed to the virus. One was a woman in a designer dress with a large diamond necklace and the other woman wore a maid's uniform. Every one of them was a different race. She realized in that moment that this virus could have been in anyone, anywhere, and once infected, the carriers could spread the deadly disease far and wide.

"Ladeja? You all right?"

She looked over at Manny, saw the deep lines in his furrowed brow as he watched her, and imagined what he must see. She'd stopped breathing, the implications of what they were truly up against too much to grasp. She returned her attention to her driving, watching the SUV in front of her to make sure they didn't lose it. "I'm fine. I just have some deep thoughts rolling over in my head right now."

"You and me both," he said softly. "I've seen a lot of shit growing up where I did, but I never thought I'd see the day I had to kill people who were already dead but apparently didn't get the memo they were supposed to stay the fuck down."

Ladeja took a peek in the rearview mirror, checking on the boys. Mateo sat behind her, staring at the locket he turned reverently in his hand. He'd held up pretty damn good for a kid who'd been in the very next room while a sick man ate his mother. She didn't know how long he'd be able to stay that strong, but she knew in her heart that when he lost it, it was going to be damned hard getting him through it. Cory sat on the other side, behind Manny, staring out the window. She saw the indentation in his cheek from where he clamped his jaw tight, the anger in his eyes. He was going to blow too, just in a different way. His father was gone, and he wasn't going to accept the fact easily. Through the back window, she could see the back of Chelle's head as she sat against the back of the cab.

"I really hadn't planned on traveling with the Camilleri family," Ladeja said as she followed the SUV through the neighborhood, dismayed by the amount of infected people she saw rambling around the streets. "I guess we can't ditch them with one in the back."

"I'm surprised you swooped in to save her."

"She might be part of the snobbiest, most air-headed family in the world, but she's still just a kid. I couldn't let her die and O'Donnell was just wasting bullets if he couldn't reach her in time. Her sisters damn sure weren't going to run to her if they didn't even bother helping her up when she fell."

"You're a good person, Ladeja Craig. You're fucking dangerous driving into the line of fire like that and I pray you never do that dumb shit again, but in all honesty, it was pretty badass."

Ladeja grinned. "You're the one who ran out to get her."

"It didn't seem like you were going to leave until I did, and like you said, they weren't going to do it. That's pretty fucked up, leaving their sister out there to die like that."

"Well, that family doesn't seem that big on appreciation so don't expect a thanks from any of them, but… thank you for getting me to my son. You didn't have to, and I got you stuck in a nightmare situation. I never expected all hell to break loose like this."

"I have a feeling hell hasn't even broken loose yet. This is just the beginning, and you didn't get me stuck in anything. I chose to be here."

"But why? You could have gone somewhere safe and locked yourself away from this mess instead of getting all up in the drama of my rescue mission."

"Girl, I wouldn't have been able to live with myself if I just let you run off on your own in this mess. I know you're not used to having a man have your back, but we're not all the kind to just leave you hanging when you need a partner."

She glanced at him, caught the serious look in his eyes as he gazed over at her, and promptly returned her attention to the road. The girls at the club had teased her a few times about how nice Manny was to her, despite his general aloofness with everyone else. He didn't tolerate any of the women being disrespected and would defend any of them without question, but he always seemed to be there extra fast for Ladeja, coming to her rescue before she even asked for help, before a situation even got bad. If she needed a ride home, he gave it. If she was having a bad day and needed to gripe, he listened like an old friend, and he never judged her for being a club companion. She'd told herself it was because he worked at the club and knew damn well the girls didn't do anything but talk to the VIPs, and she'd brushed off the added attention the other girls commented on to them just understanding each other. She was one of only a few minority girls working at the club. They'd both been raised in rough neighborhoods and had been given some tough knocks.

The way he looked at her now told a different story, a story she wasn't sure she was brave enough to read further into just yet, especially not now that she had not only her son but Mateo to care for and no idea where she was going and for how long she'd be playing it by ear while the world around her spun out of control. She knew she trusted him though, and was thankful he'd stayed by her side.

"Manny?" O'Donnell's voice came through the radio clipped to Manny's belt.

He unclipped it and pressed the button, allowing him to be heard. "Yeah?"

"Is Chelle all right?"

"I just dumped her in the back and we took off," he said, "but from what I could tell, she seemed to only have a busted ankle. I didn't see any blood. You figure out where we're headed yet? I'm sure her sisters can't wait to be reunited with her."

Ladeja grinned, picking up Manny's liberally applied sarcasm. She cut him a sideways glance, and he winked at her.

"Oh yeah. They're beside themselves with worry," O'Donnell replied in a matching tone. "We need to stay out of really populated areas. They're probably overrun with these sick bastards right now. The girls, uh, have a friend they say lives nearby. Big house, lots of land to set it apart from other residences. Gated and hopefully the gate is still up. We're going to head there. Just keep following me."

"What friend?"

"Not anyone you'd immediately think of running to during what's looking like a damn zombie apocalypse, but someone who might take us in and give us time to regroup and figure out an actual plan," O'Donnell answered. "Just stay with me and you'll see when we get there."

Manny and Ladeja shared a look as he clipped the radio back to his belt.

"Well, that doesn't sound bad at all," Manny said.

"Not at all." Ladeja sighed. "If I had to choose who to group up with during a shitstorm like this, it would not be anyone from the Camilleri family, especially not Cynda. They already left their own freaking sister to die, just ran right past her. Now we're going to someone's house who is a friend of theirs? What kind of person would be a friend to them?"

"In Los Angeles?" Manny laughed. "Anyone who wanted to drop their names. They might be selfish, stupid bitches with the survival skills of a baby, but remember those millions of Instagram and Twitter followers? That's all the people here care about. If they can remember this person's name at all, you'd better believe whoever it is has at least some modicum of fame and a shitload of money. You also better believe they're hanging with the Camilleri family to get the mentions on social media and keep their star hanging high. Shit, as long as whoever it is has four walls and a roof, I'm good with whoever it is. We can't just drive around wasting gas. We've been seeing less and less infected stragglers walking round the deeper we get into this rich and famous zone."

"How do you know they'll even allow us inside when we get there? Cynda and I don't exactly see eye to eye."

"No shit. I'm surprised she can even see out her eye after you popped her." He laughed. "No worries about getting inside. We have insurance." He jerked his head toward the back of the truck, reminding her they had Chelle.

"Again, they wouldn't even stop to help the girl when she hurt her ankle. I'm not so sure she's what I'd call insurance."

"If they left her and she died, they could spin the story any way they wanted. She's alive, and we saved her while her sisters didn't do a damn thing, didn't even try. That's a story they will not want to get out to all their followers when this blows over."

"Damn, that's cold."

"Yeah, well, they're ice cold bitches. Most people who are born rich tend to be."

"Still… they could take her and tell us to hit the road."

"We saved her. Chelle knows that. I really don't think it's going to be a problem."

Ladeja sighed. "I really don't need the added stress of dealing with Cynda Camilleri on top of everything else. I'd rather we go off on our own."

"Where to? To your apartment or mine? How many infected people do you think are crawling all over those neighborhoods jam-packed with people and businesses? You going back to Oakland? Maybe my hood, Compton? Trust me, there's plenty of non-infected people there loving this shit. You know law enforcement and the military have their hands full with this crap. The losers in our old neighborhoods are having a damn party looting whatever they can and killing whoever they want."

"You really think it's that bad back home?"

He gave her a look. “You know it is. You haven’t been out here so long you forgot what you left behind, or why.”

Ladeja chewed the inside of her bottom lip as she thought of her mother. She was a hard woman to live with, but she was her mother. When she’d left her back in Oakland to find a better life, she never thought something like this would happen. She knew her mother had grown up in Oakland and knew how to handle herself, but even on the worst days, the police were at least a threat. Now, with them busy handing the aftermath of the viral outbreak, Manny had a point. Oakland would be in total chaos.

“Who are you worrying about?”

“My mother and my brother. I never even called them. My sole concern was getting to my son.”

“I’m sure they’re all right. They’ve lived there all their lives and know what’s up, right?”

“Yeah.” O’Donnell’s SUV took a left, and she followed it, continuing as they veered up deeper into the Hollywood Hills. “My brother fell in with a dangerous crowd. His people will know she’s off limits, but I don’t know about the others, and I honestly don’t know if he’ll be there to protect her. If there’s an opportunity to loot and take out some of their enemies, he’ll probably be right in the mix.”

“All the more reason you shouldn’t take these boys there.”

Ladeja nodded. He was right. She wanted to know her mother and brother were safe, but she couldn’t jeopardize her son’s life.

O’Donnell slowed as they reached a large gate and spoke with the guard there. After a moment, there was a loud buzzing sound, and the gate opened. The guard waved O’Donnell through and motioned for her to follow.

“Well, we made it past the gate without a problem,” Manny commented as they passed the guard.

“It looks like this entire neighborhood is gated in and

there are guards. Why don't we just find another place here to stay, just us four? These are mostly celebrity homes. You know these people have like four or five mansions all over. I'm sure we could find something vacant."

"And get past the security if we did?" Manny laughed. "They probably got silent alarms and everything. Not to mention, we're getting in here because we're with the Camilleri family. Like you said, they got their own security here guarding the neighborhood. What do you think these uppity, ultra-white, rich people are going to do if they see a big, tattooed multi-racial guy and a black woman in an Oakland A's T-shirt looking around, scouting out an empty house to crash in?"

"Damn it." Ladeja hit the steering wheel. "There's sick people walking round eating people. You'd think people would be more caring, but I know you're right. We don't belong here."

"It's going to be all right. We'll figure this out."

They took a road that twisted up around a large hill before leveling out and again were stopped by a gated entry. These gates were gold with song notes and the initials "MP" in the middle.

"Who do you think lives here?" Ladeja asked as a guard stepped out of a little building next to the gate and approached O'Donnell's window.

"Michelle Pfeiffer? Maury Povich?" His eyes brightened. "Hey, he's a pretty cool dude."

"O'Donnell made it sound like it was someone kind of out there who we wouldn't imagine staying with in a situation like this. Neither of those two sound that bad."

"I can't think of anyone else." Manny shrugged. "MP might not even be the person's initials. Don't some famous people name their homes, like Elvis named his Graceland? We'll find out soon enough."

The guard buzzed them through the gate. Ladeja held her breath as she followed O'Donnell's SUV, expecting to be stopped, but they made it through. As the gate closed behind them, she felt as though it were a cell door slamming shut, locking her in with people who would offer her more harm than help.

"Relax, Ladeja. I'm right here with you."

She realized she'd been white-knuckling the steering wheel and loosened her grip, told herself to chill. They'd survived what she could only describe as a small herd of infected people, and that was after making it to the Camilleri mansion in the first place. Hell, she'd survived growing up in Oakland where hearing gunshots was a normal occurrence. She could manage this, even with the woman Thunda had thrown her away for.

The driveway ran up to the house and curved in two directions. They turned right and parked side by side in two vacant spots under a long carport.

"Here we go," Manny said, getting out of the truck.

Ladeja took a deep breath and cut the engine. "Come on, boys. We're going to stay here for a little bit while we figure out our next move."

They climbed out, grabbing their backpacks holding their belongings. Ladeja realized she had nothing. She'd left work and went straight for Cory, never thinking she wouldn't make it back home to her stuff. Just what she needed while depending on the shelter provided by the rich and famous, nothing but the clothes she wore and a cell phone.

Manny helped Chelle out of the back of the truck and walked her over as they met up with O'Donnell and the other Camilleris.

"Chelle!" Cynda ran up to her younger sister, pulling her into a hug. "We were so worried!"

"You ran right past me," Chelle said, standing ramrod-straight with her arms at her sides, not bothering to return the hug.

"We thought you were getting back up," Cynda said,

pulling back to look her in the eye. "You're the best runner out of all of us. If we'd stopped, then those people could have attacked us, and we would have just slowed you down."

Chelle angled her head sideways, her brow furrowed in disbelief. "I twisted my ankle, and you thought that helping me would have slowed me down?"

"Well, we didn't know you twisted your ankle. We're not doctors." Cynda laughed, waving a hand in the air as if to say it was all just so silly before sliding her arm through Chelle's and pulling her along. "Let's get you inside so you can relax, and maybe someone will know what to do about your ankle. At the very least, there should be a stocked bar and that can do wonders for any pain."

"Oh good," Ladeja muttered. "We're trying to survive whatever is going on out in the world and their plan is to get drunk because everyone is so much better at protecting themselves when they're wasted."

"Where are we?" Manny asked O'Donnell.

"A safe house away from all the undead shit walking out there," O'Donnell said, gesturing with his head toward the direction they'd come from before following the Camilleri family as they walked to the double doors at the side of the mansion, the closest entrance to the carport.

"I hope she's not on a bender," Cara said after ringing the doorbell.

"If she's on a bender, she might sleep more," Cheyanne advised.

"Or she might sing nonstop like she did the last time." Cara rolled her eyes. "She's really losing her voice. It's kind of sad."

"Don't let her hear you say that," Cheyanne warned. "She's just been going through some stuff."

Ladeja glanced over at Manny and he shrugged, neither of them yet having figured out whose property they were on.

The doors opened and a short, thin, light-skinned black man in a tight black silk T-shirt and skinny jeans opened the door. His hair was cut short and bleached white, and his eyes were too blue to be natural. "Hey, girls! Come on in, Mimi will be right down. We're just hanging out."

Mimi.

Ladeja and Manny shared a look before piercing O'Donnell with withering glares he seemed to shrink under. Ladeja shook her head. They couldn't be where she thought they were. O'Donnell couldn't have brought them to the home of one of history's biggest divas, a woman who'd reigned at the top of the charts, broke more records than any other female singer, but had grown notorious for her attitude, temper and sporadic mental breakdowns.

"Dahlings!"

Ladeja's fear was confirmed as she recognized the voice of Miranda "Mimi" Perry before the woman even appeared on the staircase beyond the door.

They entered the mansion as the legendary singer came down the stairs in clear stilettos with little pompoms on them and a tiny, white silk negligee that fell just below her bottom and barely covered anything, particularly her breasts which looked about to spill out of the tiny spaghetti straps struggling to support a chest that seemed much larger than Ladeja remembered it to be when she was a kid and Mimi Perry was plastered on her bedroom wall. She'd loved the biracial singer when she'd first hit the scene, inspired by her rags to riches story and in awe of her talent, but over time the woman had become full of herself and obsessed with appearing young. She was pushing fifty years old but still poured her maturing body into clothes suited more toward young, svelte bodies and singing more hip-hop influenced dance tracks, her signature R&B sound and crazy high octaves strategically placed for maximum effect in her power ballads all but forgotten.

"Come in, come in. I'm so sorry to hear about what

happened, and poor Thunda." Mimi and Cynda did the rich people greeting where they air-kissed each other's cheeks. "How are you holding up?"

Cynda started crying the horrible ugly cry she'd become known for on the family's reality TV show and Ladeja couldn't help rolling her eyes. Manny elbowed her softly in her rib and shook his head as he looked down at her, his lips twitching.

"Oh sweetheart, you're going to be all right after some time passes. Until then, I have plenty of alcohol." Mimi passed Cynda over to the man who'd answered the door. "Toddy, honey, take the Camilleris in to the bar."

"And you must be the security guard who saved their lives," Mimi said, turning toward Manny. She eyed him up and down, her gaze lingering on his muscular chest and biceps. "How fortunate they had you there to protect them, and now you're here to protect us."

Manny's eyebrows shot up into his hairline and he took a step back, nodding his head toward O'Donnell, who stood at his side. "This is the Camilleri family's security guard right here. I'm *her* guard."

Mimi looked Ladeja over, her brow scrunching a bit before she grinned. "I don't believe we've met, dahling."

"I'm not famous, or rich. I just had to get my son from the Camilleri's property and I kind of got stuck in a bad situation with them," Ladeja explained as she saw the wheels turning in Mimi's head while the woman tried to figure out who she was and in what way was she possible competition. "I'm nobody."

"Seems like you're a pretty important somebody to him." She looked Manny over again and sighed before she noticed the boys who'd been standing behind them. "Oh! You're the mother of Thunda's son."

"I'm the mother of our son," Ladeja blurted out, not liking the title Mimi had just given her. She'd done and put up way too much to be relegated to just a breeder for someone a celebrity thought was more important than her, a lowly average person.

"Of course." Mimi smiled brightly. "I like you. So then you are the security guard?" She looked over at O'Donnell and ran a hand down one of his muscular arms. "You must all be tired. From what Cynda told me before the call dropped, it sounds like you've been through hell today. Follow me and I'll show you where you can get food, what bathrooms to use and where you can sleep if you choose to stay, then you can join my friends and I."

"Friends?" O'Donnell huffed out a frustrated breath. "Look, I know our call dropped, but I distinctly heard Cynda tell you what happened at her party and surely you've seen the news. It's been running nonstop. There are sick people all over and now is not the time to be having parties."

Mimi rolled her shoulders back and pinned O'Donnell with one of the best 'I don't know who the fuck you think you're talking to' faces Ladeja had ever seen before blinking several times and held her hands up, palms out as she closed her eyes and took a deep breath through her nose. When she opened her eyes, she smiled too sweetly for it to be genuine.

"Dahling, I appreciate that you were able to safely deliver these people to my door so I can offer you shelter in my little home away from home in the hills," she said slowly as if she carefully chose each word and was restraining herself from using more colorful language. "While I am graciously hosting you and your friends here, I assure you I will treat you all with the utmost respect and I'm sure you will return the courtesy. As I was saying, some friends and I are just hanging out here since it sounds as if it's gotten absolutely crazy in the city. My friends came here with me and will be with me for the duration of my stay. Would you like to stay here with us, or will you be leaving?"

Ladeja fought a grin as O'Donnell's face flooded with red and he stammered out an apology. Mimi had a reputation for not taking shit from anyone, and it was a little awe-inspiring watching her in action.

"Wonderful." Mimi clapped her bejeweled hands and turned. "Follow me, dahlings!"

They did as told, following her through a dining room with the longest dining table Ladeja had ever seen, and a large kitchen, just as shiny and spotless as the one in the Camilleri mansion had been, but this one actually had food in it, from bowls of fruit to boxes of snacks on the counters and what looked like a whole basket of fresh baked muffins next to the stove. A petite black lady in a maid uniform entered the kitchen and smiled at them before sliding her hands into oven mitts and removing a tray of what looked like tiny little pizzas out of the oven.

"This is the kitchen, of course." Mimi spun around, her hands out in the air, presenting the room like one of the women on *The Price Is Right*. "Sarah here is a wonderful cook, so if anyone is hungry, she can make you pretty much whatever you want. I requested the kitchen be fully stocked before my arrival last night. Sarah takes care of all the domestic duties in the house, so anything you need, she's your girl. Boys? Are you hungry?"

Ladeja looked down at the boys. Cory's eyes were fixed on Mimi's breasts, which weren't exactly covered behind the skimpy negligee, but Mateo looked at the tray of food Sarah had just removed from the oven like he hadn't seen food in days.

"The boys can stay with me in the kitchen and I'll feed them anything they'd like," Sarah offered, smiling.

"Thank you." Ladeja prodded Mateo and Cory forward until they pulled out bar stools along the black marble island in the middle of the kitchen and settled in to be fed.

"Follow me and I'll show you where you can clean up and, of course, where you can sleep if you choose to stay, then you're free to move about as you please." Mimi turned and led them up a flight of stairs. "The whole second floor in this wing is guest bedrooms. The three rooms on the end there are free, so if you stay, you can decide who goes where and the one on the very end has a private bath. There's also a bathroom just off the kitchen and another next to the gym and off the theater room. Now that you know where you can eat and stay, you're absolutely free to explore. I only ask that no one enter my bedroom uninvited. It's the master suite on the first floor off the piano room."

"Wait. So if we stay, we have these three bedrooms to split between the nine of us?"

"Nine of you? Oh!" Mimi waved her hand in the air, laughing. "No, dahling. I'm putting Cynda and her sisters out in the pool house far, far away from everyone else. The rooms are yours if you want them. You can figure it out. I have people to entertain and wine to drink, and I should fit in some cardio today. TMZ has been absolutely horrible to me lately."

And with that she sashayed away, the see-through jacket of her negligee blowing behind her as she hastened down the stairs to find liquor and people to adore her.

"So we're in an enormous house with who knows how many people and a diva who is aware of what's happening out there and sees no issue with everybody inside getting drunk and sloppy?" Manny clapped his hand on O'Donnell's shoulder. "Good scouting, man. How soon do we roll out?"

O'Donnell ran a hand through his short hair. "As bad as this seems, do you know of a better place to go right now? The Camilleri party was an all-nighter, by the way, which means I didn't sleep last night and I haven't eaten anything substantial either. I lost all my men, men I've worked with for a long time and hung out with on my days off. I just need a minute of calm quiet to think."

Manny squeezed his shoulder and nodded. "Cool, bro, and nah, I can't think of anywhere else to head to right now. The last thing I heard about the rescue sites was that we shouldn't go to them. We're supposed to wait on the military to come get us or whatever. I figure they'll come rescue people from this neighborhood before they do any of ours."

"True," O'Donnell said. "Man, I gotta hit the bathroom. I'll take this room right here. You two figure out how to split the other two and meet me down in the kitchen. We'll get some grub in our stomachs and start spit-balling a plan."

Manny nodded his agreement and turned to Ladeja as O'Donnell left them. "You and the boys take the bedroom with the private bath. I don't want them or you getting up in the middle of the night to go use the restroom and bump into something bad."

"You think someone here could be infected?"

Manny shrugged. "I don't know who all is here yet, but they have to be rich, celebrity types. That type tends to sleep around and anyone who had ever slept with an infected person in the past five years would be spreading it around."

Ladeja's heart started beating faster. "I need to get to the boys."

They quickly made their way down the stairs and into the kitchen to find the boys eating huge stacks of pancakes loaded with whipped cream and fresh strawberries at the kitchen island.

"I guess you were hungry," Ladeja said, admiring the height of the fluffy pancake towers.

"I can make you something," Sarah offered, looking over at her from where she loaded the dishwasher.

"I don't want you to go to any trouble," Ladeja said as she pulled her cell phone free from her pocket. She'd wanted to call her mother from the moment she'd discovered Cynda had been able to get a call through to Mimi.

"It's my job, and honestly, cooking is my favorite part."

"Anything will be nice," Manny advised as he lowered himself onto a barstool across from the boys.

"Hell, I'll take a sandwich," O'Donnell said, entering the room, "or even leftovers warmed in the microwave. I just need food."

Ladeja walked into the dining room to get a little privacy and dialed her mother's number. The phone rang three times before her mother answered.

"Ladeja?"

"Hey, Mama."

"Where are you?"

Ladeja laughed a little as she realized exactly where she was. "You wouldn't believe me if I told you, but I'm safe right now. How are you? How are things in the neighborhood?"

"Bad. I'd tell you not to come here, but I guess I don't have to. You ran away a long time ago and left us behind for good."

Ladeja took a deep breath through her nose as she ground her teeth together and reminded herself this could be the last time she ever spoke with her mother if things went sideways. "I don't want to argue with you, Mama. It's really bad out there. I just picked up Cory from his father's house and I've lost count how many infected people we had to go through. I think Thunda is dead. He was at a studio doing a movie and we saw news footage when the studio was overrun. I think he got trampled to death. I don't think he made it and now I have to raise Cory on my own, and I have another boy with me who just lost his mother today. I'm waiting for him to break down and I'm waiting for Cory to deal with the fact that his daddy is never coming home to him and I'm waiting to see if we live long enough for any of that to happen. I did not call to fight with you."

"Why did you call? It sounds like you have your plate full."

Ladeja wiped her eye, finding wetness. "I needed to know that you and JJ were all right. Is he there with you, or is he running around with his crew?"

"Don't judge your brother, Ladeja. He's stayed with me through a lot of hard times. It's easy to judge us here when you're staying with movie stars."

"I'm not staying with—" She remembered whose house she was in, and how many movies Mimi Perry had been in and chose not to finish that sentence. "I live in an apartment in Hollywood, Mama, and it's just me and Cory, and a ton of other tenants struggling to pay bills just like me. You could have come too."

"I don't leave family. Your brother and I are all right. You've made your phone call so you can put your conscience at ease."

"It's not about that, Mama." Ladeja heard gunshots in the background. "What's going on there?"

"The neighborhood is taking care of the neighborhood. Don't worry about us. We have our people and you have yours. Take care of your son. You already lost your man to money and big dreams. Kids grow fast and if you're not careful, they forget what you did for them and they leave."

The line went silent, and then Ladeja heard the dial tone. She wouldn't kid herself into thinking the call had dropped. She'd had a clear connection and her mother had ended it abruptly, fully aware of what was going on in the world and fully aware that she could be talking to her daughter for the last time. She didn't even ask how Cory was doing, just warned she could lose him while sliding in a dig at her.

"Good luck, Mama," Ladeja whispered as she slid the phone back into her pocket, dried her eyes, took a deep breath and returned to the kitchen to find the boys still working their way through their pancake towers while Manny and O'Donnell sat opposite them, turned around in their seats to watch the small flat screen TV affixed to the underside of a kitchen cabinet next to where Sarah scrambled eggs and fried bacon on the stove.

"Hey." Manny gave her a considering once-over as she took a seat on the stool next to his. "You reach your mother?"

"Yeah. She's alive."

"She okay?"

Ladeja nodded.

"You okay?"

She just gave him a little half-hearted smile, not willing to open up that much yet. He took the hint and gave her hand a quick squeeze before changing the topic. "We're watching the news to see how bad it's gotten and get an idea of where to go from here. Sarah's cooking up some bacon and eggs so we can refuel. It's been a rough day."

"Understatement. What have I missed?"

"They're urging people to stay inside if they have a secure location," O'Donnell advised. "They don't want people traveling at all, and although they have announced military bases, they said people should wait to be rescued and transported there by the military."

"The expressways are jam packed with people," Manny added, "and there have been attacks on some because people are stuck in their cars, or they're wrecking trying to get away."

"How many infected people are there?"

Manny shrugged. "They don't have a firm number, but it's a lot, and they've had reports in every state. Entire hospitals have been shut down, and they have grounded all flights. Taxi services, busses, the subway, even the railroad is closed. They shut the whole damn country down."

"This just started yesterday," Ladeja said. "How could it have gotten so bad so quickly? Mad Cow, Bird Flu…

Nothing ever hit like this."

"This isn't like anything we've ever seen because it was specially manufactured to hit us fast and hard," O'Donnell explained. "It's a genetic bomb created in some evil genius's science lab. The Russians implanted it in their own women so they could smuggle it over here like a bunch of damn Trojan horses. They didn't plan and carry out this whole operation just to make a few people sick and give us a little trouble. They did this to wipe us off the map."

"So why haven't we just nuked them? Has Obama said anything yet?"

"I haven't seen or heard anything about an official statement from him yet," Manny advised.

"Maybe he's infected," O'Donnell suggested. "Or dead."

"Obama is not infected," Ladeja stated with complete conviction. "Obama is the only president I would bet a whole year's income never stepped out on his woman. Michelle is a queen, and he knows it."

"There are other ways to be infected," O'Donnell reminded her. "There's a lot of staff in the White House. Any of them could have been infected and attacked him. If he has been infected, they're going to hide that as long as they can. The country is scared enough as it is."

"Hey, Sarah, you have any more of those special brownies?"

Ladeja and the others looked over to see Terrell Houston, an actor famous for playing rough, deadly gangsters and drug dealers, enter the kitchen and walk over to the refrigerator with his hands in his pockets. Light-skinned, tall, and powerfully built with short, dark hair and green eyes, he was easily recognized as one of Hollywood's most attractive men, but in the years since he'd made it big he'd become more known for his volatile temper than his acting roles. The rumor was he didn't really have to stretch his acting muscles in his darker roles.

"Hello, kids," he said, noticing Cory and Mateo. He slid his gaze over to Ladeja, his mouth widening into a devilish smile as he studied her. "Hello, miss."

"There are more brownies in the refrigerator. Top shelf. Red saran wrap," Sarah answered as she busied herself scooping eggs and bacon onto plates.

"Thanks, babe." Terrell winked at her and retrieved the brownies from the refrigerator. He turned back toward them, looking straight at Ladeja as if the two men with her did not exist. "We're having a good time in the rec room. You should definitely come join us, but I would get the kids tucked in first. We're playing grownup games tonight." He winked at her, held her gaze long enough to be uncomfortable, and left, chuckling to himself.

"You were saying everyone is scared?" Ladeja arched an eyebrow at O'Donnell.

"Well, most normal people. We just happen to be in an area heavily populated by people who think they can't be touched by the same dangers that plague the less wealthy."

"Were those the kind of special brownies I think they were?" Ladeja asked Sarah as she deposited the plates on the island.

"Don't let the kids have any," Sarah cautioned them by way of answer and grabbed silverware.

"Yeah, I just keep feeling better and better about this haven we found." Ladeja glanced over at Manny, noting his jaw was still clenched as it had been from the moment Terrell Houston had locked his pretty green eyes on her.

"If the two of you want to try to find somewhere else, I can't stop you, but I strongly caution you against taking those boys out there again. You saw how many infected were on the Camilleri property and that wasn't anywhere near as populated as the rest of Los Angeles. We might be with a bunch or airheaded, over entitled celebrity jackasses who are either currently or on their way to getting high and drunk, but we're inside and we're protected by a pretty big gate."

"Hopefully, no one drives through this one," Manny said. "He's right, Ladeja. The news is just clips of people being attacked. That's the only thing out there for us."

Ladeja's call to her mother replayed in her mind, and she bit her bottom lip to keep her emotions reined in. Manny had no idea how accurate his words were. She had absolutely nothing out there. Everything she had was in that very room with her. Her son, another child to care for, a man who had feelings for her and who she could someday admit feelings for if she got past all the hurt Thunda had caused her, and a new friend to watch her back as she did everything she could to protect her son.

She stabbed her fork into her eggs and took a bite. As she did, she looked across the island at the two boys. Cory twirled his fork in a puddle of whipped cream, a faraway look in his eyes. She knew he was thinking of his father who would never return to him, and it was now completely her job to raise him into a good man. Mateo looked at her, smiling at her despite the horrible heartache she could see in his eyes, grateful for her protection.

They would stay and despite however many drunk, high, superficial celebrities were currently partying it up in Mimi Perry's rec room and no matter that she would have to share breathing space with the woman who'd taken her child's father from her and her repugnant sisters, she would protect these boys with her life.

"So what's the verdict?" O'Donnell asked.

"We stay here," she said. "Until the military can reach us and take us somewhere more secure, we hold tight here."

Loud music spread into the kitchen, followed by high-pitched squeals and hearty laughter. They looked at each other as Mimi's voice rose above the music, singing one of her hits complete with her signature glass-shattering high octaves.

"We're all gonna die," Ladeja muttered.

5

Justain jerked awake, quickly scanning the room for whatever had woken him. He hadn't meant to fall asleep and was surprised he'd even been able to while sitting on the floor with his back against the foot of the bed. Images of car jams and attacks still rolled across the television screen, but the volume was off. That hadn't awakened him. The door was locked. Beyond it, he heard nothing.

Maybe that was what woke him, he thought. The quiet. Or the pain of falling asleep sitting straight up. He rubbed the back of his neck, trying to relieve the aching knot caused by his head falling back on the foot of the bed as he'd slept for however long. The sky outside was dark, indicating it had been no little nap. He looked for a clock, finding one on the nightstand between the two double beds. It was three in the morning. He hadn't realized he'd been so tired, or that watching nonstop violence on television could be so incredibly boring.

No one had come to help him. The news kept saying everyone should stay inside and wait for help to arrive, but he hadn't seen or heard one police car, fire truck, ambulance, or military vehicle. He was a very important man in Hollywood. If there was a list of people to evacuate, he should be at the very top. Even if he wasn't at home, his assistant would know where to send help. Unless she'd been killed.

He hoped she wasn't that incompetent.

He reached into the pocket of his silk bathrobe and extracted his cell phone. No new messages or notifications of voicemail appeared on the screen. Cursing under his breath, he tried his assistant again, surprised to actually hear the phone ring.

"Yes! Finally!" He got up from the floor and paced as the phone continued to ring. "Pick up, pick up, pick up."

"Hi, you've reached Meredith Johnstone, personal assistant to Harry Justain—"

"Damn it!" Justain's hand tightened around the phone as he listened to the rest of Meredith's voicemail greeting, wishing he had her neck in his hand instead.

"This is your boss, the man who enables you to pay your rent," he announced from between gritted teeth after the long-awaited beep. "I'm at the hotel, but not my room. My room was invaded, and I had to practically scale a fucking building to get to a safe room several floors below it. My phone is now working, which means yours should be working. I'm going to need you to send help right away to get me out of this fucking nightmare and you're going to need to come up with a damn good excuse why that has not happened yet." He started to hang up, then changed his mind and added an additional message, his voice elevating on each word until it reached a full shout. "Unless you're dead, which in case you better wake the fuck back up, crawl out of whatever underworld hole you landed in and get me the fuck out of here right fucking now!"

A startled gasp caught Justain's attention. He turned toward the sound, realized it was coming from the balcony or somewhere outside the room. He disconnected the call and crossed the floor, carefully stepping around the broken glass he'd never cleaned up from when the door had been broken into.

He stepped out into the cool night air and found an unexpected sight on the balcony to his left. A young girl, somewhere in late childhood or her early teens, with long, wavy blonde hair and blue eyes so bright he saw them clearly in the moonlight, stared back at him. She wore skinny jeans with a dark T-shirt and black leather ankle boots. Her hands trembled as she clasped them before her chest, those blue eyes wide with fear.

"I'm not infected," he assured her, trying to place where he'd seen her before. She wasn't the age range he tended to work with, but she was someone noteworthy. He rarely gave two thoughts to anyone under the age of sixteen, so the very fact she seemed familiar at all to him said she was pretty big in some way. "Are you alone?"

She glanced into the hotel room she stood outside of before returning her gaze to him. Her hands still trembled, but she lowered them to her sides and straightened her shoulders. "My mother is somewhere in the hotel. She told me to stay locked in until she came back."

"How long ago was that?"

The girl looked away, focusing on a spot in the street. Justain followed it, relieved to see that the group of zombies that had been hanging out beneath the balcony had left, not relieved to see what looked like a trio of them at the end of the street, shuffling toward the direction of the hotel, and absolutely no one else to provide any sort of help. He turned just enough to check out the car museum where he'd seen Misty Waters and the Asian go in to, afraid the girl would run off if he completely took his eyes off of her. Everything on the street looked abandoned, dead. He wondered if the playmate and her rescuer were just as dead. Just as dead as the young girl's mother.

Justain returned his attention to her. "You're the first

person I've seen alive and uninfected since this morning. I was stranded here by someone I was with. I know it must hurt you to admit, but I think you're stranded here too, even if it wasn't intentional."

Fresh tears spilled from the girl's eyes and she wiped them away without a word, reminding Justain of the scene he'd seen her do that in.

"You were in that movie with the horse, and you're on one of those preteen shows now. I remember watching you in a scene and thinking you'd be great for one of my movies in a few years, when you're older."

She looked up at him, frowning.

"I'm Harry Justain," he introduced himself, not expecting her to recognize him as other actors and actresses would. Child actors weren't as knowledgeable of producers and directors as adults were, and he barely worked directly with them. "I'm a producer."

"I'm Emma Whitman."

"You and your mother were staying here at the hotel while you film locally?"

She nodded. "We always stay in hotels during filming. We live in Maine and my parents don't want to disrupt my brother's life while I'm filming. He's involved in a lot of sports and programs at his school and it's his senior year."

Justain noted she still used present tense while discussing her mother and chose to not acknowledge it. If there was any chance this girl could be remotely helpful in helping him out, he didn't want her to be a crying, emotional mess.

"I'm sure you've noticed what has been happening around here."

She nodded, her eyes watering, no doubt thinking her mother had been eaten alive but still not willing to admit it.

"I had to escape out of my room by climbing down the side of the building, or the balconies, to be exact. I didn't have any time to get clothes on. This room is empty. You didn't have any men's clothes in that room, did you?"

"My security guard stays in the adjoining room on the other side. You might be able to fit some of his clothes."

"Is he there?" Justain asked, perking up. A security guard wasn't as good as a police helicopter or a firetruck ladder, but one could certainly help him out of this mess.

She shook her head, pouting. "He went out early this morning, to the gym, probably. We haven't heard from him, but his stuff is still in his room."

"Okay then. I see I have an adjoining room with you too. I can unlock my side and you unlock yours and I'll come through your room to get to his. Once I'm dressed, we'll go out looking for your mom."

She nodded and ran back into her room, clearly pleased with the idea of finding her mother, not that Justain gave two shits about the girl or her family, but if no one came to save him he'd rather find his way out in pants.

He walked back into the hotel room and unlocked the connecting door on his side to see Emma standing there, having already opened the connecting door from her side. He offered her a friendly smile before stepping into her room, which was a much better room than the one he'd been taking refuge in the past several hours. It was, in fact, a suite, with a sitting area and a small kitchenette. He recalled her saying the bodyguard slept in the adjoining room, but he saw no beds in the room he stood in. A glance toward the hall door explained why. A staircase started between it and the kitchenette. "This is a bi-level suite?"

"Uh huh." She stretched her arm out toward the bodyguard's room. The door was already standing open. "You can check Roberto's room to see if any of his stuff fits you. He's pretty tall like you, so you might get lucky. It has to be better than walking around in that."

"I'm sure it will be." Justain walked across the suite and entered the bodyguard's room, an identical room to the one he'd been stuck in. He didn't see a suitcase, so he went to the closet and found several black T-shirts and slacks in the same color. He grabbed a shirt and a pair of slacks and checked the sizes. Not quite his size, but he'd make it work. A pair of black and gray running shoes rested at the bottom of the closet. To his relief, those were exactly his size. A quick search of the dresser turned up a pair of black socks.

He took the clothes into the bathroom and squeezed into the slacks. He'd have to go commando because wearing another man's boxers wasn't happening. The slacks fit him tight in the thighs and he had a few near catastrophes with the zipper and his crotch, but managed to get all his bits and pieces tucked in. He had better luck with the T-shirt, although it appeared to be tailored for a trimmer waist, so it fit him like a glove, stretching over his belly. Once he had the socks and shoes on, Justain looked in the full-length mirror on the shower door and grimaced. It definitely wasn't his most flattering look, but it beat running around in a silk robe with his balls hanging out. If he came in to contact with any infected people, he didn't want them to have easy access to his skin. From what he'd gathered from the news, they didn't have to eat a person to harm them. Just a bite could infect him and he would still die, albeit slower.

He stepped out of the bathroom and crossed the floor to reenter the suite. Emma sat at the bar separating the kitchenette from the rest of the room, eating an orange. Justain's stomach growled.

She gave him an odd look as she took in his attire. "I guess that's better than the robe until you find something else. Are you hungry?"

His stomach growled again, and he was pretty sure he might be drooling. "Yes. I haven't had anything to eat since last night, actually."

Her eyes widened. "There's food in the fridge and the

cabinets. Mostly snack stuff and microwaveable food. I stay pretty busy while shooting and Mom hates cooking full meals just for herself. Plus, we eat at restaurants or on set a lot."

Justain nodded as he moved to the kitchenette, not caring about her and her mother's eating habits. He pulled open the refrigerator and nearly cried with joy when he saw the contents. He hadn't realized how hungry he was, but with food in front of him, he felt like cramming it all into his gullet.

He pulled out the makings for a club sandwich and searched for a plate, also grabbing a mug for the Keurig he spotted on the counter. Although all the rooms had them, the one he'd been stuck in had only had one K-Cup pod, which he'd used shortly after Misty had ditched him.

"So since this is a bi-level suite, is there a hallway door to the upstairs as well? I'm not familiar with this layout."

"Yeah. My mom went out that one earlier. The laundry room is on that floor."

He looked up from the sandwich he currently piled high with ham. "You know what's going on out there?"

She nodded. "I watched the news until I heard screaming and then I turned the TV off so no one would hear me in here."

"That was very smart. I've been watching the TV on mute all day. Well, after I climbed down to the room next door. I climbed down because infected people were breaking down the door to my suite. They were in the hall."

She looked at the orange she held, rolled it over in her hand a few times and set it down on the counter before her, appearing to have lost interest in eating it. "My mom's not dead. She's smart. She would hide if she saw them in the hall. She's hiding until it's safe to come back to the room. Besides, Ricardo was out there. They're probably together. He'll protect her."

"You said he went out early this morning and never came back?"

"He was gone when we woke up. He's really into working out and he likes to use the gym when it isn't packed."

"He's your security guard, and he just leaves you alone sometimes? Is that normal for him?"

"He keeps his phone on him at all times and he doesn't leave us long or if we're not secure. We've been staying at this hotel over a month since shooting started back up and no one has figured it out. He wouldn't have left unless he was one hundred percent sure we were safe."

"But he didn't come back."

"He left before my mom. They both left before the screaming. They'll be back when they can make it back safe."

He started to ask if it was possible her mother and bodyguard had been the ones screaming, but thought better of it.

"I know what you're thinking. They're not dead. They're just hiding like we are, and everyone else in this hotel."

He thought of that as he finished preparing his sandwich and slid on the top piece of bread. He'd heard too much screaming for everyone in the hotel to have survived, but it was possible some had. They had. Granted, he'd had to scale a building, and he doubted many others had done the same. It had been quiet for a while though. Maybe the infected people had given up on finding anyone else and left the building. "Did your mom take a cell phone with her?"

"I've called her a bunch of times. Phone calls won't go through."

"I had the same trouble, but I finally got through to my assistant's voicemail right before I discovered you."

"That's why you were yelling."

"Yes. I was angry. I'm ready to leave this place."

Her eyes widened, hopeful. "Maybe I can get through to my mom."

She quickly slid off the barstool and ran up the stairs to the second floor. Justain grabbed his mug of freshly brewed coffee and moved it and the plated sandwich over to the coffee table, choosing to eat while seated on the sofa rather than the bar. He picked up the remote and turned the TV on, quickly pressing the mute button. He may not have heard anything in the hall for a while, but he wasn't taking unnecessary chances.

A video of a woman tearing into a man's chest filled the screen and Justain's stomach started to protest the sandwich he'd just taken a bite out of. He scrolled through channels, but they were all filled with the same thing, except for the weather channel and the Disney Channel. He opted to watch a muted children's show featuring what looked like a talking dog while eating.

Emma came down the stairs with a cell phone in her hand. The frown on her face told him the call hadn't been successful.

"You didn't reach her?"

"It dropped without even ringing like it's been doing all day long."

Justain retrieved the cell phone he'd transferred from his robe pocket to the back pocket of the borrowed slacks and attempted to call his assistant. The call immediately dropped. "Damn it. Well, it worked earlier. I guess you just have to keep trying until you get through. It should be easier this time of night, or morning, whatever part of the day you would consider this to be. Most people should be asleep."

"We aren't." She plopped down in the chair to the left of him. "I haven't slept in almost twenty-four hours. I can't. There were infected people outside right on the sidewalk for hours today. My mom and bodyguard are out in the hotel hiding from however many of them are out there. I can't sleep until my mom's back here."

Justain finished up his sandwich and rubbed his hands together, ridding them of bread crumbs, and took a big sip of coffee. He studied the girl out the side of his eye as he considered his next move. He'd planned on just getting clothes from her and had lucked into food and coffee. He'd not intended on being a babysitter and it was looking to him like her mother and bodyguard were dead. His own mother had spent the majority of her time traveling with her lovers and when she was around she was drunk, but from what he gathered from television, most mothers would walk through fire for their children. He didn't think a mother would stay away from her child a full day while the equivalent of zombies were lurking in the hallways right outside that kid's door.

Emma was on the young side, he guessed somewhere between twelve and fourteen, but she was a very pretty girl and had the beginnings of what looked like would blossom into a really nice figure. If this disease spread as easy as the news made it seem, the pool of uninfected women could be scarce really soon. It was in his best interest to keep this girl with him in case he needed a woman.

He powered off his cell phone to preserve the battery. There was food in the room and they had television, even if nothing good was playing and his clothes were uncomfortable, so he couldn't fully enjoy anything, but it could be worse. They'd wait. If the girl's mother and bodyguard came back, fine. Maybe the mother was young and attractive.

If they didn't, someone else might come save them. The news said someone would, and he had to believe the city officials would know better than to screw over their most important people. Money bought everything in this town and he had plenty to throw around to those who were loyal. The city was going to need a lot of cash to fix the damage caused by the viral outbreak. There was no way he'd be forgotten. He just had to wait.

Worst-case scenario… he had to spend time alone with a pretty, young girl while waiting long enough to make sure any infected people in the hotel cleared out.

Misty popped another Reese's miniature into her mouth and watched the television screen as footage of military vehicles flooding Washington D.C. was shown. Of course, the military was going to protect the president and other government officials before anyone else. The president had released a statement that a full investigation was being conducted on the virus implanted in the mail-order brides from Russia and they were working with the best scientists and health professionals to counter the deadly attack on the American people.

All government buildings were on full lockdown and hospital emergency rooms were closed. Military and police personnel heavily guarded hospitals and the only people allowed admittance were health professionals and women in labor. Anyone else had to call an emergency number running along the bottom of the screen to get preapproval for treatment and have their names added to a list, but with people flooding the phone lines, barely anyone could get through. Of course, this enraged people and they disregarded the order to stay at home unless absolutely necessary. People flooded their area hospitals and clinics, demanding to be treated and caused riots which attracted the attention of infected people.

Misty jumped as she detected movement behind her. Relief set in as she realized it was just Mike. His clothes were wrinkled, and he attempted to smooth his mussed hair with his hands, indicating he'd slept, but his eyes didn't seem to agree with the rest of the visual.

"Rough night?"

"A lot of tossing and turning." He sat near her on the sofa and yawned, looking up at the screen. "Any good news?"

"No. It's only getting worse."

"Wonderful." He looked down at the assorted wrappers littering the floor. "Did you sleep at all?"

"I dozed a little here and there, but bad dreams never let me sleep long."

"Yeah, I know what you mean." He ran his hand through his hair and stood. "I'm going to look out front and see if there's anyone on the street."

Misty sat straight up. "I'll come with you."

"I really don't think anyone else is in here with us. We would have heard something by now."

"Are you willing to bet your life on that?"

"Good point." Mike looked around, frowning.

"What is it?"

"I'd feel a lot better if I had a weapon, just in case."

"I already looked while you were sleeping, or I thought you were sleeping. They kept the Xbox and TV, even have them functioning, and some framed pictures and stuff, but that's about all in this display. Did you check the bedroom?"

"Yeah. Toothbrushes, but no toothpaste in the bathroom. Bar of soap, but no water hooked up. Some baseball jerseys from one of his tours. Nothing in the way of a weapon. I was hoping for at least a baseball bat or something."

"Were there any cars belonging to baseball players out there?"

He shook his head. "I don't remember any. I saw a car belonging to some gangsters. It's possible they'd use guns as part of their display, but they'd be fake, I'm sure. Did you see anything in the gift shop we could use?"

"No, other than snacks and drinks, it was all just posters, T-shirts, books, and toys like remote control cars and stuff." She thought back to when they'd entered the museum and what all they had passed. "Wait. Wasn't there a car from the *Zombie Huntress* movie out there?"

Mike looked like he was about to roll his eyes, but had just barely stopped himself. "Unless the Zombie Huntress comes with it, I don't think the car is going to be much help."

"Follow me." Misty slid her feet into the house shoes she'd found in the gift shop and walked to the door. With the handle in her grip, she suddenly lost her nerve. "Okay, you go out first and then I'll direct you where to go."

He grinned before moving over to the door. "So you're willing to sacrifice me to whatever waits outside the door, huh?"

"Didn't you come to Hollywood to be an action hero? I'm just the sexy eye candy. That's why the men get paid more. Time to earn it."

He laughed, but didn't protest. He quietly unlocked and opened the door, sticking his head out to scan the area before fully stepping out of the vehicle. "Come on. The coast is clear as far as I can see."

Misty stepped out and waited as he quietly closed the door behind them. She considered going back into the tour bus to grab her tote bag in case they ran into trouble, but she didn't exactly have any lifesaving supplies in it.

"Okay, where was the *Zombie Huntress* car?"

"This way." Misty gestured with her head in the direction they should go and waited for Mike to move that way before she fell into step next to him.

"And here I thought you were going to walk behind me so I'd be the first to come face to face with anything we might have missed in here."

"No. I might be a chicken-shit, but I'm not a complete witch."

Mike smiled. "If we're being honest, I'm scared too. I just know we can't stay in the tour bus forever. For starters, with no water hooked up, I am not using the bathroom in there and for another, I wasn't able to sleep last night worrying about my parents and that young girl I saw across the street at the hotel."

Misty hadn't slept either, worrying about the girl. She hoped Justain hadn't discovered her. She knew firsthand what a villain he was, but she'd heard dozens of stories about powerful men in Hollywood thinking every woman looking for a big break wanted to sleep with them, even if they said no. It was a game to them, or maybe they just couldn't comprehend a woman actually refusing what they considered a great honor. Those were grown women who came to them seeking fame though. She hoped the man wasn't low enough to stoop to doing to that girl the same thing he'd done to her. At least she didn't think he still had the drug he'd used on her in his possession. He'd started down the rope she'd made of bedsheets only a minute or two after her and she'd heard the door to his suite come crashing down right before looking up to see his dangling bits as he swung a chubby leg over the railing to start the climb down so he had had little time for grabbing anything.

"Where's your mind at?"

Misty jumped, her face flushing as she caught Mike's steady gaze on her. She hadn't really paid him much attention before, other than to just be thankful the guy had literally saved her life moments before she would have become a zombie piñata, but he was a pretty good-looking guy and not in bad shape either. He was slim but fit, with strong arms and long legs. "I always thought Asian men were tiny," she said, her face immediately warming as she realized she'd just spoken her thought out loud.

"Oh wow, I'm so sorry," she blurted, but he was laughing.

"I'm a bit on the tall side at five-foot-eleven, but the average height for South Korean men is five-foot-eight, so we are not as short as many stereotypes portray. Also, we are not Chinese or Japanese who, on average, are a little shorter in general, but we tend to all get lumped together. There are exceptions, of course. There are many Asian men over six feet tall and many short men who are white, black, Native, or Hispanic."

"I didn't mean anything by that. I just—"

"I know. It's cool, but that wasn't what you were thinking of when I asked."

"It wasn't." She looked ahead for the *Zombie Huntress* car, but they still hadn't reached it. "I was thinking about the people you saw in the hotel. I definitely think the girl should be saved if she's alone or with someone who could hurt her."

Mike frowned. "You think she could be with someone who'd hurt her?"

They turned a corner and the *Zombie Huntress* display loomed before them, taking up its own corner section in the room they'd entered. "Look, there it is."

Misty quickly climbed over the red velvet rope that kept the public away from the vehicle and moved to the open trunk. The car, a black Malibu, had been parked so that viewers could see the open trunk and all the goodies it contained, but only if they moved around to the left of the display, which they had not done while checking the place out the previous day.

"Is this for real?" Mike asked, joining her to look down into the trunk. It was full of weapons from the movie, everything from axes to spiked baseball bats.

"They're just props, but that ax looks pretty real."

"That would be because it is real." Mike pulled the ax free of the trunk and gasped with excitement. His eyes lit up as he handed her the regular ax in favor of the battle axe he'd discovered. It had two curved blades, one on each side, and a staff about three feet long.

"Would the two of you like a little privacy?"

He laughed, testing the battle axe out. He smiled ear to ear as he whipped it around, spun it in circles, and sliced through the air. "This will work just fine."

Misty tested out the weight of the ax, found it a little heavy, and looked back in the trunk for something more her style. She found fake grenades and guns, and a crossbow that looked real, but she didn't know if it would be as effective in her hands as it was in Daryl Dixon's or the Zombie Huntress. She figured if an infected person was far enough away that she'd have time to line up a shot, they probably weren't much of a threat to her. She needed something quick and effective for the ones who might pop up on her out of the shadows. She eyed the studded bat. It would be easy to swing, but she could just picture the damn thing getting stuck in someone's head.

"Didn't the Zombie Huntress have a compartment or something inside the car?"

The front car doors were already open so people could see inside, so Misty ran to the driver's side and slid into the seat. The custom hidden pull-out compartment between the two seats was already pulled out as part of the display and it held two of the Zombie Huntress's most often used weapons: a sharp dagger and a hatchet.

"That looks more your size," Mike commented, leaning down to peer into the passenger side of the car. "What are you going to use?"

Misty tested out the weight of each weapon, both of which were very real and not the fake ones used in actual fight scenes. She stepped out of the car and swung the hatchet. "This isn't as light as the dagger, but I like that I can swing in an arc and not have to be as close as I'd have to be with the dagger to actually do some damage."

"You can take both and just carry one as a back-up in case anything happens. I'm taking this bad boy right here."

"Yeah, the two of you had a little bonding experience." She grinned but quickly sobered as she looked at the hatchet and imagined it sinking into flesh. "Do you really think we'll have to use these?"

"I don't know, but it's best to be prepared just in case." He rolled the battle axe over in his hands. "Not even a week ago, none of this stuff was real. A virus that kills people and then reanimates them, sending them on some psycho mission to eat everyone they come across? The news says the military and police are supposed to be handling it, but do you really think they ever had an action plan for this? Nuclear bombs, cyber-attacks, terrorists, deadly diseases that wipe out millions of people but leave them dead… That's what they plan for. This isn't something anyone plans for. This is a horror movie that came off screen."

"Can you do it? Can you kill one of those people?"

"I can and I will." He held her gaze over the roof of the car between them. "I almost did right before I found you. I had been running for hours, trying to find a place to hide, but nothing was unlocked. Every time I tried to stop and rest, here came someone infected, sometimes alone and sometimes a small group. Soon I had a small army of them following me, so I ducked down that alley and one came out of nowhere and damn near got me. I can tell you that having been that close to one, whoever those poor bastards might have been before the virus, that's not them anymore. They are dead."

"Are you sure about that or are you just assuming it because these people are like zombies now and in the TV shows and movies they're always thoughtless monsters?"

"I know the man who popped up and tried to kill me didn't have a single thought in his head other than I was dinner and he was starving. I didn't succeed in killing him, but if I had, I wouldn't feel a bit of regret." He sighed. "If the military doesn't find us, if the government doesn't eradicate this disease before it's too late, you're going to be put in a situation where it's kill or be killed. I really hope the slight chance that there might be some part of a person's mind still in these monsters' heads doesn't make you think too long which way to go."

She looked at the hatchet in her hands and hoped she didn't take too long to think about it either, whether she found herself up against one of the infected, or Harry Justain.

"Okay, well, now that we are armed, let's head back up front. I really have to use the facilities and I want to check out what's happening outside."

"Okay." Misty retrieved the dagger, deciding to keep it as a back-up like Mike suggested, and followed him as he made his way toward the front of the building, suddenly aware of increasing pressure in her own bladder.

Misty used the bathroom faster than she ever had in her entire life, washed her hands in the blink of an eye, and walked out into the lobby to find herself alone. She tightened her hand around the hatchet and scanned left to right while waiting for Mike.

He finally stepped out of the men's room a moment later and stopped, looked at her, then back at the bathroom, then returned his gaze to her. "That is the first time a woman has ever beaten me out of a bathroom." He grinned. "You were scared, weren't you?"

"Hell yes, I was scared," she snapped. "Have you ever seen a scary movie? Do you know what psychos can appear out of nowhere to get you when you're in a stall with your panties around your ankles?" She blushed, realizing what she'd said. She'd never actually discussed using the bathroom with a man before, preferring to pretend she didn't do such dirty unavoidable tasks.

He laughed. "I guess we didn't really have to use separate bathrooms. It's just us here."

"We hope," she said. "I kept imagining someone grabbing my ankle beneath the stall or rushing at me once I opened the door."

"You're safe. Even if something happened, you would have screamed and I would have come running." He started across the lobby, ducking down as he reached the glass door.

"Are the infected people from yesterday still out there?" Misty wrapped her arms around herself. If infected people were out there, she didn't want to see them. Watching them all night on the news had been bad enough, and she still had flashbacks from the scene she'd stumbled upon in the hotel hallway.

"Those ones are gone, but there are others. They're just shuffling around out there." He walked over to the admissions counter and picked up the phone. He dialed a number, waited a moment, and cursed, slamming the phone back down.

"Your parents?"

He nodded, clenched his jaw a moment, then returned to the front where he sat on the floor, hidden from view behind the enormous poster covering the floor to ceiling window next to the door.

"Are they in Korea?"

"No. My family moved here when I was about five years old. They live in Nebraska."

"There's a base there! I think a big one. They probably made it there very early on before all the traffic jams." Misty suddenly became very excited, unsure why. She didn't know Mike's parents. She barely knew him.

He smiled at her, but it didn't reach his eyes. Without saying anything, he went back to watching the street, his gaze fixed on one point.

"You're looking for the girl?"

He nodded. "I don't know if my parents made it to the base or locked themselves in at home. I don't know if they're alive or dead and there's not a damn thing I can do for them right now, but if that girl is alive in that hotel, I'm going to save her."

Ladeja jerked awake, sitting straight up. She looked around, searching for what had made the loud noise that had ripped her from precious sleep. A large shadow loomed in the connecting doorway between her and Manny's room and she sucked in a hefty dose of air, but could not expel it to produce the scream she felt trying to tear out of her.

"It's just me." Manny stepped into the room. "Sorry. I didn't mean to startle you. I was just checking on you two."

"Two?" Ladeja looked down at the bed and found Cory sleeping next to where she'd been lying. Just Cory. Her heart leaped into her throat.

"Mateo is in my room. He said he kept getting squished. I wasn't sleeping anyway."

"Oh." Ladeja placed her hand over her racing heart just as someone squealed from downstairs. "What are they doing?"

"They've been doing it all night," Manny complained. "Telling them there's infected people out there who follow loud noises and try to eat any uninfected person they come across won't get them to shut up either. Fortunately, this house is a pretty good distance from the others."

"Yeah, but if you really felt secure, you'd have slept, at least a little before they woke you up. Do these people ever sleep?"

"Probably during the day. They're down there playing pool, drinking, and dancing, except for Mimi. I actually saw her in the gym. She's working out on the stair climber in that same thing she was wearing when we got here last night."

Ladeja blinked at him. "She was wearing a negligee."

"Yup."

"She's working out in a negligee?"

"Yup." He grinned. "And those heels."

"Wow." Ladeja laughed. Despite the dangerous situation they were in, she had to chuckle at the image of Mimi Perry on a stair climber in that ridiculous attire.

"She's sipping from a wine glass too."

"Lawd." Ladeja leaned forward, laughing until she snorted, which caused Manny to join in. "These people are freaking crazy. Wait a minute. You said since we got here last night? What time is it?"

"About seven in the morning," he answered. "These curtains are pretty damn thick, and block out all the light. I imagine it helps them sleep during the day whenever they stop the partying and settle down."

"Yeah." Ladeja yawned, rolling her eyes when another loud whoop came up the stairs. "I don't know how the boys are doing it, but I don't think I can sleep through all their fun. You should try though. I'm up now. I'll keep an eye out for anything weird."

Manny shoved his hands into his pockets and stood straighter, defiant.

"Come on, Manny, I know you want to keep us safe, but if something goes down and you haven't slept at all, how effective do you think you're going to be? Get some rest. I will be fine. You know I wouldn't do anything to jeopardize my son's life."

He nodded. "I know. Okay, I'll try, but anything strange happens, anything at all, even if you just get a bad feeling in your gut, you come get me and O'Donnell immediately."

"I promise."

He turned toward his room but stopped, looking back over his shoulder. "And stay as far away as possible from Terrell Houston."

"Oh, you didn't even have to warn me about him."

Manny eyed her closely for a moment, nodded, and left, hopefully to get some sleep.

Ladeja kicked the covers off of her, stood, and stretched. She padded across the bedroom and stepped inside the bathroom, leaving the door cracked as she brushed her teeth and combed her hair. She found everything she needed in the bathroom and assumed rich people kept toiletries available for their guests in case they didn't bring their own, and it wasn't cheap stuff either.

She finished in the bathroom and tiptoed over to the bed. She smiled to herself as she pulled the cover up around Cory's shoulders and tucked him in. He looked so angelic in sleep, like when he was a little boy and she was his world. She missed those days before middle school started and his father became rich and famous. Suddenly, she wasn't good enough for him, but she still loved him. She hoped it was a phase and he'd come back around to being the sweet boy who adored her as much as she adored him.

Loud laughter drifted up the stairs, and she sighed. Mimi Perry might know how to make her guests feel welcome, but she wasn't that great at making them cautious. She glanced at the chair she'd left her folded clothes on and opted to stay in the borrowed pajamas Mimi had loaned her. Not a negligee, thank goodness, but drawstring yoga pants and a Mimi Couture T-shirt.

She stepped out of the bedroom and closed the door behind her. She stood there for a moment, afraid to move, but she was hungry and didn't know how long it would be until Cory and Mateo woke up. She definitely didn't want to wake them before they were ready. With everything going on she didn't know when or if they'd get another good night's sleep and they'd both lost so much, maybe sleep would gift them a dream of a life where they still had both parents and monsters weren't walking the streets.

Manny was right there with him. Even though the rooms were separate, the connecting door between them was open and Manny would protect her son. She thought of all he'd done for her since the outbreak was announced and smiled to herself. A moment later, her mouth turned down into a frown. Thunda had been there for her once too. Now she was raising his child on her own because instead of being with her, he'd dropped her for a reality star and died trying to get even more fame and money.

"Food now, men never again," she murmured as she turned and made her way down the stairs, headed straight for the kitchen. She'd met Mimi's guests the night before and wasn't in any rush to mingle with them again. In addition to the Camilleri sisters, Terrell Houston, and Mimi's hair and makeup guy, Toddy, she'd met Mara Monet, Terrell's co-star in the movie he was working with Mimi on and possibly his girlfriend. Whether he was aware of that or not, Ladeja wasn't sure, but the woman definitely didn't seem to like any females in the house.

Ladeja entered the kitchen and found O'Donnell and Chelle sitting at the kitchen island. O'Donnell nursed a cup of steaming hot coffee and Chelle sat across from him, her leg stretched out over the two barstools next to her. The TV between them was on broadcasting news.

"Hey!" O'Donnell greeted her. "Please tell me you're a whiz in the kitchen because we are hungry and, well, I pretty much live off of drive-thru food."

"I live off of food made by staff," Chelle mumbled, picking at the bagel and cream cheese on the plate in front of her.

"I don't want to wake up Sarah," O'Donnell continued, lowering his voice. "I caught her sleeping in the laundry room. Poor woman looked knocked out."

"I imagine so," Ladeja replied, moving over to the refrigerator. "Those people have probably been running her ragged all night."

She looked in the refrigerator and pulled out a carton of eggs and a package of bacon. "Bacon and eggs?"

"Never can go wrong with that," O'Donnell said. "I

appreciate it."

"That's like a million calories," Chelle said. "Does Mimi have egg whites? Our cook made egg white omelets with spinach and peppers."

Ladeja studied the girl for a moment. She also wore Mimi Couture pajamas, but hers were silk instead of cotton, and she wore makeup despite having nowhere to go. "You do know that all eggs contain egg whites? You just have to separate them."

She frowned. "How do you do that?"

Ladeja shook her head, wondering how people could make it through life without knowing the simplest things. "Maybe you'll find out someday, but not today. I don't have time to give cooking lessons, nor do I have time to separate out egg whites to make you an omelet. I'm going to scramble up a bunch of eggs and fry up this package of bacon. If you want some, good. Otherwise, you're on your own. I'm sure you'll burn off whatever calories you take in if those idiots in the game room keep whoopin' and hollerin' and we find ourselves running from the infected they attract."

Chelle's gaze dropped to her bagel, and she continued picking at it in silence. O'Donnell arched an eyebrow at her as if to question her snippiness, but Ladeja told herself she didn't have time to worry about the poor little rich girl's feelings. She found frying pans and went to work preparing the breakfast food. Her conscience nagged at her a bit, pointing out that she could have responded to Chelle in a nicer way, but she argued back with it that she didn't have to make anyone anything. Just a quick glance around the kitchen told her there was an abundant supply of muffins, cookies, breads, and fruit. She was sure the cabinets would provide several other ready to eat snack foods. Mimi was known to struggle with her weight, so she was pretty sure egg white omelets weren't the main things on her regular menu. She had to have a stash of Twinkies or something somewhere. She would have just grabbed something simple herself, but she couldn't shake the feeling that this might be one of the last times she could enjoy a hot cooked meal.

"Has there been any good news at all?" she asked O'Donnell.

He sipped his coffee and shook his head. "It's a damn mess. Cell towers are still overloaded, hospitals are a damn nightmare, and the military is too busy with them and government buildings to really get out and help people. They won't stay inside like they were told to, and it's just causing this shit to spread even faster. The president did make an announcement before they secured him away from it all. They're running an investigation, however good that does at all right now, and they say they've got the brightest minds working around the clock on a vaccine."

"A vaccine?" Ladeja flipped the bacon strips over and poured the eggs, yolks and all, into another frying pan. "That would work to prevent the virus, but what about the people already infected? Are they saying they can reverse the virus in the people already sick?"

"All they said was they were working on a vaccine. I think we all know that won't do shit against the people already infected, but they won't broadcast that to an already panicked country. While a vaccine is good news, we still have to stay alive and uninfected long enough to get it."

"So what are they planning on doing with the already infected?"

"They haven't said. They just keep reiterating that people need to stay inside and off the streets. They quit telling people with symptoms to come to the hospital because hypochondriacs, senior citizens, overprotective parents and generally anyone with the damn sniffles overran them. The military is turning people away from the hospitals unless they're pregnant women in labor or they're on a pre-approved list they're supposed to call in for but people keep flocking to the hospital because they can't get through when they try the number."

"So what are the sick supposed to do?" she asked as she turned the stove off and grabbed dishes out of a cabinet.

O'Donnell shrugged. "I'm afraid to even answer that. If someone truly has the virus and turns into what we saw back at the Camilleri mansion and out walking the streets, the only thing their family members can do is kill them, which I imagine most family members won't do."

"So if they can't escape them or keep them confined somehow, they'll get eaten alive or infected themselves."

"Yeah. It's pretty fucked up and I don't see how this is going to get any better anytime soon. They released numbers on how many mail-order brides were brought over from Russia in the past five years, and that number alone is staggering. Throw in the number of them that divorce within a couple of years and sleep with others, infecting them, how many of those people who carried the virus without knowing slept with other people, how many of them donated blood… It's a living nightmare."

Ladeja's hands shook as she transferred the food onto two serving dishes and placed them on the kitchen island. She took a deep breath, trying to calm herself, before she grabbed three plates and silverware.

"I didn't mean to scare you."

"I know." She passed out the plates and silverware and took a seat next to O'Donnell. "We should stay a little scared though. I'm afraid that getting comfortable could be the difference between life and death. I have two boys to take care of."

"You're a good person for taking in Mateo. I'll help you any way I can."

"I couldn't leave the boy. No one else would take care of him." She eyed Chelle and noticed her blush.

"I imagine when they get this under control, there will be some sort of process for abandoned children. There's bound to be a lot of them displaced."

Ladeja picked at her food. She couldn't imagine dumping the boy off at some shelter. "Hopefully they'll make the adoption process easier. I'll keep him as long as he wants to stay with me. I can't stand the thought of him being abandoned another time."

"Was Mateo's mom infected at the party?" Chelle asked.

"She was killed. An infected man ate her while Mateo and my son hid in the next room in the guesthouse where he was told to stay in because your family didn't want him seen. I'm surprised you know his name."

"I didn't until just now." Chelle's eyes watered a little. "I know what people outside my zip code think of my family. I know that to a point, they're probably right. We are shallow, and spoiled and we have more than we'll ever need and we still want more. I'm not proud of it."

Ladeja and O'Donnell both sat silent, staring at the girl. Ladeja would have never expected those words to come out of the teen's mouth.

"Why do you continue acting in a way you're not proud of?" she finally asked, genuinely curious.

"Why does anyone do anything?" Chelle shrugged. "Training? Expectation? Ignorance? All I know is I have three older sisters who are gorgeous and if they had any flaws, they got them fixed because our mother criticized anything less and our dad was really only a dad when it came to photo ops. He cared more about his clients' lives than ours. We were just to be pretty pictures when needed. Growing up in that family, you learn to be beautiful and to be popular and to topple anyone you can convince yourself is inferior to you. You do it because you know you have to be perfect to get your parents' love and you do it because you're desperate for someone to love you, even if it's strangers on the internet who you'll never meet or people who line up for hours to get your autograph just to talk about you once they're out of the line."

"That's why you got plastic surgery? So your family would love you?"

"Sometimes I look in the mirror and I don't even know who is looking back." She looked at the bacon and eggs in the serving dishes and licked her lips. "That smells fantastic."

"You've never had bacon and eggs before?"

"With all the fat? Of course not. Obesity is the worst disease anyone in my family could get."

"Really? Worse than cancer or HIV?" Ladeja scooped up a small heap of eggs from her plate and put them in her mouth.

"Yes. If you get cancer or HIV, you can get a lot of sympathy and your posts about it would definitely go viral. Sales from our products would explode and our show's ratings would go through the roof. If you get fat, well then you're just pathetic and ugly and you become the worst kind of tabloid fodder."

Ladeja slowly chewed her food and swallowed, amazed how Chelle could go from really deep to beyond shallow in just a few seconds. As she watched, the girl almost started to visually salivate, still eying the food.

"Oh, for crying out loud, eat the food." She heaped a pile of scrambled eggs onto the plate she'd set out for the girl and tossed some strips of bacon on it. "We're all probably going to die soon anyway and if by some chance we do survive this, we'll probably be starving so you and your sisters can quit obsessing over calories and public image. You'll probably be bean poles with big, sagging fake boobs and asses anyway. Enjoy the bacon while you can."

Toddy burst through the door, startling all three of them. "Where's Mimi?"

"I think she tired of my sisters," Chelle answered. "I

thought she went to bed."

"Manny saw her in the gym," Ladeja said, her gut twisting as she noted Toddy's wide eyes and rapid breathing. "What's wrong?"

"It's Mara. I think she's infected."

6

Mara was a bitch. She'd done nothing but give stank-eye to every woman in the house, but Ladeja still wouldn't wish the infection on her. She wouldn't even wish it on Cynda and that was saying a lot because she'd definitely wish a case of inflamed ass herpes on her. In fact, she had. Several times.

"I don't understand why she's in my bed," Mimi screeched, pacing the floor in her heels and sweat-soaked negligee, all her goodies clearly on display through the flimsy wet material.

"We put her away from people so she wouldn't get them sick," Terrell explained, his eyes fixed on Mimi's body as she continued sashaying back and forth, totally unconcerned with the peepshow she was giving.

"We put her away from people so she wouldn't eat them," Toddy corrected him, earning a lethal glare.

"She's not infected," Terrell said. "She's just not feeling good."

"None of the infected people are feeling good either," Toddy shot back at him, hiding behind O'Donnell when Terrell took a step toward him.

O'Donnell narrowed his eyes at the shorter, skinnier

man until he got the point and stepped away from him.

"Everyone needs to calm down," O'Donnell addressed the group standing outside Mimi's bedroom, which included everyone except the kids, Manny, and Chelle, who said she didn't want to walk on her sore ankle unless absolutely necessary. Ladeja had a suspicion she'd stayed in the kitchen so she could hog the bacon and eggs without judgment. She'd seen her expression when she'd tried her first forkful of scrambled eggs and the only word she could think of to describe it was orgasmic. "What exactly happened? What symptoms is she showing?"

"She just got sick," Terrell answered, shrugging.

"There's a lot of ways a person can be sick," O'Donnell snapped. "She seemed just fine when we met her yesterday and she's been partying it up with you all down here all night long, so what happened to make you think she needs bedrest all of a sudden?"

"Look at her!"

"Yeah, I did." O'Donnell cast another glance in the room at where the woman lay supine in Mimi's bed, her sweat soaking into the rose-colored silk sheets. Her skin was flushed, her eyes, when opened, were red-rimmed, and tears silently spilled from the corners.

"I'm looking at her right now," Mimi added. "I'm still trying to figure out why she's in my bed. I gave you two a perfectly good guest room upstairs."

"She couldn't make it up there and she needed to get to a bathroom quick, so we rushed her in there. After she threw up, she needed to lie down and she couldn't make it farther than your bed."

"And this hit suddenly right out of the blue?" O'Donnell asked.

"Yeah, man." Terrell coughed. "I told you that."

"Why the fuck did you just cough?" Toddy asked, pointing at him. "He's infected too! He's been sleeping with her and they been slopping that nasty virus all back and forth! They both need to go!"

"I'm not sick!" Terrell yelled. "People cough all the damn time. It's dusty!"

"First you put your sick girlfriend in my bed then you call my house that I graciously shared with you dusty?" Mimi planted her hands on her hips, pulling the wet thus completely sheer fabric taut across her chest. "The only thing dusty is your career. You haven't had a hit movie in years!"

"Hooker, you been lip-synching for at least the past ten!"

"Who are you calling a hooker?"

"The old ho standing in front of me with her breastesses hanging out for attention! Who the fuck works out in a nightie and hooker heels? A desperate ho getting attention the only way she knows how, that's who!"

Mimi gasped, her face growing redder as she struggled to come up with a response.

"Maybe you should put the titties away," Toddy softly suggested. "At least take a shower and put on something more suitable for running in case this bitch gets up and decides to have us as appetizers."

"Motherfucker, I done told you—"

"Hey!" Ladeja yelled in her mama voice, effectively silencing the two arguing men and gaining the group's attention. "O'Donnell and I have been out there in this shit. It isn't a joke."

"We were out there too," Cheyanne cut in as she and her sisters gave Ladeja serious stank-eye.

"Yes, I know. I saw you run right past your sister when she needed help," Ladeja replied. "As I was saying, the situation out there is serious and if there's even a chance that anyone in this house is infected, we have to be extremely careful. She needs to be watched, and Terrell, you should be too, because if she's infected, you're infected."

"I told you we—"

"And I told you this ain't shit we're gonna play with!

You might play a badass thug in the movies, but I have two real badasses with me and they will drop your ass easily if you push them. I have children here and I'm not jeopardizing their lives so you and your ego can just shut the hell up now, and Mimi, seriously, you need some real clothes on and some shoes you won't break your damn neck in. If shit hits the fan, we're going to be running for our lives."

"Ugh, it's not like I don't have security," she exclaimed, rolling her eyes.

"Honestly, so did we," Cara advised. "O'Donnell is the only one who survived."

"Well, dahlings, there's a lot to be said for quality employees."

"Mimi, just put some real clothes on," Ladeja snapped, hoping to get her out of the way before yet another argument broke out within the group. "Please, for your own good."

"Ugh, fine!" She whipped the negligee over her head and flung it behind her as she sashayed into her bedroom in nothing but a thong and yanked open the door to the walk-in closet. The door banged against the wall as she disappeared inside the large closet Ladeja figured would probably be as big, if not bigger than, the one she'd seen at the Camilleri mansion.

"Did she really just storm off buck-ass nude like that?" Ladeja asked as Mara moaned, not appreciating the sound the door made when it hit the wall.

"Wasn't she pretty much naked already?" O'Donnell asked.

"What's the deal? It's just a human body," Cynda said. "I guess no one has ever seen your angelic ass naked before?"

"Not as many as have seen your fake ass naked."

"Jealous?"

"Why would I be? I didn't have to pay anything for my body and I don't have to flaunt it to strangers to feel better about myself."

"Ladies, that's enough." O'Donnell glared at them both, but the corner of his mouth twitched when he looked at Ladeja. "Has anyone else shown any symptoms of illness? Any symptoms at all?"

They all looked at each other and shook their heads.

"Terrell, you just coughed," Ladeja reminded him, "and from the way Mara has given every woman here death glares, it's obvious the two of you are sleeping together so you need to stay in the room with her."

"And get sick if I'm not sick?" He shook his head. "Hell no, that ain't right. You just want me to come down with something."

"No, we just want to make sure we don't come down with what the two of you have. If she really isn't infected you have nothing to worry about. Whatever it is will pass, right?"

"Can someone explain why there seems to be a negotiation going on down here when this man should just be taking his ass on where you told him to?"

Ladeja turned to see Manny walking into the room, a dark scowl on his face making him more attractive than usual. She heard the Camilleri women murmur their appreciation and bit the inside of her jaw to keep from telling them they'd better not even think about it, then immediately wondered why. She'd already decided men were off limits. Still, the thought of Manny with one of them boiled her blood.

"We were trying to play nice," O'Donnell told him as he reached the group. "This guy doesn't make it easy though."

"Do you know who the fuck I am?" Terrell asked, his voice elevating with each word. "I have cars that are worth more than your whole damn life."

"Will any of that shit really matter when you're dead?" Manny stepped closer, invading Terrell's space. He didn't stop until he was less than a breath away and looking down at the tall man.

"Are you threatening me?" Terrell held Manny's gaze, but his voice cracked as he asked the question, his nerves slipping through the false bravado.

"I am tired. I was trying to sleep after a long fucking day of saving rich dumbasses and a few people I care about. I came here and found even more rich dumbasses and they're really fucking loud and it's really fucking grating my nerves. All I know is there are real monsters outside and your ungrateful ass is in here disrespecting my girl, Ladeja, when she told you nicely that you need to get in that room with your sick girlfriend. Now, you can walk your ass on in there or I can dropkick it all the way down the hill where the monsters are probably still loitering and you can be their all-you-can-eat jackass buffet. What is it going to be?"

Ladeja held her breath as Terrell stared up into Manny's eyes, his nostrils flaring. Manny stood completely still, his face a blank mask. She'd seen him go blank like that before. Someone usually got his ass handed to him after Manny went blank. Terrell held his gaze and she could see in the set of his body he was struggling to stay strong before the man he damn well knew could reduce him to a drop of blood if the right buttons were pushed.

Terrell finally smiled, his eyes narrow and shady as hell as he backed up a step. "Whatever, man. Everybody in here all worked up over nothing. I'm gonna sit with my girl and make sure none of you crazy hypochondriacs try to put a bullet in her over a damn cold."

He walked into the room, muttering "Andre the Giant-sized Jason Momoa looking-ass motherfucker," under his breath and pulled out a chair from Mimi's vanity to set beside the bed. He plopped down in it, slouched, and crossed his arms as he glared at the woman in the bed. It was the same posture Ladeja had seen Cory adopt after being scolded.

"Wow, you certainly handled him well." Cara moved to

Manny's side, looking up at him all doe-eyed as she placed a hand directly over his bicep and gave it a little appreciative squeeze.

He glared down at her for a moment before his mouth gave way to a small, amused grin. "You heard the part about rich dumbasses, right?"

She stepped back, made a face like she'd been slapped and narrowed her eyes before growling and walking back to her sisters, who both glared at Ladeja as if she were the one who'd made the comment.

"I told you to get me if anything happened," Manny told her, stepping close to her.

"Nothing really happened, and O'Donnell is here. You needed sleep."

"Hard to sleep with all the yelling." He looked down at her a moment before looking over at O'Donnell. "The bitchy one with the nasty case of stank-eye is sick?"

"Yeah, and she's not looking too good at all," O'Donnell answered. "She's sweating a lot, man. She definitely has a fever."

"It just came on suddenly?" Manny looked back at Mara a moment, studying her as Sarah dabbed her face with a cool rag.

"That's what they said," Ladeja told him. "O'Donnell and I were in the kitchen with Chelle, eating breakfast."

"Which is probably almost cold now," O'Donnell said. "Can we get back to the kitchen now?"

"You can. I have to get back to my son and Mateo. They shouldn't be alone, even if it seems like everyone is down here. I don't want them alone at any time."

"I'm going back up," Manny told her as O'Donnell left them. "Finish eating and if you get tired again, wake me. We'll sleep in shifts, so someone is always awake and ready to protect the boys."

"Sounds like a deal."

"Is this better zombie apocalypse attire?" Mimi asked, stepping out of her walk-in. Her hair appeared to be freshly washed, indicating she had yet another bathroom within the walk-in, and anger made her shower pretty damn fast. She turned in a circle with her arms spread out, showing off her outfit. She'd traded the skimpy negligee and heels for a tight, hot pink tank top with a neckline that damn near plunged into her naval and skin-tight jeans with a hot pink leopard print pattern and black lace-up boots that stopped at just below her knees. They, of course, came with a skinny heel.

"Is she planning on running from the infected or trying to attract them on Tinder?" Manny asked, his face scrunched a bit as he scrutinized her and shook his head in disapproval.

Ladeja laughed. "Hey, at least she has a weapon. That giant-ass belt buckle can probably bash a skull in."

Manny eyed the heavy-looking gold hearts and music notes belt buckle accented with pink gemstones, possibly diamonds, and nodded his head in agreement. "Well, I'm going to get back to the boys and try to get a little sleep. I mean it, Ladeja. Wake me if anything happens, even if they're just bitching at each other again. That could have escalated."

"Aye aye, sir." She saluted him, earning a dirty look in return before he shook his head and walked away, muttering.

Ladeja returned to the kitchen to find the only bacon and eggs left were what she'd already scooped onto her own plate earlier and Chelle was eying them as she rubbed her hand over her belly.

"All those calories were worth it, weren't they?" She grinned as she sat down and stabbed eggs onto her fork, not caring that the food had started to go cold. She trusted Manny, but she still didn't want to be away from the boys.

"I couldn't help myself," Chelle answered, her voice full of defeat.

"Well, you'll be able to work it off if Mara and Terrell turn and we have to get out of here quick."

"Fuck that," O'Donnell said, lifting his coffee mug. He took a sip and grimaced before walking over to the sink to pour it out and grab a hot refill from the coffeemaker. "If one of them turns, I'm shooting both of them in the head. Problem solved, quick and easy. I don't want to go out there on the run again unless absolutely necessary. Those two aren't going to ruin this for us."

"You really think they're infected?" Chelle's eyes grew wide as she looked between them.

Ladeja and O'Donnell shared a look before she answered. "She's sweating a lot and a sudden high fever is one of the top symptoms the news has been warning about."

"What's are the other symptoms?" Chelle asked.

"Chewing on people," O'Donnell answered.

Ladeja rolled her eyes. "High fever, chills, delirium, and a sudden onset are the symptoms, and Mara has two of those, for sure."

Chelle visibly shivered. "At the party, the infected model looked and seemed fine when I saw her like two hours before she started attacking people. I didn't even see the others before they started. It was just chaos out of nowhere."

"Well, the news said some people get sick, appear to die, and wake up infected pretty quick," O'Donnell said, leaning back against the sink. "Some take longer."

"So she could, like, die, wake back up, and try to eat us before anyone even knew she'd turned into one of those things?"

"We kind of ordered Terrell to stay with her and keep watch," Ladeja advised. She turned to O'Donnell. "Of course, if he's infected he could change quicker than her, so we need to have someone watch over both of them."

"I'm going to go down to the gate and talk with the security guards, check out what they're doing to secure the property, and see if there's been any infected near the gate. If they can spare anyone to watch the house itself, I'll bring one back. If not, Manny and I will have to take shifts. I wouldn't trust anyone else, but you're going to have your hands full with the kids, and I know I don't even have to tell you to keep them far away."

Ladeja nodded her head, thinking the plan was good. "I told Manny to go upstairs and try to get some sleep. I think he watched over me and the kids all night. Did you sleep any?"

"Yeah, I was tired as hell when we got here, but all I really need is four hours and I'm good for a while. I'll trade off with Manny if I get tired. Between the two of us, we should be just fine watching Mara and Terrell. Watching over them and making sure there are no outside threats is where it gets more complicated. That's why I'm going to talk to security. If they can't spare a man, they can at least work out a communication system with me. I'm sure they report directly to Mimi, but I'm not comfortable putting the fate of our lives in her hands."

"I hate to wake up Manny now, but someone needs to watch over those two while you talk with security."

"Can't we just lock them in Mimi's room?" Chelle suggested as Toddy walked in and started rooting around in the refrigerator. "Then you can go check with security and Manny can sleep. He wouldn't need to get up unless one of them turned and tried to get out or attack the other. Anyone could watch them from outside the door and scream if they needed help. I guess even I could, so Ladeja can stay with the boys."

"What are you all talking about?" Toddy asked, sniffing food in a container he'd found.

"O'Donnell is going to the gate to talk with security and see if any infected have tried to get onto the property," Chelle told him, "but we need someone to watch Mara and Terrell in case they are infected."

"Why don't you just call the gate and talk to them?" Toddy asked. "And you don't have to go down to the gate to see what's happening. The security cameras show everything out there."

"Mimi has access to security cameras?" O'Donnell set his coffee mug down with a heavy thunk, clearly annoyed he hadn't been told about that, and possibly mad he hadn't thought about it himself.

"Of course she does. You're in the Hollywood Hills, honey. You never know when some crazy, obsessed stalker is going to jump a gate and go swimming butt-naked in your swimming pool. Everyone has security cameras."

"You sure you got enough sleep?" Ladeja asked. "That seems like something you would have thought of."

"It's usually something I'm told about right away when I introduce myself as security, and I haven't seen her look at any security footage."

"She was entertaining guests," Toddy explained. "Mimi likes to keep things festive and didn't want to kill the mood with all the yuckiness going on out there, so she hasn't been watching the news or the security footage. She figures if something happens, the guards will call her."

"Of course. We wanted to be downers with all the yuckiness," O'Donnell muttered. He stood up. "Can you take me to where I can view the footage and hook me up with how to contact the front gate?"

"Sure."

He looked around the room, focusing on the ceiling, and shook his head when he located the tiny camera in the corner. "Is there a camera recording in Mimi's room?"

"Yeah, security cameras in bedrooms are really popular. Makes it a lot easier to get flattering angles for sex tapes."

"TMI," Ladeja said as she started stacking the dishes they'd used.

"Oh, I'll clean up," Sarah said, rushing into the kitchen and grabbing a clean washcloth. She opened the freezer and grabbed a bucket of ice cubes to place inside it. "I'm sorry if you cooked that. If you're still hungry, I can fix you something."

"Girl, you are already being overworked," Ladeja

advised as she took the dishes to the sink. "Please be careful around Mara and Terrell. If they're infected, they can attack you. You shouldn't be in there with them at all."

"I can't let her suffer," Sarah said as she put the ice bucket back in the freezer and picked up the cold compress she'd just made. "She's burning up and moaning like she is in absolute agony."

Ladeja sighed, knowing in her gut the woman was jeopardizing her life by caring for a starlet who'd been nothing but nasty to all of them. "Just make sure you're protecting yourself. The sudden onset of fever definitely sounds like the virus that's changing people into those flesh-eating monsters. If she starts talking out of her head or she even looks like she might be dead or about to kick it, get your ass out of that room and lock the door behind you. I'm pretty sure taking a zombie bite isn't in your job description."

Sarah nodded and rushed off with the compress while Ladeja finished rinsing off the dishes and placed them in the dishwasher.

"I think that went in one ear and right out the other," she muttered.

"You can't save people from themselves," O'Donnell told her. "You don't need to worry about anyone but the boys. Toddy and I are going to check out that security footage. I'll keep one eye on the perimeter and one eye on what's happening in Mimi's room."

Ladeja nodded her agreement as he walked out of the room with Toddy, then turned to leave the room herself.

"I can help you watch the boys," Chelle offered, stopping her.

She turned and raised an eyebrow. "Why would you want to do that?"

"Don't my sisters and I kind of owe it to Mateo? His mother died on our property. I owe you too." She looked down and seemed to gather herself before continuing. "When I hurt my ankle and fell, I heard my sisters running behind me. Then I felt and saw them run right past me and suddenly it was like everything went quiet except for the shuffling. I was too scared to turn my head at first, so all I saw was all three of my sisters running past me, leaving me, while the shuffling behind me got closer and closer."

Fresh tears silently slid down her cheek. "I saw my life flash before my eyes and all it consisted of was social media numbers, sales figures, *Entertainment Tonight* interviews, photo shoots, surgeries, and a lot of nights spent alone while surrounded by people I barely knew but cared way too much about their opinions. It hit me how pathetic it all was right about the same time it hit me that my older sisters were leaving me to die."

She wiped the tears away with her hand and sniffed, straightening her shoulders. "Mimi put us in the guesthouse. She said it was because we deserved the best accommodations, but I know it was because she doesn't really like us. Mimi doesn't really like anyone she thinks is prettier, younger, or thinner than her, but she plays nice to get our mentions. Mentions in the Twittersphere and on Instagram are currency and she'll pretend to be the gracious hostess to get them just like my sisters will talk her up to get their names out there with her too. I don't want to be out there with them, away from everyone else, and I don't want to be in here with them either. They've already shown me I can't count on them if anything happens. If Mara and Terrell turn or any other infected people get in here, they would probably shove me right into them to buy them time to escape."

"Damn, that's fucked up." Ladeja shook her head and considered what to do. It hadn't even been twenty-four hours since she'd decided the whole Camilleri family was worthless and she didn't want them near the boys, but Chelle was growing on her. If anyone in that family could possibly become a normal, decent, caring person, it would be her. Also, once she looked past the makeup and all the glitz, Ladeja had to remember she was dealing with a teenager. "Yeah, I didn't get much sleep myself with all the carrying on down here. I imagine you didn't sleep at all. We can take shifts, so someone is always awake with the boys."

Chelle slid off the barstool and slowly started to walk, favoring her right ankle.

"Did anyone ever look at that?" Ladeja asked, comparing the two socks-clad feet. They appeared about the same size, which she supposed was a good sign.

"Sarah did. She said it's probably just a sprain. She gave me some Tylenol. Now it just hurts a bit when I walk on it, but the pain shouldn't last that long. Don't worry. If any of those things get in here, I'll run whether it hurts or not."

Ladeja helped her up the stairs, hoping she was right about being able to run if the time came. She already had two boys to protect. She didn't need a third child added to the mix.

Emma stepped out onto the balcony and looked around. A trio of infected people hobbled in her direction, but they were too far away down the street to be a real danger. A moment later, she saw a car appear behind them. It drove right over one, not stopping as it hit the hood, rolled onto the roof and flew off, landing behind the yellow sports car.

Emma waved her arms back and forth to get the driver's attention. "Hey! Up here!"

Justain appeared behind her, clamped a meaty hand over her mouth and pulled her back inside. "What are you doing?" His words came out tight, growled from behind clenched teeth. "Are you trying to get those things up here?"

"There was a car," she explained, wrenching herself out of his grip.

He looked at her for a moment before quietly moving

out onto the balcony, where he appeared to scan the street below. He shook his head, muttered, and stepped back in, closing the balcony doors behind him. "Whoever it was, they're long gone now and two and a half infected people are creeping this way."

"Two and a half?"

"Yeah, one bastard left his legs behind him and is pulling his torso along with just his arms. Apparently, stopping these nasty animals isn't going to be easy."

Something thudded heavily into the front door of the suite and was immediately followed by the same moaning sounds she'd heard from the infected group that had been on the street below earlier that morning, right by the sheets that had been used as a rope.

Justain gave her a dark look and placed one stubby index finger in front of his wide, thin lips, cautioning her to stay quiet. He jerked his head toward the staircase. She looked at it and froze. The stairs were way too close to the door for her comfort. Another loud thud sounded and this time she thought the door actually shook.

Apparently deciding she'd waited too long, Justain grabbed her arm and pulled her up the stairs. Once they'd reached the second floor of the suite, he pushed her onto a bed, did the hush gesture again, and went down the stairs.

Emma rubbed her upper arm, still sore from his tight grip around it. She heard him rooting around in the kitchen area and then his heavy footfalls on the stairs. He returned, carrying a couple of steak knives.

"Stay very quiet," he whispered as he sat on the bed opposite hers. "They might go away."

"What if they don't? What if they eventually get in?"

"We go out that way and hope none of them are on this floor." He nodded toward the door.

"I have to stay here so my mom can find me."

He looked at her and rolled his eyes. "Your mom's dead, kid, or worse, she's one of them. Hell, maybe it's her and your security guard ramming into the door."

Emma's jaw dropped open as tears burned her eyes. "She's not dead!"

"Shhh!" He came off the bed and stood over her, his face a mottled shade of red. "Shut up before you draw them to this door too. Are you trying to get us both killed?"

"My mom isn't dead," she said, not as loud, but just as strong. "She isn't infected. She'll come back for me."

"She would have come back for you a long time ago if she could, kid. The sooner you deal with the fact that she's gone, the sooner you can get over it and take care of yourself. You can't stay in this suite forever and there hasn't been a single siren out there. No gunshots. Nothing. If no one comes to help us before we run out of food, we're going to have to leave."

Emma folded her arms over her chest and shook her head as she willed her tears to stay put. She would not cry in front of this man. She would not believe him. Her mother was alive. She was smart. She would hide. She would never leave her.

Emma pulled her phone free and tried her mother's cell again, gritting her teeth as it continued to ring. Eventually, she heard her mother's voice requesting the caller leave a message. Emma hung up and closed her eyes, fighting through the bad thoughts trying to trick her.

"I hope she didn't have the ringer turned on."

Emma looked over at Justain. He'd reclaimed his seat on the other bed and watched her with no emotion. "What?"

"The ringer on her phone. If she was by a group of infected and you called, the sound of the ringer could have drawn their attention. I heard a lot of screaming yesterday. They attacked someone in this hotel. We might be the only survivors. Did any of those women screaming sound like your mother?"

Emma sat there, blinking, stupefied by such a cruel question. Once she found her voice, she asked, "Why would you say something like that to me? You're telling me you think I got my mother killed by calling her?"

"I'm just being completely honest with you," Justain said. "You're not a little girl, Emma. You're a beautiful young woman on your own. Your mother can not help you anymore. I'm sure she loved you, but she left you and they killed her. There's no way she could survive what is out there. She's dead and your father and brother are in another state. They'll never make it to you in this mess. Your family is gone, but you don't have to be alone. I will help you, but we have to be smart and survive this together. You need to let your mother go and work with me. Can you do that, sugar?"

Emma pulled her knees to her chin, wrapped her arms around them. She suddenly felt very vulnerable. Something was wrong with Harry Justain. She didn't like the way he looked at her, his eyes seeming to travel the entire length of her. She didn't like the way he called her *sugar.* She didn't like the way he seemed to want her to feel as if her mother was dead and it was her fault. She was young, but she wasn't stupid. Her mother had taught her there were certain types of men in Hollywood that she had to stay away from and she had the sinking feeling she'd let one of those very men into their suite.

"Emma? Are we going to get through this together?"

She looked between him and the door, and tried to decide whether she had a better chance at safety with the sick man in the suite or the sick people outside of it.

Mike jumped to his feet when he saw the yellow sports car race down the street, but it whipped right past the museum before he could even think about opening the door and flagging whoever it was down. He glanced up at the hotel balcony just in time to see a heavyset man clamp a hand over the young girl's mouth and pull her inside the room. "Damn it."

"What is it?"

He jumped, not having heard Misty reenter the lobby. The fuzzy slippers on her feet muted her steps as she walked across the dark linoleum, a backpack slung over her shoulder and another one in her left hand. She gripped the hatchet in her right.

"I saw a car, but it sped right past. Where'd you get the backpacks?"

"I've been looking around the exhibits, seeing if there's anything we could use. I figured these backpacks I found in one of the displays would come in handier than the totes from the gift shop."

"Yeah, I guess so." He looked back at the hotel and saw a man on the balcony the girl had just been pulled away from. "Isn't that the guy who was in the bathrobe?"

"He's still alive?"

"If that's him, yeah. He made it over to another room from the inside and squeeze into clothes." Mike strained for a closer look as the man turned and closed the balcony doors behind him. The moment the doors shut, it clicked in his head why the man seemed so familiar. "Wait. I think that guy is Harry Justain! I thought he looked familiar but couldn't place him. Of course, I got a better look at his under-uglies than at his face earlier. I was supposed to have a meeting with him this week."

Misty appeared next to him and pressed her face to the door, looking at the hotel. "Was he in the same room as the girl?"

"Yeah. She was just out on the balcony again, yelling and waving her hands when the car roared past. He pulled her back in, probably to make sure their location wasn't given away to any—" He muttered a curse as the trio of infected people came into view. A man and woman shuffled right up to the hotel, followed behind by what looked like only the top half of another man. They stopped under the balcony and looked around for where the noise that had drawn them had gone.

"Oh, gross." Misty turned away, her hand covering her mouth.

Mike took one look at the greenish pallor of her skin and walked her over to the front desk, where he gently eased her into the chair and pulled out the small wastebasket to set by her feet. "Try not to think about what you just saw."

"How do you not think about just seeing half a man crawling in the street with all his yucky innards hanging out?"

"Think about something else."

"Like what?" She lowered her head, but still appeared squeamish.

"I don't know. Puppies and kittens?" He threw out the first cute thing he thought women liked to look at.

"Oh, now I'm thinking of all the poor puppies and kittens being eaten by those infected people, or worse. Is anyone even taking care of the shelter animals now?"

Mike hung his head and cursed himself for mentioning puppies and kittens. "I'm sure someone stayed with the animals in the shelters, and the zoos too."

He stayed with her for a moment until the green tint faded from her skin and she took a deep breath. "I feel better now. That was just really gross."

"Yeah, it was. I need to see what's happening." He walked back over to the door, careful to look out of it while keeping his body hidden behind the posters plastered to the windows next to it.

The three infected people continued to stand on the sidewalk beneath the balcony the girl and the man he was pretty sure was Harry Justain had just been on. He watched them for several minutes until another group joined them. This one had a kid. The thought that some poor kid had been violently attacked by one of the monsters and changed into one of them sucker-punched him in the gut and made him even more determined than ever to reach and rescue the young girl he'd seen on the balcony.

Another straggler approached them, another younger infected girl, but he didn't think this one had still been a kid even though she was incredibly thin and appeared to have had a young face. "Wait a minute."

"What is it?"

He pressed his nose to the glass and peered closer, taking in the newest infected person's short blonde buns. "I might be losing my mind, but I think an infected Miley Cyrus is hanging out by the hotel."

"Seriously?"

"If it's not her, it's a damn good lookalike." His stomach sank. "Man, I would have figured her to be heavily protected by armed security. This sickness can really reach anyone, can't it?"

Misty joined him at the door again and looked, narrowing her eyes as she scrutinized the infected girl in question. "I don't know if that's really Miley. I mean, everyone is doing that stupid mini-bun style now."

"Really?" Mike frowned, then shrugged. He supposed it wasn't the worst hairstyle he'd ever seen. Every boy band had at least one guy with a really stupid hairstyle at some point in time.

More infected people appeared, grouping together with the others already under the balcony. Mike quit wondering whether Miley Cyrus was one of them and concerned himself with the young girl still alive, or so he hoped.

"They all just appeared after that car sped down the street," he told Misty. "The girl was waving her hands and yelling. I think she was trying to get the driver's attention."

"So she got all their attention instead?"

"Looks like it." He looked at the hotel and noted all the windows and balconies on that side of the building alone, imagining an equal or near number on the other side. That was a lot of rooms. "You were staying in the hotel. Did it seem very busy?"

Misty shrugged. "I guess the lobby was fairly full when I went in, and they have two restaurants inside, and probably an executive conference room. Most of these hotels do."

"And you had to climb down the balconies because there were so many in the hall, and you weren't safe in your room once they knew you were in there?"

"Yeah, why—oh." She looked up at the closed balcony doors. "The girl was yelling."

"And it brought all those bastards from the streets right to the balcony and they're just hanging around because that's the last place they heard the dinner bell."

"So if there's any left inside the hotel…"

"She called them right to their room. If that is Harry Justain, I don't know how much of a fighter he is, but I'm afraid it might just be the two of them up against however many infected people still roam that building looking for snacks."

Misty looked at him, studied his face. "You look like you're about to say something I'm not going to like."

"I can't let people die if I can help them."

"Can you help them?"

"We found weapons. They might not have. I fought one of those bastards off with just a metal bar earlier. I can fight more with the battle axe."

"Ok, so you have a battle axe and I can pretend I'm Lizzie Borden with my little hatchet, but just that group in front outnumbers us and we can't even see all the way down the street from here. What if we step outside and a freaking horde of them close in on us?"

"Those things might be banging down that girl's door right now as we stand here debating this. I'd rather die a hero saving a young girl than live as a coward."

Misty rolled her eyes. "Good grief. Spoken like an action hero. I'm sure you'll gain many parts once this is over."

"Yeah, because all the white actors taking Asian parts

will be dead."

"Keep trying to live your action movie dreams and you might die too. Can we at least wait until that group leaves?"

"There was a group there for hours after we first found this place. She might not have that much time. They're attracted to noise. Maybe we can just be really quiet as we walk out and throw a brick or something down the street. While they go after it, we'll run into the hotel."

"That's it!" Misty grabbed his shoulders, jumping up and down excitedly. "Genius!"

"What?"

She ran into the gift shop, leaving him to stand there confused until she came back holding a boxed remote control car. "The best part is, they also sell batteries here," she said, beaming.

"Hell yeah," he said, eying the remote control car like it was made of gold. "Let's clear the way and go save that girl."

7

Misty took quick inventory of her backpack. Unsure if they'd be returning to the museum, or hell, if they'd even be alive to worry about shelter anywhere, they'd busted the glass out of the vending machines and crammed the snacks and drinks into the two packs. They'd grabbed the first aid kit too, and Misty busted the pad and tampon dispenser off the bathroom wall before emptying its contents into her backpack.

They'd grabbed everything edible or drinkable they could find in the gift shop and packed up seven of the smaller, unboxed remote control cars. They'd also unboxed and juiced up two of the larger ones, planning on using them first since they didn't have to worry about carrying them in their packs which were loaded to the brim with food, drink, batteries and other necessities.

"Be very careful and watch your step," Mike reminded her for the second time, looking at her fuzzy, slipper-clad feet. "Even a sharp rock might hurt you through those things."

"I think there are a couple of stores in the hotel and there should be a gym. Maybe they carry tennis shoes?"

"We'll grab you some if we safely can. If not, I guess

we'll just have to hope for the best and make do until we can get you something better somewhere not infested with diseased cannibals."

"Ew. I hadn't thought of them that way, but I guess as far as descriptions go, it isn't all that bad."

Mike tugged at the straps on his backpack, making sure it fit against his back snugly, and picked up the remote to one of the radio controlled cars he'd lined up near the door. He tucked the battle axe under his arm, careful to make sure the blades weren't close enough to his body to cut him, and waited for Misty to get ready.

She zipped up her own backpack, making sure not to fully zip it, just as Mike had shown her so they would have easy access to the small cars when they needed them and adjusted the straps so the pack would stay settled in place when she ran. She picked up the other large remote controlled car and its controller, needing both hands to do so. Unable to hold the hatchet or dagger, she'd slipped the hatchet through a belt loop and tucked the dagger into the backpack's side pocket.

"Walk me through this plan again so I can make sure I'm not being incredibly stupid walking out into whatever's waiting for us out there with a freaking kid's toy in my hands instead of weapons."

"I use this car to lure all the infected far enough from the hotel for us to run right over to it and get inside trouble-free. Once inside, I'll ditch this remote and switch to the battle axe. You'll leave that car and its remote in the lobby so we can use it when we leave, the same way we're using this one now, and you can then access your hatchet and blade. While inside the hotel, we'll still have the smaller cars to use if we need to lure groups of infected away."

"And if there're hundreds inside and those cars go quick?"

"We have weapons."

She took a deep breath and willed her hands to stop

shaking. "I came here to make it into movies, not do this action crap for real."

"There's a girl over there and maybe other children. We haven't seen any cops or military and have no idea when we will. I'll do it by myself if—"

"No. You're not playing superhero all by yourself. I'm in this with you, but I'm warning you, I'm going to be pissed if this is the outfit I die and come back to life in."

Mike looked at the outfit in question: black slacks, a black T-shirt with Elvis and his pink Cadillac and the silly, fuzzy Herbie the Love Bug slippers, and grinned. "It could be worse. Wait until you see what Harry Justain is wearing. It looks painful."

"I'd rather not. I just want to grab the girl and go. Are we doing this?"

Mike studied her a bit, something niggling in the back of his mind. Something about her attitude seemed off, but he shrugged it off. He didn't really know Misty and even if he did, how could one actually determine what constituted as weird behavior in what was looking like the zombie apocalypse? "Yeah. You ready?"

"I'm not going to get any readier. Let's just do it."

Mike nodded and unlocked the door. Slowly and carefully, terrified the slightest sound would draw the attention of the group congregating beneath the balcony across the street, Mike gently placed the truck on the sidewalk and closed the door.

"Here goes everything," he said as he positioned himself behind the poster next to the door and used the remote control to move the truck. As with all remote controlled cars, it made a lot of noise the second it started moving, but safely hidden by the poster, they were overlooked as the infected group zeroed in on the small truck headed toward them.

"It looks like it's working," Misty observed.

"Yeah." Mike navigated the truck toward the group and looped it around in circles until they started shambling toward it. "Yes, you bastards. There you go. Follow the truck."

He turned the truck and sent it on a straight path down the street, away from the hotel and, more importantly, away from them, as Misty quietly opened the door and they slipped out.

Mike took a quick glance to their left, making sure there weren't any stragglers that way, before fully walking out of the safety of the museum entrance. He edged his way out onto the street, where he could see the backs of the infected group performing the slowest chase scene ever, but it was working. The few stragglers he saw up ahead fortunately noticed the loud truck before catching sight of him and Misty and joined in with the others to chase it down. He held the lever down, running the truck farther away until the infected group following it nearly disappeared in the distance.

"Let's go!" He shoved the controller into the side pocket of his pack and took off running for the revolving door at the front of the hotel, Misty behind him with the other big truck in her hands.

He held the battle axe in both hands as he entered the revolving door and waited for Misty to fit into the slot next to him before he pushed forward.

"Maybe this won't be so bad," he said, finding the lobby empty as he stepped out of the door. Misty immediately set the big truck down against the wall next to the door and grabbed her hatchet, raising it in a defensive stance.

"Try not to jinx us," she whispered, her eyes seeming to look in all directions at once.

"Right." Mike took a deep breath and looked around the lobby. There were two different hallways he could choose to go down, or he could take the elevators right in front of him. "What do you think?"

"What? I thought you had this all planned out?"

"I know the girl looked to be on the fifth floor, so we

need to get up there. I don't know which way is more dangerous, elevator or stairs?"

"Great." Misty huffed out an irritated breath. "Infected people could be in the stairwell, but I know they can also be in the hallways. If we're in an elevator and it opens right by a group of them, there's no way we're fighting through them before they hop inside with us in that small enclosure. On the stairs, we might have a chance of fighting through them unless there's a lot, then we're probably just as screwed. I mean, if we fall down, it's all over. They'll be on us in a second."

"What if we can ensure they aren't waiting right outside the elevator?"

She frowned, thinking. "The cars?"

Mike nodded and grabbed one of the smaller cars out of her backpack, along with its controller. "We'll send it up first and roll it out. They'll follow it like the ones on the street did."

"Will it work if you're operating it from down here?"

"We'll find out soon enough. We gotta try." Mike walked over to the elevator, keeping alert for any infected creepers just waiting to pop out of somewhere unexpected, and pushed the Up button. The elevator doors opened, and he placed the car inside with its front pointed toward the doors, and pushed the button for the fifth floor before stepping back out.

He held the battle axe under his arm, keeping his hands free for the remote, and watched the numbers above the elevator light up one by one until the five lit up.

"I hope this works," he mumbled as he estimated how long it would take for the doors to open and pushed the lever forward on the remote. He had no way of judging how far a length of floor the car would have available to travel so he held the lever down as the elevator started its descent back down to the lobby, figuring that even if it had hit a wall, the commotion of the wheels whirring as it was stuck in place would keep the attention of anyone or anything that it had attracted and keep them away from the elevator.

"What if something got into the elevator before the doors closed?" Misty asked.

"Shit." Mike handed the remote to her. "Keep the lever pressed down."

He tested out the weight of the battle axe in his hand, gave it a swing to prepare himself and held it against his shoulder like a baseball bat as he angled his body as if he were about to take a swing from home plate. "Keep that lever pressed down, but open the door and jump out of the way."

Misty nodded and stepped forward, her thumb on the lever. She flattened her back against the wall and, with one hand holding the small remote, reached over with the other to quickly hit the button to open the elevator doors before leaping out of the way.

The smell of death and rotten ass hit Mike the moment the doors separated, warning him of the danger before the milky-eyed man in tattered clothes lurched toward him. Already keyed up for the swing, Mike let it fly. Unlike the movies where zombies get beheaded in one swing, the blade wedged under the man's jaw and sent him crashing into the wall, head still intact, and body still moving. Fortunately, the infected man appeared to be the only one to have hitched a ride down in the elevator.

"Hold him!" Misty yelled as she extracted her hatchet and stepped toward the man.

Mike used all his strength to hold the struggling man against the wall while she danced around him.

"Are you pushing the lever?" He looked at the controller in her left hand.

"Yeah, yeah, I'm holding it." She raised the hatchet in her right hand and made to lower it. The undead and refusing to lie down man snapped at her, eliciting a shriek out of her before she jumped back.

"Shit," Mike cursed, his muscles straining to keep the

man in place. "Just keep your thumb on the lever."

He slid his hands up the pole of the battle axe, shortening the distance between the target and himself, and kicked the infected man in the stomach, pinning him in place with his foot before he yanked the battle axe out of his neck and brought it back down with as much force as he could muster, slicing straight down into the deadly man's brain and splitting the top of his head all the way down to the tip of his nose. He turned his head to avoid getting blood spray in his face just in time to see Misty bend over at the waist and vomit on the floor.

"Sorry," she apologized before retching again.

"No problem." Mike pulled the battle axe free, his own stomach turning at the sickening *shlupp* sound it made as it pulled free of the man's head. "You still holding down that lever?"

Misty answered nonverbally by raising the controller, her thumb firmly pressed on the lever, as she took deep breaths through her mouth and gathered her wits.

Mike stepped into the elevator and held the doors open. "Come on."

"You really want to go up there? You don't think he was the only one?"

"I don't know how many are up there, but I know there's a girl. Are you coming with me or not? No offense, but between his nasty-smelling ass and what you just spewed all over the carpet, I'm going to be sick if I stay down here another minute, so I gotta go now."

She turned a soft shade of red and quietly entered the elevator, her shaking hand clenched around the handle of her hatchet.

"You're going to have to actually use that thing, you know." Mike glanced at the hatchet as he pressed the button to deliver them to the fifth floor. "It won't always be two against one in our favor."

"I know."

"You holding down the—"

"I'm holding the damn lever," she snapped. "I'm not completely useless here."

"I didn't say you were," he spoke calmly despite feeling anything but, as he watched the floor numbers over the elevator door light up as they ascended. "The only reason I'm not pissing my pants right now is because I have hope that the car is doing its job of keeping those diseased freaks away from the elevator. I'm asking you about it so much because it's keeping me from completely losing my shit and running out of here with my tail tucked between my legs and if I seem harsh about you using the hatchet, it's just because I don't want to see you die."

"Sorry," she said softly. "I'm not usually so snippy."

"Yeah, it's all good. Everybody gets a pass in the zombie apocalypse." The Five lit up as the elevator came to a stop. "Here goes everything. Do whatever you gotta do. Just stay alive."

The elevator doors opened, revealing a long corridor. The sound of the remote control car's tires whirring as it repeatedly hit the wall at the end of the hallway could barely be heard above the frustrated moans of the group of infected people gathered there, knocking into each other in an effort to get their hands on the object making so much noise. If it weren't for the sound of the bell chiming as the elevator doors opened, or the motion itself, they probably would have been able to slip right out unnoticed, but the toy car trick only worked to buy them a little distance and time.

Two infected people at the back of the group turned as they stepped out of the elevator and peeled away from the group, chomping their jaws as they shuffled toward them.

"Run," Mike commanded as he turned and sprinted down the hall, away from where the infected group congregated. Misty followed on his heels. Her soft shoes made no noise on the floor, but her labored breathing let him know she'd followed his instruction.

"How do we find the girl?" she asked between heavy

breaths. "She could be in any of these rooms!"

"Hey!" Mike yelled. "Is anyone in here alive?"

"Oh, okay," Misty said. "I see we just capture the attention of every fucking thing in here!"

"Any better ideas?" He turned, having reached the end of the hallway. At the other end, the infected group blocked any chance they had of getting back on the elevator, leaving them with only the stairwell at their end unless a door opened up on the floor.

"We need to get off this floor. There's too many to fight."

"Yeah." Mike looked at the rooms and tried to judge which one would belong to the girl, but other than knowing it would be on the right of him, he had no idea. "If anyone is alive in one of these rooms, call out now!"

"Maybe it's the wrong floor," Misty suggested. "Sometimes the insides of buildings don't line up with the outside. I stayed at a hotel in Baltimore like that. It had a split level."

"Fuck," Mike growled as the small army of infected approached. There couldn't be any more than ten, but against two of them and in such a narrow space, ten was dangerous. "Let's go up."

Misty opened the door to the stairwell and ducked inside. Mike quickly followed her, and ran up the stairs two at a time, unsure if the infected could open the stairwell door or not.

He nearly ran into the outstretched arms of a diseased man on the sixth floor landing, but ducked just in time, sliding underneath the man's arms before he could get his bony fingers on him.

"Shit!" Misty screamed, stumbling as she too almost ran into the man.

Mike grabbed the man's hair from behind and yanked him back, ramming his head into the wall before delivering a few well-placed kicks to the midsection that crumpled the man to the ground. Once he had him down, he used the battle axe to slice through his head, making sure he wouldn't be getting back up again.

"That was close," Misty said, bent over with her hands on her knees as she caught her breath. A second later, they heard the fifth floor door open and slam against the wall as the infected group from that floor followed them into the stairwell.

"No time to rest," Mike said, shaking as much blood as he could off the battle axe. He opened the door to the sixth floor and stepped through, cussing as he was met with the sight of four infected people shuffling toward him. Two men, a woman, and a teenaged girl. "We have to fight our way through these."

"Oh, yay," Misty muttered, stepping onto the floor behind him. "Let's hurry before the ones in the stairwell get us from behind."

"Good idea." He raised the battle axe and brought it down square in the center of the leading man's head. The blade sliced through easily enough, but Mike was met with resistance when he tried to pull it back out. Panic squeezed around his heart, sucking the breath out of him as he struggled to pull the blade free, but only managed to puppeteer the infected man now attached to it. The other infected man came around the man stuck to his axe, mouth wide open and ready to chomp down on him.

With a squeal that could raise the dead, Misty rammed her dagger into the second man's ear, and fortunately, her weapon didn't get stuck. She pulled the small blade free just in time to dive between Mike and the zombie puppet and embed it into the infected woman's right eye, effectively reaching the brain and taking her out of the equation.

They were left with the teenaged girl and the man still stuck to his axe.

"Oh, man." Misty's eyes watered as the young infected girl in the One Direction T-shirt approached, snarling. "She's so young."

"Take him," Mike said, all but shoving the pole end of the battle axe into her hands as he grabbed the hatchet out of her belt loop and brought it down in the center of the young girl's head. Blood splattered down all over the faces of the boy band on her T-shirt and there seemed to be something very wrong with that image, but Mike couldn't think about the age of the girl he'd just killed or how innocent she might have been. Whoever she had been, he was pretty sure wasn't there anymore and if it came down to it, he'd slice his way through the entire Mickey Mouse Club if it meant he made it through the day alive.

"Mike!"

He pulled the hatchet free from the girl's head as her body fell to the floor and looked back to see Misty struggling to do the same with the battle axe stuck in the leading man's head. Behind her, the sound of bodies hitting the stairwell door sent a clear message that they didn't have much time. The infected might not seem that smart, but all it would take was a lucky combination of one of them pressing against the door handle while the other bodies pushed against the door for it to open and allow them access.

"Hold him down by the shoulders while I pull," he ordered, dropping the hatchet to wrap both hands around the pole of the battle axe. "Do it now."

Misty made a sound in her throat that sounded like she might have vomited a little and swallowed it back down but she did as told and walked behind the man, pushed him down to his knees, and held him firmly by the shoulders as Mike put his foot on the pole and used his entire body weight to send the battle axe slicing through the guy's head, until it sliced clear of his body.

"Hardheaded bastard," he muttered as Misty let go of the man's shoulders, allowing the rest of his body to fall forward, and picked up her hatchet.

"They're almost in," she said, as if he hadn't noticed. "What do we do now?"

"We get what we came for." Mike checked the hall. It was clear as far as he could see, and there was an elevator. He just needed to find the girl behind one of the many doors on both sides of the hallway. "Let's start knocking and see who opens. I don't think these infected people have enough sense left in what's left of them to grasp the concept of door handles. If the ones in the stairwell don't figure out how to get that door open, it looks like we'll have a clear path to the elevator."

"All right." Misty shoved the hatchet back in her belt loop and wrapped her hand around the dagger. "You take that side and I'll take the other. If anyone is alive and they don't answer, that's on them. We can't stay here much longer."

"Yeah." Mike knew she was right, but it still didn't sit well with him. He did not intend to leave without the girl.

He started with the door closest to the stairwell on his side, knocking loud enough to be heard but hoping not loud enough to really rile up the group in the stairwell. "Anyone alive in there? Open up and we'll get you to safety."

He didn't know if what he was saying was true, but he knew anyone alive wouldn't stay that way long if they didn't leave. Misty copied him on the other side of the hall, but after they'd both knocked on four doors each, we had only met them with moans, growls, and the sound of bodies thumping against the doors, or silence. They continued down the hall, a ball of dread growing in Mike's gut as each knock was met with more of the same until finally he knocked on a door and instead of growling or moaning, he heard whispers.

"Is someone in there?" he asked, pressing his ear to the door. It seemed to be about where the room belonging to the girl would have been, and hope bloomed in his chest at the thought that Misty had been right about them misjudging the floor. "I'm not infected. It's safe out here right now, but it won't be for long. This hotel is crawling with infected people. If you want to survive, you need to get out now while it's clear."

"We have no money," a man replied. "There's nothing here you can take from us, so if you're looking to loot—"

"There are infected people in the stairwell, and once they get on this floor, you're stuck. Whatever you do or don't have will run out and you will die. Like I said, this building is crawling with them. They're on the street. We have a clear shot off this floor right now and an escape plan, but you have to come right now."

Mike waited for a response and glanced down the hall to check on Misty. She continued down the hall, knocking on doors. She looked over at him, saw him watching, and shrugged. Apparently, she wasn't having much luck finding other survivors.

"Who sent you?" the man asked.

"Who sent me?" Mike turned back toward the door. "No one sent me. It doesn't look like anyone has been sent to save anyone, at least not here. I was hiding across the street and saw there were people here and thought I could help. We created a diversion to clear the front of the hotel so we could come through and sweep the floors in search of healthy people who need a way out."

"Who's we?"

"My partner and I. Just two healthy people trying real hard not to get infected or dead. Look, this floor is clear now, but I don't know how long it'll last and we have a way out of the hotel. Once we leave, that escape route goes with us. You're welcome to leave with us, but if you choose to stay and try to get out later when you run out of food and water, it might be too late for you then. I've heard a lot of infected people moaning and thumping into shit behind these doors. There are a lot of floors in this hotel and multiple stairwells. You're already in a critical situation, but that doesn't mean it can't get a hell of a lot worse. I don't think the military is too worried about sending people to hotels. They're pretty busy with the hospitals and government buildings right now."

The door opened a sliver and a ruddy white face with a large nose peeked out.

"Harry Justain?" Excitement filled Mike's chest, not at the sight of one of Hollywood's leading producers, but at the realization this had to be the room with the young girl.

Justain's eyes brightened, and a small smile formed on his wide lips. "The one and only. You'll have to ignore my current dress. I had to leave my room in a bit of a hurry, in nothing but a bath…" His eyes narrowed as his words trailed off. "You were outside yesterday."

"Yeah." Mike felt color flood his face. All he could offer was a sheepish shrug. "I was running away from a group of infected after almost being eaten by one. I saw a woman hanging off a balcony and was just barely able to help her down before they were on us. We took shelter across the street. We almost didn't make it."

Justain straightened to his full height. "She's with you now?"

"Yes, she's my partner." Mike glanced down the hall to where Misty continued knocking on doors, inching closer to where he stood. "We wanted to come back and make sure we could help anyone who might still be trapped inside this building."

"How thoughtful." Justain stepped back, allowing entrance.

Mike stepped into the room and immediately locked eyes with the young girl sitting on one of the double beds with her knees pulled to her chin. This close to her, she looked really familiar. "Hey. I've seen you. You're an actress."

She looked between the battle axe in his hand and him, and nodded. "Emma Whitman."

"Yeah, you're in some Disney stuff. Pretty cool. Well, Emma, we've come to help you out of here and we can all look for somewhere much safer to wait this thing out."

"Have you seen my mom?"

Justain rolled his eyes and muttered something under his breath as he went about the room, looking in drawers and closets for items to take.

"Your mother is here in the hotel?"

She nodded. "Our bodyguard went out and didn't return. She went out to find him and she hasn't come back."

"How long ago?"

"A couple days."

All the excitement and hope Mike had felt upon finding the girl spiraled down into a sickening lump in his stomach. He didn't have kids, but he knew how ferocious parents were when it came to protecting their children. A mother wouldn't leave her child alone in this kind of danger for that long unless something had prevented her from returning.

"Don't you tell me she's dead too. You don't know that. My mother wouldn't leave me. She wouldn't!"

"Oh, now you got her started up again," Harry complained, walking out of the bathroom with his hand shoved into a bag, stuffing something inside it. "I told her we're going to have to eventually leave, but she's been digging her heels in, convinced her mother is going to make it past all that's out there to find her."

"Hey." Mike didn't say anything further to the man, allowing his eyes to issue the warning. Big-shot producer or not, there was no call for speaking that way in front of a scared young girl. He looked back at Emma. "Get together whatever you need. Medications, food, a change of clothes is fine but not too much. Just pack necessities."

"I'm not leaving without my mom."

"I didn't see her in the lobby or the two floors I've been on." He swallowed hard, hoping that was true. She very well could have been the woman whose eye Misty had rammed her dagger through. "Pack what you need and dress in your very best survival clothes. We'll check the other floors before we go. If she's here, we'll find her."

"Are you crazy?" Justain asked. "You said you have an escape planned out. Let's go before we can't."

"Chill. I said I have a plan and I do. Part of my plan includes taking whoever has survived so far in this hotel with me when I go and I'm damn sure not leaving a young girl here all alone, so we will check every nook and cranny of this hotel if we have to. If you don't like the plan, you're welcome to form one of your own, but the girl is going with us."

"What makes you think you can just barge in here and take my—"

"Is he your father?" Mike asked the girl, already knowing he wasn't. Justain had been dangling off the side of the hotel half naked the day before and somehow wormed his way into the room. He was well known in the industry as a bachelor who liked a lot of women and had no children, or if he did, they were dirty little secrets he denied.

She shook her head vigorously. "My daddy's back home with my brother."

"Do you want to go with me?"

She nodded her head with even more enthusiasm and jumped up from the bed. She grabbed a leather duffel bag from under the bed, quickly grabbed a few things from the dresser, and ran into the bathroom.

"I know you," Justain said, studying him. "That Asian actor from the high school zombie movie. I had an appointment set up with you for this week."

"And look how punctual I am." Mike spread his arms wide. "I managed to arrive early, even in a real zombie apocalypse, and I even brought my own props." He tilted the battle axe back and forth a bit in his hand, too tired to give it a full twirl. He'd already decided to replace the thing with something lighter as soon as he could. It might have looked pretty badass, but the battle axe was a bitch on the biceps and he hadn't even spent that much time working with it.

Justain didn't seem to find him amusing. "There's food downstairs. I'm going to grab it."

"This isn't personal, Justain. I came here to save everyone, but that girl is pretty young. I'm going to protect her more than anyone and I can't just not look for her mother. What if you were separated from your mother in this place? Wouldn't you look for her before leaving?"

"My mother's a bitch," Justain said as he started to turn for the stairs, but stopped, his gaze locking on something over Mike's shoulder.

Mike turned and found Misty in the doorway, pinning Justain with a dark glare.

"Hey."

She blinked and turned her attention to him, the deadly look in her eyes gone. "I knocked on every door on both sides and all I heard were the sounds of the obviously infected, if anything at all. Is the girl here?"

Mike nodded at Emma as she emerged from the bathroom. "This is Emma Whitman, Disney star. Emma, this is Misty Waters."

Something slammed in the hall and Mike heard the moans and groans as Misty turned her head toward the stairwell and cursed. "They're on the floor!" she announced before stepping into the room, slamming the door closed behind her and throwing the bolt.

Emma let out a shriek and looked to Mike for help as Justain muttered under his breath, something about incompetency and stupid sentiment.

"Everyone relax," Mike said calmly, but firmly. "This suite is a bi-level, so it also opens on the floor beneath us, right?"

Emma nodded. "We came up here because they were at our door."

"After she drew them all to the room by yelling on the balcony."

Mike glared at Justain and considered leaving his ass. "She's a kid, not a professional survivalist. She did nothing wrong. Besides, the infected in the stairwell came from that floor. We drew them to the stairwell and they probably all crammed right in to it so the floor below should be clear. If not, we'll do the same thing we did to get through it before. We got this."

"You'd better," Justain warned him. "Get me out of here alive, and I can guarantee you the role of a lifetime. If I die, that opportunity dies with me."

"Yeah, I'm used to not getting the big breaks. I'm Asian. I'll get everyone out because it's what I came here to do. It's the right thing to do." He looked at Misty, saw the disdain in her eyes as she held Justain in her sights. "Hey, Misty, help Emma get ready for the road. I'm sure she and her mother wouldn't mind if you borrowed some better clothes too, hopefully some shoes. I'll go downstairs with Mr. Justain here and we'll pack up the food." He took the bag from Emma's hand. "You grabbed a change of clothes?"

She nodded. "And socks. Whenever my family went camping, my mom always made sure we brought a lot of socks."

"Smart." He offered her what he hoped was a reassuring smile. "Misty will help you pick out something good to travel in, and I'll fill this up with food. Just come downstairs when you're ready, all right? Don't worry about what you hear out there in the hall. As long as you don't make a lot of noise, they won't bother you at all."

She straightened her little shoulders and gave him a firm nod. "Don't forget to check our bodyguard's room. He kept a lot of water in the mini-fridge in there."

"Thanks." He winked at her, nodded to Misty, and took the stairs Justain had already started moving down. He didn't trust Justain not to take all the food if left alone for long. The man had too much attitude for someone who'd just been rescued, or at least was in the process of being rescued. He definitely didn't care for his harshness with the girl, and Misty seemed to be picking up some sort of bad vibe as well.

The stairs led down to an open sitting area and a small kitchen. He headed straight for it and started opening cabinets, figuring whatever he found in there was better for travel than whatever currently occupied the refrigerator.

He emptied the cabinets of Pop-Tarts, cheese crackers, canned tuna, canned sauce and boxed pasta. The pasta might have to be cooked, but he figured it wouldn't be too hard to boil water, even if they had to camp out somewhere. With that in mind, he grabbed two small pots.

"Why are you grabbing pots?" Justain asked.

"In case we need to prepare food," Mike answered, looking over to see Justain finish doing something with his cell phone and raise it to his ear. "Who are you calling? The phone lines have been jammed since this started."

"My assistant, and they're not completely jammed. They're just overloaded, but the chances of getting through go up with every dead body that drops, I'm sure. The more dead there are out there, the less are left to overrun the cell towers." Justain cursed before pocketing the phone. "Voicemail. If she's not dead, she's fired."

Mike shook his head. He'd spent some time in Hollywood rubbing elbows with the rich and entitled, but the man before him still surprised him with the degree of his self-centered, insensitive jackassery. "Why are you calling your assistant at a time like this, anyway?"

"To see what's taking so long to arrange transportation out of here!" Justain answered in a tone that implied the question was stupid. "A car should have already been sent."

"You know we're in the middle of what's looking like a freaking real-life zombie apocalypse, right?"

"Look, buddy. I'm a very important man. I make and break careers. I'm too great a man to be left in a situation like this."

"Yet, here you are." Mike finished packing up the food

found in the kitchen and made his way to the bedroom off the side of the living area, figuring it to be the bodyguard's room. He located the mini-fridge and added the water bottles inside to the duffel bag before looking around the room.

"I'm still here because my assistant is a moron," Justain said, following him into the room. "Maybe the driver got lost. Someone, somewhere, is an idiot, but it'll all get straightened out and believe me, someone will pay for making me wait around here this long in these conditions."

"They've probably already paid," Mike assured him as he started moving around pillows and checked under the mattress. "I'm pretty sure everyone else is either in as big a mess or dead."

"What are you doing?"

"Bodyguard's room. He must have had weapons. Hopefully, he didn't leave with everything on him."

"I didn't see anything when I had to borrow clothes, and you've already got a weapon."

Mike's fingers hit something under the mattress and he pulled out a sheathed Ka-Bar. "This is lighter and easier for travel."

"How much travel? On foot? I thought you had a plan, and I thought that plan would include a vehicle."

Mike tossed the battle axe down on the bed and clipped the sheathed Ka-Bar at his hip, his muscles more than happy to make the trade. "I was on set when a bunch of infected overran the studio. I ran out on foot and managed to make it here. I don't know how to hotwire cars and I haven't come across any with keys inside. Since you were trying to contact your assistant about transportation, I'm going to assume you don't have a vehicle either?"

"Damn it." Justain ran a hand through his thinning hair. "So, what's your brilliant plan? Walk out there among the cannibals?"

"My plan is to get everyone out of this dangerous

building and find a more secure shelter. If you would rather wait in this infested building of impending death hoping the military is going to leave the hospitals and government buildings which have become infected hot zones, you are more than welcome to. The girls and I will be on our way to find somewhere safer."

Mike grabbed the duffel bag and stepped out of the room, entering the living area as Emma and Misty came down the stairs, both dressed in blue jeans and gym shoes. Emma wore a dark colored T-shirt while Misty had kept the one she'd found in the gift shop. They both had hoodies tied around their waists. Misty's hoodie appeared to serve as a tool belt for her hatchet and dagger.

"You gave him your battle axe?"

Mike turned to see Justain holding the heavy weapon he'd left on the bed. The idea that maybe he should punch the jackass in the nose and take it struck him, but he didn't feel threatened. Anyone who would think to call his assistant for a ride during an apocalypse probably wasn't much of a fighter, and he didn't appear to have any hired goons with him.

"If you're going to leave it, I might as well take it," Justain said, testing the axe's weight in his hands. "Since your bright idea is to go out there with all the monsters."

"Sure. Protect yourself." Mike turned back toward the girls. "We're going to go out into the hall now and check each floor. If your mother is still in this hotel, Emma, we will find her."

He handed the duffel bag to the young girl. "How's that? Too heavy for you?"

She tested its weight and shook her head.

"Good. You hold on to that and stay between Misty and me. We'll make sure nothing gets to you." He looked back at Justain. "You can bring up the rear."

"Bring up the rear?" Justain's eyes bulged. "Are you crazy? What if something comes up behind us?"

"You have a battle axe. Swing it." Mike moved to the

door, quietly unlocked and slowly opened it, peeking out and scanning the hallway before taking a step. "Coast is clear."

They traveled toward the elevator, moving in silence. Once they reached the elevator, Mike motioned for the rest to stay put as he moved down the hall and picked up the remote control car they'd used when they'd first traveled to the floor, seeing no use in taking a new one out of their pack if they could reuse the first one. After picking it up, he knocked on the doors in the narrow hall, getting nothing but silence or the gargled sounds of the infected in return.

"I don't think anyone is alive is in those rooms," he said, rejoining the group. "Our first run-through on this floor, we hooked a right and got chased up the stairs. We need to check the left side and see if anyone needs help."

"We need to get out," Justain snapped. "You're wasting time!"

"You're a grown man and you have a weapon. You are free to go on your own if you don't like our plan." Mike turned and led them down the part of the hotel they'd skipped the first time. "Stay close and stay alert."

Emma and Misty stayed close at his back as Justain begrudgingly walked behind them, mumbling about idiots, incompetence, and toy cars. Mike tuned him out, his ears picking up a rustling sound. He placed his free hand over the hilt of the Ka-Bar as he turned the corner at the end of the hall, finding only empty space. The rustling had to be coming from behind one of the closed doors.

"Anyone alive on this floor in need of help?" Mike called out, realizing they'd now covered every inch of the hall on that floor and no infected were in it. "Speak now if you need help!"

Something made a raspy, growling sound from behind the door to his right and a hard thump shook the frame. Emma gasped and grabbed the back of his shirt.

"It's all right," he assured her. "They don't really seem

to know how to work doors that well."

He walked down the hall, called out again, and turned. If anyone was alive, they weren't speaking. If they died, it wouldn't be on his conscience. Satisfied he'd done all he could do for that floor, he led the group back toward the elevator.

"Let's just start from the top and work our way down," he suggested.

"No point going to the top," Justain said. "I had one of the two penthouse suites. Nothing up there now but infected people and chewed-up bodies."

"Okay." Mike sent the car up to the floor beneath the penthouse.

"Why are you sending a toy car up there?" Justain asked after the elevator doors closed.

"Diversion," Mike explained. "If there's anyone infected up there, we don't want them waiting right outside the elevator when we step out."

Misty worked the controller as they carried out the same routine they had earlier. This time, Justain and Emma joined them in the elevator. Mike would rather Emma handle the controller, allowing Misty to keep both hands free and able to better protect her, but she was carrying the duffel bag. He'd tell Justain to drop the axe and take the duffel bag, but he figured the man would run off with it if things went south. The elevator reached its destination, and he braced himself, more scared than he was the first time he'd done this trick. Having a young girl and a wild card with him wasn't good on the nerves.

The elevator stopped, dinged, and the doors opened.

As had happened on Emma's floor, the remote control car had lured a group of infected people away from the elevator. This group seemed to consist mostly of infected people in spandex and bathing suits. Mike was willing to bet they'd find the fitness center on this floor.

He placed a finger before his lips, urging the others to remain quiet as they followed him out of the elevator.

Misty continued holding down the lever on the remote, keeping the infected completely focused on the whirring sound of the toy car's tires as it repeatedly rammed into the wall at the end of the hallway and drove straight out of their hands when they managed to grab it.

Emma gasped as they cleared the elevator and the doors closed behind them.

"Quiet," Mike whispered, reaching for her arm to move her down the empty hall to their right, but she'd locked on to something, or someone, he realized as he turned to follow her gaze.

"Mom?" she questioned.

A blonde woman in jeans and a blue blouse turned her head at the sound, along with a few others near the back of the group. A chunk of her neck was missing and her eyes had clouded over. If they hadn't, Mike was pretty sure they'd match Emma's exactly.

The young girl let out a wail of despair loud enough to attract every infected person on the block before the entire group in front of them turned and forgot about the car in favor of live prey.

"Run!" Mike yelled, grabbing Emma before following his own advice. "Head for the stairs!"

Misty took the lead, sprinting ahead, the controller forgotten. Four feet from the stairwell, a door opened and two arms reached out to snatch her.

8

"Hey."

Manny looked up from the multitude of screens in front of him and smiled as he straightened up from the slouched position he'd been in when Ladeja entered the small room. "Hey yourself. That for me?"

"Yep." She handed him the mug of hot coffee and pulled up a chair next to him. "You look tired, but I don't want to get O'Donnell up until he's had at least his minimum four hours of sleep. Do you want to take a nap? I can watch the screens and scream unholy hell if something happens."

This got a chuckle. "Oh, I know you can make some noise when you want to, but I'm sure what you're seeing is just plain boredom. I'm not much of a sitting and watching monitors kind of guy."

"Not even that one?" Ladeja nodded toward the monitor showing the video feed from Mimi's gigantic closet where the three oldest Camilleri sisters were practically doing stripteases, fully aware a camera was on them as they tried on Mimi's clothes.

"Rich bitches too stupid to stay clothed and ready to run during the middle of a fucking viral epidemic do nothing for me, babe. Especially not that one who should be mourning her husband."

Ladeja shook her head as she watched Cynda sashay through the closet naked as the day she was born before turning and winking at the camera.

"That's what Cory's father chose over me."

"He did you a favor, the ignorant bastard."

"Yeah, sure. Meanwhile, every man in the world still prefers something like that over a good wom—"

Manny leaned over and cut her off by sealing his mouth over hers and delving inside, kissing her so deep her toes curled and she forgot all about the infected people she was supposed to be worried about.

"Not every man," he said as he pulled away. "For the record, I'm pretty sure those bitches know I want you and Cynda's so jealous of you she's resorting to prancing around naked in a desperate attempt to win. She wouldn't feel so threatened by you if she'd really ever had that asshole's loyalty. Don't ever give that skank any power over you when you are so much damn better than her."

Ladeja stared back at him, still feeling his kiss on her lips, and replayed his words, trying to unjumble them through her clouded mind. "You want me?"

"Yeah, girl, and apparently it's obvious to everyone but you." He chuckled, shaking his head in amusement as he glanced back at the monitors. His entire body stilled, and the laughter fled. "What the hell?"

Alerted by his sudden change in demeanor, Ladeja leaned forward and watched the monitor he'd zeroed in on. The front gates were a wide open, mangled mess and the guards were in a panic, most of them running after a large van that had just plowed through them, taking out at least two guards in the process.

"Are they dead?" Ladeja asked, focused on the two men she saw sprawled on the ground, watching a couple of other guards check them out.

"If not, they probably wish they were." Manny rose

from his seat but kept his eyes glued to the monitors, following the speeding van until it stopped outside the front of Mimi's mansion and an overweight guy in sweats and a baseball cap ran to the front door and started pounding on it.

"Get O'Donnell up and watch the kids while I see who this asshole is and how screwed we are now that the jerk bashed right through the fucking gate." He grabbed Ladeja by the back of the neck, gave her a quick kiss, and scooped his gun off the desk before running out the door of the small control room.

Ladeja took a quick glance at the screens, noticing that the man at the door had captured the attention of those downstairs. Mimi and Toddy were at the door and the Camilleri sisters appeared to be quickly trying to pull on clothes as they left the closet to see what was happening. Mara appeared to sleep in the bed and Terrell sat slumped over, still in the chair at her bedside.

She started to leave to get O'Donnell, but stilled as she noticed Mara raise her upper body off the bed, her movements odd and stiff. Mara's head turned just as Cara exited Mimi's closet, her vision compromised by the shirt she was still in the process of pulling over her head. Mara lurched forward, knocked Cara to the floor and clamped her mouth on one of her arms.

"Oh shit!" Ladeja ran out of the room, screaming, "O'Donnell, wake up! Chelle, lock yourself in with the kids! Mara's attacking!"

She ran past the bedroom the kids were in as Chelle slammed the door closed and clicked the lock in place, and took the stairs down. "Manny! Mara's infected! She got Cara!"

She realized she probably didn't need to warn him as the sound of screams reached her on the stairs, but she'd done it without thinking, fueled on fear at the thought of him walking into unknown danger, distracted by the gate-rammer.

She reached the bottom of the stairs, O'Donnell close behind her, and saw Mimi and Toddy at the front door, yelling to the man beyond it.

"Go away, Larry!" Mimi yelled. "You're violating your restraining order, you crazy ass!"

Not seeing Manny, Ladeja headed toward Mimi's bedroom, her heart nearly stopping as a gunshot rang out. "Manny!"

"Stay behind me!" O'Donnell ordered, pushing her behind him as he advanced, running toward the bedroom and the sound of the gunshot.

"What the fuck?" Terrell bellowed, his voice seeming to bounce off the walls as they reached the room to see Cynda and Cheyanne, half dressed, kneeling next to their sister, who writhed in pain, screaming, as blood poured out of her wounded arm.

Mara's lifeless body rested next to her, what was left of it. The top of her head had a large hole in it and what Ladeja assumed to be brains stuck to the wall behind her. Manny stood a couple feet away from her, his arm extended, gun pointed at Terrell, who stood on the opposite side of the bed between them, his hands up in the air.

"You gonna kill me, motherfucker? What the fuck? That crazy bitch did that shit, not me!"

"You've been sleeping with her. You're infected, and it's just a matter of time before you turn."

"What, you think you're a doctor now? You don't know shit! You shoot me and you're a fucking murderer!"

"Everybody calm down," O'Donnell said, stopping just outside the room. He'd went to bed wearing his clothes and boots, so he'd responded to Ladeja's call immediately, but his eyes reflected his confusion. "Manny, catch me up on what the hell's going on here."

Manny turned toward him, his eyes widening as he saw Ladeja. "I told you to stay with the boys, Ladeja. Go lock yourself in the room until I tell you it's safe."

She bristled at his tone, aware he only wanted to protect her, but she'd been on her own for long enough since Thunda had left to just obey an order from a man. Plus, she was afraid to do as he said. "Chelle is locked in with the boys. I'm staying here until I know everything is all right. You have a dead woman on the floor, one wounded, your gun is out on someone, and Mimi's hollering at that guy about a restraining order through the door. Meanwhile, we no longer have a gate."

"We no longer have a gate?" O'Donnell swiveled his head, looking at them all. "What the fuck did you people do while I took a nap?"

"A van ran through the gate," Manny told him. "I was on my way to check it out when Mara turned and attacked Cara."

O'Donnell looked down at Cara and paled. "She got bit."

"Yeah," Manny said. "That means we have two infected inside with us and nothing to protect the perimeter should any more show up."

They shared a look and Ladeja picked up on the silent communication. Neither Terrell nor Cara were going to make it out of the mansion alive. She looked at the young girl and a ball of nausea rolled around in her stomach. She didn't like any of the three women before her, but she would have never wished such a fate on Cara.

"Hell no, motherfucker," Terrell said, breaking Ladeja out of her thoughts. "I see the wheels turning in your heads. You're not gonna put me down. You can shoot that bitch, but I'm not infected."

"You slept with Mara," O'Donnell said, placing his hand over the gun at his hip. "You're infected, and so is Cara."

Cynda and Cheyanne quickly moved away from their sister and huddled together in the corner, pure terror in their eyes.

"Cynda! Cheyanne!" Tears poured out of Cara's eyes as

she reached toward them, only to see them turn and run out of the room, headed for the back door. They opened it and rock music entered the house.

"What the hell is that?" Manny asked, not taking his eyes off Terrell in case the man made a move for him.

"Music from somewhere outside," Ladeja answered as the healthy Camilleri sisters closed the door and locked it. Even they appeared to have enough brain cells to realize what a danger the music was.

"That's probably Junior Flint," Mimi said, arriving with Toddy and a security guard in tow. "He was supposed to have a party later tonight. They can get really loud and last for hours. He must have started up early."

"We're surrounded by idiots," Manny growled. "Ladeja, get the boys and Chelle dressed and ready to run, then stay on the monitors until I say otherwise. Do it now. For Cory's sake," he added, knowing what magic words to use to avoid confrontation.

Ladeja turned and ran for the bedroom, knowing the proverbial shit was speeding toward the fan. They had no gate, two infected people were in the mansion with them, and some ignorant redneck rocker was blasting music that would surely draw every infected person within hearing distance right to their area.

"Open up, it's me," she said as she banged on the bedroom door.

"What's happening?" Chelle asked, opening the door. She was already dressed in a Mimi Couture T-shirt and velour sweatpants she'd borrowed and the gym shoes she'd worn when leaving her home. The boys were also dressed and their backpacks packed. Chelle wasn't as dumb as she'd originally thought.

"The gate is down and that moron, Junior Flint, is blasting music from his house, which is apparently close enough we can hear it over here and if we can hear it, any uninfected in the area can hear it." She grabbed the clothes she'd arrived in off the dresser and headed for the bathroom. "As if that's not bad enough, we have two infected in the house."

Ladeja closed herself in the bathroom and quickly traded out the clothes Mimi had given her to sleep in for her jeans and Oakland A's T-shirt. Once finished, she stepped out and sat on the edge of the bed to put her shoes on.

"Mara was infected like we thought, and she turned," she said, quickly lacing up her shoes. She took a deep breath and decided to just blurt out the worst of the news before she lost her nerve. "She bit Cara. Cara's infected."

Chelle stiffened, and her lips parted, but she said nothing.

"You understand what this means?"

"She's going to turn into one of those things."

Ladeja nodded. "I'm sorry."

"It's not your fault. I shouldn't care at all. I mean… she ran right past me when I needed help. They were going to let me get eaten by those things." Her eyes grew dark. "Where are Cynda and Cheyanne?"

"They were with her until they realized she was infected."

"They're leaving her to die alone."

"Pretty much. I think it's more humane to put her down before she turns," Ladeja said, trying to offer some words of comfort as angry voices carried up to the room. "I have to get in the control room and monitor what's going on. Whatever happens will be on the monitors and I don't think the boys should see that."

"I'll stay with them." Chelle straightened her shoulders. "There's nothing I can do for her, and I don't want to see what happens."

Ladeja nodded her understanding and searched for words, some form of condolence, but she came up empty, and she was wasting time. "Lock the door."

Ladeja ran down the hall, confident the boys were safe in the room with Chelle. A gunshot rang out as she entered the small control room and she jumped in response. She braced herself as she lowered herself into the chair and looked at the monitors, doing a quick assessment.

Terrell was on the floor, dead. O'Donnell stood over Cara, his gun pointed, ready to shoot, but he couldn't seem to pull the trigger as Cara, still aware, seemed to beg for her life. Manny was talking with Mimi and the security guard she'd brought in with her while Toddy and Sarah packed food in the kitchen. Cynda and Cheyanne quickly finished dressing in the walk-in closet and huddled together on a chaise. The van remained outside, backed up to the front of the house. Its back doors were open, and she saw a pair of feet sticking out. The intruder was dead or unconscious. She guessed unconscious, based on the fact they had left someone in place to watch over him. The other security guards had split up between the front gate and walking the perimeter.

Ladeja studied the controls, hoping to be able to pan out and see if the cameras on the property gave any access to Junior Flint's house. She had no idea how close the property was to them and after a cursory glance of the controls, she resolved herself to just not knowing. She had no idea how to work any of it, so she watched the feeds that were already up in front of her and prayed she didn't miss anything important. She had her cell phone in her back pocket in case she needed to call Manny and alert him to something quick. If the call would even go through.

She divided her attention among the monitors, trying her best to watch all of them at once. She knew there were cameras on the second floor but didn't know how to work the system to see those feeds. She figured if anything got in the house, the downstairs would be the point of entry anyway, so thankfully those were the feeds Manny had been looking at when he'd left the room.

O'Donnell lowered his arm and turned away from Cara, shaking his head as he said something to Manny.

Manny said something to him as he left Mimi and the security guard, stood over Cara, and raised his own gun.

Ladeja braced herself, not wanting to watch the man she cared about pull the trigger and end a young girl's life. She knew it needed to be done, but she didn't want him to be the one to do it. She didn't want that image in her head, knowing she'd forever see him as the man who took a young woman's life while she pleaded with him not to, but she couldn't look away.

Minutes passed, his arm wavered, and finally the security guard who Mimi brought in from outside walked over to the bed, grabbed a pillow and placed it over Cara's face before unholstering his gun and shooting through it. A splash of color exploded on the wall behind Cara's head and her body fell sideways.

Ladeja wiped away tears that she had shed reflexively and took a deep, cleansing breath that caught in her throat as she caught a frenzy of action on the feed from the yard. She wasn't exactly sure where it was, but the feed was labeled North Side Left. The security guards ran toward the edge of the screen, guns drawn. As they raised the guns to shoot, she noticed a group of shambling people pop into view on one of the other feeds. Then another feed. Then another.

She pulled her cell phone free and called Manny, praying the call would go through.

"Yeah?" he answered quickly.

"They're on the property." She saw multiple security guards fall prey to the uninfected as the one left to guard the man in the back of the van seemed to catch notice and walked out of the frame. "They've just taken out most of the outside security."

"Get the kids, get your shit, and get down here now." He disconnected.

Ladeja ran toward the bedroom, screaming for Chelle to open the door before she reached it. The three of them were up with their packed bags together by the time she set foot inside. Chelle handed her bag to her.

"Is Cara dead?"

"Yeah, and the infected have started pouring onto the property."

Chelle didn't say anything as Ladeja led them down the stairs to where Manny and Mimi were waiting at the foot.

"What's the plan?" Ladeja asked him.

"Stay close to me. O'Donnell is getting Sarah and Toddy from the kitchen, and Forrester's getting Cynda and Cheyanne."

"Forrester?"

"Security guard. We have to leave. We're compromised here."

A scream sounded from the kitchen and gunshots rang out.

"Shit," Manny cursed, looking around. A tall man in all black appeared with the older Camilleri sisters. "Watch them," Manny ordered before moving toward the kitchen, but O'Donnell ran toward them, carrying the duffel bag of food Sarah and Toddy had packed.

"Stragglers got in the kitchen and were on Sarah and Toddy right before I could reach them. Fuckers tore her damn throat out and got Toddy right in the stomach."

The front door burst open and a tall sandy-haired man with piercing green eyes, also dressed in black, stepped in, gun at the ready. "We gotta move, people. That dumbass redneck's party drew these fucking bastards out like cockroaches and we're gonna be surrounded.

"Let's go," Manny ordered, taking the lead.

Ladeja grabbed Cory and Mateo's arms and followed the others as they rushed out the front door, O'Donnell and Forrester covering the rear.

The security guard at the door jumped into the back of the van and pulled the heavy man who'd run through the gate's body deeper into the vehicle as they all piled inside. Focused on getting the boys out of danger, Ladeja didn't take her gaze off the inside of the van. Whatever was happening around them, she didn't want to know.

The back doors slammed shut, she heard the driver's door open and close, and the engine turned over. The van lurched forward, and they all fell. A large, strong hand clamped onto her arm and helped her straighten up as light from the dash filled the vehicle, allowing them to see.

Forrester crawled forward and awkwardly climbed into the passenger seat. "Any of the other guys make it?"

"I don't think so," the other security guard said, swerving around a cluster of infected people entering Mimi's property through the gaping hole where the gate had once stood.

"Fuck, Teague!" Forrester hit the dashboard.

"Where are we going?" Cynda asked.

"Away," O'Donnell said. "We can't stay here. Obviously."

They all looked outside the van as they sped off the property, noting all the shadowy forms shambling on it.

"This is your fault, you crazy psycho!" Mimi hit the chubby man lying in the van, getting a moan out of him. "What's wrong with him? Did you kill him?"

"I already told you we tased him," Forrester said.

Mimi slugged the man again. "Get up, you fat freak!"

"Who is he?" Ladeja asked.

"My number one stalker," Mimi answered. "His stupid fat ass came here to save me, ramming through my gate in the process."

"He certainly didn't help things," the security guard driving the van said, "but in all fairness, there was a weak spot in the perimeter fencing because they didn't all come through the downed gate."

The man groaned and sat up. "What happened?"

"You tore my gate down and my men tased you, you stupid jackass." Mimi smacked him in the head. "You got my maid and my best assistant killed and we're on the run in this stupid van of yours now. What are we supposed to do now, Larry?"

The man smiled. "Don't worry, my angel. I came to take you to my yacht, where we'll be safe!"

Mimi sat back in surprise. "You have a yacht? You? How can you afford a yacht when your profession is following me and driving me nuts?"

"Well, I never had to actually purchase it," he said, wiping at the drool spilling from the corner of his mouth, a result of the earlier tasing. "I had to find a safe place to take you before I came to rescue you so—"

"Kidnap."

"Rescue."

"Kidnap."

"Clearly you're not a child." Larry ogled Mimi's breasts swelling over the plunging neckline of her pink tank top so lasciviously Ladeja involuntarily shuddered.

"Abduct."

"Rescue!"

"Do we need to ask the police?"

"Sure. Find one. They're not busy at all right now."

"Can you two stop arguing over semantics and get to the point?" the guard driving the van asked. "I'm driving with no direction at all right now. If you actually know of a good spot, spill it, Larry."

"Who are you?" Larry asked.

"Teague. I was the third guy that tased you."

"You tased me three times? How dare you! I oughtta sue."

"You're a husky guy, Larry. It was kind of like knocking out a baby elephant."

"You would knock out a baby elephant, you animals!"

"Can we get back on track?" Manny asked. "What about this yacht?"

Larry looked at Manny and gawked before turning angry eyes to Mimi. "Who's the big hunk of sex? You're cheating on me with another chunk of eye candy?"

"What the hell did he just call me?" Manny asked, clearly revolted, earning a shrug from Ladeja.

"I can't cheat on you if I've never been with you," Mimi said, rolling her eyes. "Just tell us about the yacht, weirdo."

"You could ask nicer."

"We could just beat it out of you," Ladeja snapped, her nerves already shot and only growing worse as she noted all the infected people shambling around aimlessly as Teague drove them out of the Hollywood Hills.

"Geez." Larry turned toward Mimi. "Your friends aren't very friendly at all. Is she even important? I've never seen her in anything."

Manny gripped Larry by the throat and pulled him close until they were nose to nose. "As far as I'm concerned, Ladeja and these two boys are the most important people in this van, and if you don't get to the fucking point, I'm going to throw you out to the infected. Do you understand?"

Ladeja gripped Manny's shoulder, trying to calm him as Larry bobbed his head up and down as best he could, despite Manny's strong fingers wrapped around his neck. The pudgy man's eyes watered from the pressure, or maybe he was crying. Ladeja couldn't tell and only she seemed to be concerned as the rest of the van's inhabitants appeared to not care about the man's fate. Teague's eyes showed actual amusement as he glanced back at them through the rearview mirror.

"Speak," Manny ordered, releasing his hold.

"I commandeered a yacht," Larry choked out, rubbing his throat as he scooted closer to Mimi as if she could protect him if Manny went for another throat grab. "The infected are all over. The bases the military has set up for survivors filled up pretty quick and it's not that easy getting to them anyway. The military was supposed to send out soldiers to collect the uninfected, but things got bad too quick."

"The yacht," Manny reminded him.

"I'm getting to it!" Larry inched farther away from

Manny until he pressed against Mimi and she shoved at him in disgust. "I couldn't find a single building I thought would be safe, so I started thinking outside the box. Where could I take my angel and not have to worry about an invasion?"

"I'm not your angel." Mimi's nostrils flared in disgust.

"Nobody cares," Ladeja snapped. "Let him finish."

"Thank you." Larry gave Mimi a smug look before continuing. "I figure if these infected people can't even walk normally, there's no way they can swim, so we need an island, but to get to an island, we need a boat. I went to the coast where a lot of boats were docked and saw the military there, barring people from getting on their boats. There's a beautiful yacht there we can take because the owners were all made to leave. I'm sure most are probably even dead by now."

"How are we supposed to get on a yacht if the military isn't letting people pass?" Ladeja asked, her voice raising several octaves. Manny moved forward, but she grabbed his shoulders and urged him not to kill the guy.

"Idiot." Mimi smacked Larry in the back of the head.

"Hey! This is the thanks I get for rescuing you?"

"I was safe before you drove through my gate and that redneck moron, Junior Flint, blasted his music, bringing all those nasty devils to my property." Mimi folded her arms beneath her ample bosom and settled back to pout. "I didn't even have time to lock up. I just know more psychos like you are going to steal my stuff."

"Seriously? That's what you're worried about right now?" Ladeja rolled her eyes and leaned in to Manny. "What do you think?"

Manny looked at O'Donnell. "A yacht would be a hell of a lot safer place to be than any building we could find here."

"I can hotwire anything," O'Donnell said, his brow scrunched in thought. "We have guns. If we make the most of what ammo we have between us…"

"You guys actually think we can get past the military and steal a yacht?" Ladeja asked, looking between the two men. "Are you crazy?"

"Crazy about staying alive," Manny said as the van swerved to miss a cluster of infected people and Teague struggled to avoid spinning out as they took a hard curve too fast. "It's too dangerous out here. We have to try."

"And if we're shot down by the military?"

"It's better than getting eaten," Chelle answered her. "We had armed security and our home was overrun. I nearly died only to make it to Mimi's, another guarded property, and we lost Cara inside the walls. A quick death would be better than suffering the pain of getting attacked by one of these monsters."

"How do you even know what happened?" Cheyanne asked. "You were upstairs with *her*."

"I was upstairs with the woman who saved my life when my sisters left me for dead and you know what I was doing up there?" Chelle asked her sisters, neither of whom had the courtesy to look ashamed. "I was watching over the innocent kid whose mother died in our guesthouse. She was out there alone checking on him because we didn't want the help's kid seen at our party."

"Yeah, our party," Cynda said. "We're family. We're supposed to stick together, not fraternize with the enemy."

"Again, you ran right past me and left me for dead," Chelle reminded her surviving sisters. "I'm sure you didn't do a damn thing to help Cara or even stand by her in her last moments."

"Neither did you," Cynda shot back. "You were with the enemy."

"Cara already abandoned me, and what exactly makes Ladeja the enemy, the fact that Thunda would have stayed with her if she hadn't kicked his cheating ass out and you'll never get over the fact that you know damn well you would have stayed just a side ho if she hadn't, and he wanted your fame and money more than he wanted you?"

A sound Ladeja could only describe as a rage-fueled screech erupted out of Cynda as she launched herself at her younger sister, grabbing two fistfuls of Chelle's hair before straddling the teenager.

Ladeja acted on reflex, drew back her arm and delivered a solid punch right between Cynda's eyes before anyone could stop her, sending the woman toppling back into her other sister's arms, blood seeping through the fingers now covering her nose as she wailed.

"Remind me not to piss you off," Manny said, laughter in his voice.

"I second that." Approval laced O'Donnell's words.

Teague and Forrester looked at each other and shook their heads, grinning while Larry and Mimi looked at Cynda in shock and Cory scooted back into a corner, away from everyone. Ladeja tried to ignore the angry accusation in his eyes as she pulled Chelle back into a sitting position and moved her over to the side of the van she, Manny, and the boys were on, opposite the other two Camilleri sisters. Mateo looked at Cynda, smiled, and lowered his head to hide it.

"So now that the ladies wrestling segment of the evening is over, are we headed to the coast to steal a yacht or what?" Teague asked.

"Yeah," Manny said. "It's the best option we have."

"Do we have an actual plan, or are we just going in guns blazing and hoping to get on board by the skin of our balls?" Teague asked.

"Just get us as close as you can without being noticed," O'Donnell advised. "Once there, we'll check it out and if it's still guarded, we'll have to create some sort of diversion. The women and the boys can get on board along with at least one armed guard who will provide cover fire for whichever one of us creates the diversion to get to the yacht."

"Or we could create the diversion," Cheyanne suggested. "The soldiers are probably mostly men. Cynda and I can just flash them or something."

"Do you really think there are men left on this planet who haven't already seen both of you completely naked?" Chelle asked.

"Hellooooo," Mimi cut in before either of the older Camilleri sisters could respond. "I'm Mimi Perry. I'm a superstar. I can just walk right through them. No one's going to stop me."

"Angel," Larry said. "I saw them turn away Beyoncé."

"And? I'm far more important than Beyoncé."

"Yes, my angel, to me you are everything."

"Wait. Are you saying you think Beyoncé is bigger than me? I thought you adored me!"

"We're going to die surrounded by narcissistic idiots," Ladeja whispered as she rested her head on Manny's shoulder, defeated.

"No, I promise we won't," Manny whispered back as he reached up and patted her head. "One of us will probably end up shooting them first."

9

"Hey! Stop!" Mike yelled as the door started to close.

It opened again and a gangly young man in thick-framed black glasses poked his head out, eyes growing wide as he took in the scene in the hallway.

"Hurry!" The guy urged, motioning with his hand for them to pick up the pace.

Already running as fast as he could with the added weight of Emma in his arms, Mike reached the door within seconds and dove in, followed by Justain, who sounded like he was about to hyperventilate.

"That was close." The young guy slammed the door shut and threw the bolt. "I really thought you guys had a cool system set up with the remote control cars. That was genius."

"How did you know about the cars?" Mike asked, lowering Emma to the floor while simultaneously checking out the room.

It was a two-bed room with a small sitting area, a desk with a laptop open displaying video feed from the hotel security cameras which answered his question, and an extremely famous actress standing before the balcony doors, staring disapprovingly at Justain, who'd plopped down on one of the beds to catch his breath.

"You're Betty Meadow," Misty said, her voice full of awe.

"I'm aware of who I am," Betty said. "This is Watts, that jackass stuffed into ill-fitting attire over there is Harry Justain and who might the rest of you be? For chrissakes, quiet the child so those murderous beasts out there go away."

Mike pulled Emma close, burying her head in his chest as he stroked her back and tried to shush her. "She just saw her mother out there. She's infected."

Sadness flittered through the award-winning actress's eyes before they hardened and she visibly gathered her stern composure. "Yes, well, as tragic as that is, silence her or we will all be infected. Watts has been monitoring the hotel's security footage looking for an opportunity for us to get out of here. We have a real chance if we keep our heads."

Mike glared at the curvy, red-headed older woman as he continued trying to soothe Emma. "She's extremely upset. She can't just turn off her emotions after what she just saw."

"Then take her into the bathroom until she gets the worst of the sobbing out of her system," Betty suggested, motioning with her hand for Misty to take the girl away.

"She kind of has a point," Misty said, pulling Emma away. "I'll sit with her in there so the sound doesn't keep the infected by our door. I'd rather not have to climb down balconies or bedsheets again."

"Did she say she climbed down balconies?" Betty asked as Misty ushered Emma into the bathroom and closed the door.

"Yeah, that's how she escaped one of the top floors earlier. She was dangling from a bedsheet tied around a balcony rail when I ran into her and we hid out in the car museum down the street overnight."

"Why did you come back? For him?"

Mike looked over at Justain, noting the dark look he gave the actress. "No. I saw the girl on one of the balconies and I didn't know if she was alone or not, or how many people were in here, trapped. Misty and I came back to save as many people as we could."

"Very noble," she said, eyebrows raised. "Stupid, but noble. The woman … Where have I seen her?"

"Playboy," Watts volunteered, smiling from ear to ear as he sat in the desk chair and started pressing laptop buttons, moving through the various security camera feeds. "You might have seen her on the late night talk shows though… unless you check out Playboy. No judgement here!"

"I do not peruse Playboy." Betty rolled her eyes as if the idea were ludicrous. "And you … Are you in one of those music groups my granddaughter keeps going on and on about?"

"No, I'm not in a K-Pop group," Mike answered. "Not every Asian guy sings and dances."

"Oh, don't be so sensitive," Betty said. "You're in Hollywood hanging out with a Playmate. I thought you might be somebody."

"He's Mike Rha," Watts said. "He's been in a handful of movies, nothing huge, and that teen zombie show."

"Never heard of it."

"The girl is Emma Whitman, Disney preteen star."

"You seem to know all about us," Mike said. "Who are you?"

"I'm Watts."

"I caught the name earlier. What do you do, Watts?"

"This." Watts gestured toward the laptop.

"You work security?"

"Nah, dude. I'm a hacker. I hacked into the security cameras after everything went *Night of the Living Dead* and my cousin never returned from going out to get us some food."

"How'd you end up with the old bat?" Justain asked,

finally having brought his breathing down to a normal pattern.

"You wish you could have this old bat," Betty said, her nose turned up in disgust. "You certainly tried, and I'm not old. I'm mature."

Justain shook his head. "Of all the people to get stuck with."

"Nice outfit," Betty commented. "I'd ask if you've lost circulation in your balls yet, but I don't believe you own a pair."

"Guys," Mike interrupted. "We need to quiet down in here so the group in the hallway leaves us alone."

"Use the remote control car again," Watts said.

"We kind of lost the controller out there." Mike lowered his pack to the floor and opened it. "We have a few more cars. If we can get the infected to back up off the door just enough for us to stick another car out there I can guide them the rest of the way down the hall."

"Are those the same model cars?" Watts asked, leaning toward him.

"Yeah."

"You have controllers for them?"

Mike nodded.

"Dude! If they're on the same frequency we can just use one of the remotes you have to control the car you left in the hall."

Mike pushed his pack over to Watts. "What if they aren't the same frequency?"

"I'll have to work my craft and see what I can do. I'm really good with electronics and shit."

Mike stood straight and watched Watts pull out the remotes and study them. "So… you're Betty Meadow's own personal Geek Squad?"

"He saved me, like he saved you," Betty said. "I was on an upper floor at a private get together when someone started eating people and complete chaos broke out. I hid in a closet, intending to wait until the room cleared, but it didn't seem like it was ever going to. I decided I had to make a move. I barely managed to escape and run down the stairs. When I hit this floor, Watts grabbed me in the stairwell and pulled me in here."

"I was watching on the security feed," Watts explained. "At that time my floor was clear, but a group of infected were following her and a group was headed up the same stairwell. She would have been a Betty Meadow McNugget if I didn't pull her in when I did. Unfortunately, the infected got on this floor then. We've been waiting for them to figure out they can go back into the stairwell but they don't seem that great with doors. I saw you and the Playboy Bunny do your remote control trick and was hoping you'd hit this floor."

"Can we not refer to her as the Playboy Bunny?" Mike asked, looking toward the bathroom door where he could still hear soft sobbing.

"Dude, you mean you didn't know who you were with?"

"I know about the Playboy spread."

"So what's the problem? You have an issue with Playboy Playmates?"

"No, but I don't like calling her the Playboy Bunny. It sounds offensive, or like it defines her. It doesn't."

"Whatever, dude." Watts shrugged, then looked in his backpack again. "Um, so my cousin went out to get us some burgers before they started telling us to stay inside and I'm pretty sure he's dead or on the run. Either way, he never came back and the hotel staff got killed off pretty early on. You don't want to know the shit I saw on the feeds."

"You want some food?"

"Yeah, well, I see you got some."

"Sure, man. Go ahead. Sorry about your cousin."

"Eh, he was a dick." Watts grabbed a granola bar and practically inhaled it. "Sure wish he'd made it back with those burgers though."

Mike shook his head as Watts grabbed another granola bar and moved to the desk to better view the security screens displayed on the laptop.

"Don't eat all the food," Justain admonished the techie. "We're going to need it for the trip out of here."

"Relax," Mike said, looking over the screens. "It's not like any of it actually belongs to you. Everything edible in that backpack came from the car museum or Emma's room."

"Cripes. Of all the people to get stuck with in this mess, I got to get stuck with a real we are the world type. Charity won't get you far in this shit."

"It'll get you farther than pissing off everyone around you," Betty said. "I don't think there's anyone in this room you can buy, Dirty Harry, not even the Playmate despite that being just the type you usually prey on."

"Don't call me that." Harry's eyes darkened as they narrowed into slits.

"But the tabloid moniker fits so well. It's one of few things they got right."

Mike glanced up from the laptop to study the two. He could almost see the tension filling the space between them as Betty's words replayed in his mind and he recalled the way Misty had acted around Justain, the way she'd not wanted to save him at all, just the girl. His gut twisted as his thoughts went to the day before and why both of them were climbing down balconies at the same time, and why Justain was only in a robe.

"They got a few things right about you too," Justain shot back, grinning. "You really are aging."

"You don't say?" Betty rolled her eyes. "If that is the worst you have for me don't bother wasting your foul breath. Unlike many of the braindead twits in the business, I have no fear of aging. After all, I do it so much better than some." Her nostrils flared as she eyed him from head to toe. "How much weight have you gained these past few years, Juicy, darling? You used to just molest groups of young women. Now it appears maybe you are eating them, and the entire McDonald's inventory."

"Are you two going to be arguing like this all the time?" Watts asked, back to working on the remote controllers. "It's distracting, and not the best idea considering these infected people seem to hear us really well."

Betty and Justain gave one another one last withering glare before Betty turned around to look out the balcony doors and Justain focused his attention on the battle axe. Water ran in the bathroom and shortly after the door opened. Misty walked a much quieter Emma across the room and sat with her on the loveseat in the small sitting area.

"What's going on? It sounds like they're still out there."

Something, or someone, thumped against the door, as if on cue.

"Watts is working with the controllers," Mike said quietly, not wanting to rile up the infected beyond the door. "He might be able to control the car we left out there with one of them. If he can, we can draw them away from the door and continue on with our escape plan."

"What if the car is broken?" Misty asked. "Without us running it, they could pick it up, bite it, drop it, anything."

Mike looked at the screens on the laptop, zeroing in on where they'd left the car. "It looks fine on the camera, from what I can tell. We have to try it. It's the easiest way we'll get out of here."

"This escape plan you speak of," Betty said softly, her voice no longer loaded with anger and contempt. "Does it include a final destination or did you just decide to come save the poor souls trapped here with no idea where you'd be taking them?"

Warmth flooded Mike's face. "I honestly didn't think that far out. I just knew there was a young girl here and she wasn't safe."

"Genius," Justain muttered.

"You were trapped, just like us," Watts reminded him.

"If these two geniuses didn't come in here you'd probably starve to death in that room eventually, or jump just to put an end to it. And they are pretty genius. The remote control car thing is awesome."

"If you can get one of those damn controllers to work," Justain said. "Otherwise, we're still stuck, just with even worse company now."

Betty Meadow said nothing, opting to allow her raised middle finger to do all the talking for her as she remained at the balcony doors with her back to the room.

Watts slid the casing back on a controller he'd been poking at with a small set of metal tools and pressed a button. One of the cars inside the backpack made a whirring noise as its wheels turned.

Mike swiveled back toward the monitors and watched as Watts held down the lever and the car they'd left in the hall rolled back an inch. "The car in the hall is responding to the controller."

"Then we're all good, guys." Watt pumped his fist in the air before pulling the other responding car from the backpack. "We should toss this one since having two responding to the same controller at the same time won't help us much, but first I'll take the batteries. Never know when we might need them. I'm pretty sure we're on borrowed time with the electricity."

"What's our plan?" Misty asked, looking to Mike for an answer. "We didn't clear all the floors, but most of the rooms appear empty or full of people we don't want to meet. We've already had some close calls and now we have a young girl with us."

Mike nodded his head as he looked at the security camera feeds. "Watts, you said you've been watching these feeds a while?"

"Yeah, man."

"Do you think there's anyone else alive and uninfected in this building?"

"I can't say for sure, bro, but I know if they are, they're

deeply screwed. I mean, look at the floors. Almost all of them having infected people creeping around on them and the stairwells are fucked. We're going to have to take the elevator down and we should do it as soon as possible. I'm serious about the electricity, man. I've seen enough apocalypse movies to know that shit's going to get cut."

"You can't seriously still be thinking about saving more people," Justain groaned. "Keep trying it and you're going to be one of those freaks out there."

"My mom is not a freak," Emma said, a hint of a growl to her voice. Misty wrapped her arm around her and held her tighter, delivering a look of pure death Justain's way.

Justain rolled his eyes and waved his hand dismissively, not a single care given that he'd insulted the young girl's mother while she still mourned the loss. "Use your brain. That bleeding heart is going to get us all killed. You can't save everyone."

"We didn't have to save you," Misty advised, still glaring.

Justain returned the look with a matching heat, again causing Mike to recall and question the predicament he'd found the two in the day before.

"You didn't," Justain agreed. "If you're waiting on a thank you it's not coming. The two of you left me for dead and only came back today to save the girl. You have her. Now, the question is are you going to actually save her or are you going to drag her through the halls of this hotel until you finally succeed in ending her life and your own?"

"I hate to agree with the bastard but he does have a point," Betty interjected, looking over at them. "I am thankful you came back and attempted to save as many people as possible, but you have a girl with you now. I would love to save everyone, but we cannot risk her life to do so. We need to get out of this hotel and find a safe place."

Mike took a deep breath and reviewed the security camera feeds. Watts hadn't lied. Nearly every floor was infested and looking at the feed for the first floor chilled Mike's blood. They'd lucked into the empty lobby. What remained of the staff appeared to be in the banquet rooms. All of them were infected. If anyone else was alive in the hotel, they'd have to find a way to survive on their own or pray really hard that the military did actually send help. If anyone in the building was alive and uninfected he didn't know them. He didn't have their faces in his mind, but he did know Emma. He had her face engrained in his memory, and Misty and the others too. He could survive the thought of leaving nameless, faceless people behind if he had to, but he couldn't live with the images of those in the room with him haunting him if they died because he wanted to be a hero.

"You're right. The lobby is still clear so we just need to pull the car trick again and get the infected to all go left. We make a quick run for the elevator, take it down and there's a larger car waiting at the revolving doors. Once we're on the street, that's when everything goes up in the air. I have no idea where we can go. The museum was a decent hideout, but we'll run out of food."

"What about the military bases?" Betty asked.

"The last news report I saw suggested those were hard to get in to," Misty advised. "People swarmed the hospitals and the bases. Some of those people were infected and they infected others. The military isn't helping anyone because they're busy fighting off the infected there."

"There's no telling how that is going to pan out," Mike said. "I'm sure once the military takes care of the hot zones they'll send out teams to find survivors, or set up new bases and broadcast the location. We can either wait right here or move. I don't think we're safe waiting here."

"Definitely not," Watts agreed. "This is like a roach motel but the pests are freaking cannibals. We can't wait around on a news broadcast either. The power is going to go, I just know it."

"So where can we go?" Betty asked.

"A single family home would be a safer bet than a hotel or any tourist trap," Watts suggested.

"This is Hollywood, dear. Everything here is a tourist trap." Betty sighed. "I don't keep a residence here. It's too busy for my tastes. Everyone I know who lives here lives up in the hills. Not an easy journey with what's out there."

"We need to stay away from any areas full of people," Misty said. "Even single family homes are part of neighborhoods. This thing seems to be spreading fast. We need to be somewhere rural."

"In Hollywood?" Betty scoffed. "Where do you expect to find a place like that?"

"On the water," Justain said, grinning.

"Like a boat?" Mike asked, considering the idea. It definitely had merit. If the infected couldn't figure out how to open doors he highly doubted they could swim.

"Like a yacht," Justain answered. "I have one in Santa Monica and if you can all keep me alive long enough to get to it, you can board it with me."

"Santa Monica isn't that far by car," Betty said hopefully. "Does anyone have one?"

The room inhabitants looked at each other and shook their heads.

"I could try hotwiring one," Watts said. "I'm good at mechanical stuff. I'm sure it isn't that hard."

"If we can't find one and get it running we'll just have to walk," Mike said. "It probably wouldn't take more than four, five hours tops."

"Oh is that all?" Betty sighed, looking down at her clothes. She was wearing a long evening gown and heels.

"I guess you didn't happen to have a change of clothes?" Mike asked.

"I had no idea I would be on the menu when I accepted the invitation to the party or I would have skipped the evening gown and went for a more survivalist look."

"My cousin probably has something you can wear,"

Watts said, crossing the room to the closet.

"If he's built like you, there isn't enough elastic in the world," Justain commented, laughing so hard his belly jiggled, causing his snug T-shirt to ride up a few inches.

"Says the can of busted biscuits," Betty replied, turning her nose up at the image before her. "Please pull that shirt back down. You're spilling out all over the place."

"My cousin is from my mother's side. They're pretty sturdy stock," Watts said, pulling out a Nike tracksuit and a T-shirt.

"That is pretty sturdy," Mike agreed, checking out the suit. "What is that, a 2XL?"

"Yeah, I think so, not that I think you need a 2XL," Watts quickly added, looking at Betty with an apology in his eyes, or fright. "It's a track suit so it should fit well enough over your… uh… curves, and stuff, but it has a drawstring too so the pants shouldn't fall down. Hopefully."

"Thank you, Watts." Betty graciously accepted the clothing and turned for the bathroom. She paused a moment and looked down at Watts's feet. "What size shoe do you wear?"

"A six."

"What is that in women's, about an eight?"

Watts looked around the room. Mike shrugged, as did Justain.

"I think that's about right," Misty said.

"Tight squeeze." Betty looked down at her heels and pursed her lips a moment before looking back at Watts. "Would you happen to have an extra pair? I can tell by the size of the tracksuit your cousin's shoes would swallow my feet whole."

"Um, well, yeah." Watts bent down and pulled a pair of sandals from under one of the beds.

"Of course." Betty rolled her eyes before taking the shoes. "Still better than heels. Thank you."

"Now that that's finally settled," Justain muttered as

the bathroom door closed behind Betty. "What's the plan?"

"We use the remote controlled car on this floor to pull the infected away from the door, buying us time to get to the elevator."

"Us who?"

"Us," Mike said, gesturing around the room. "All of us."

"At once?" Justain's eyes widened. "You want all of us to go out there at once when we don't even have an escape car lined up?"

"What else would you suggest?"

"You and the nerd go and clear the way, get a car, get it running, and then come back for us," he said, his tone implying it was the obvious option.

"No way, man." Watts held his hands up. "I'm cool with busting out of here but once I'm out those doors I'm not coming back in."

"None of us are," Mike assured him. "We're not pulling such a dangerous stunt, not to mention doing all the work for you."

"Fine. Leave a car. The two of you head out first, find a vehicle and get it running. After enough time has passed for you to do that, we'll do the car trick and meet you out there."

"Again, that's going to be a no." Mike stood and crossed his arms. "We are going out together and watching each other's backs."

"Wonderful." Justain threw his hands up in the air. "So if we hit a wall of those monsters, we all die. Brilliant plan."

"It's better than sending two men out and expecting one of them to be able to get a car running with only one man there to watch his back while he's doing that. You do realize the sound of a running car would draw the attention of anything out there, right? We go out together, protecting each other, and if we are lucky enough to find a car and get it going we will all be there and ready to jump in and go before we're swarmed."

"Not to mention I have no intention of staying behind and Emma definitely isn't staying behind with you," Misty chimed in, tightening her hold around Emma's thin shoulders.

Mike's gut twisted again, as he noticed Emma turn her face away, uncomfortable even looking at the large man sitting on the bed in front of her. Misty's glare heated up several degrees as her hand firmly wrapped around Emma's shoulder, almost as if she were sending a silent threat to Justain. Before he could question it, the bathroom door opened and Betty Meadow stepped out.

"Look out, it's the creature from the black lagoon!" Justain quipped.

"Look out, it's a boil plucked fresh off Satan's ass!" Betty shot back as she tightened the sleeves she'd fastened around her waist, opting to wear just the T-shirt on top and wrap the jacket part around her waist as the girls had done. The bottom of the track suit billowed around her legs like harem pants and hung so low only her toes peeked out from beneath the fabric which had completely eclipsed the sandals.

"See, that looks good," Watts said, chewing his bottom lip nervously.

"The pants are tucked under my breasts," Betty said. "Just how big is this cousin of yours?"

"About the same size as the other wrestlers."

"Other wrestlers?" Mike, Betty, Misty, and Justain spoke at once.

"Yeah. He's a wrestler, but he was out here to talk about some movie deal, some action flick."

"Wait a minute." Realization struck Mike. "Is your cousin … Killa Watts?"

"Yeah."

"Dude, we could totally use a guy like him. Are you sure he isn't coming back soon?"

"I'm sure, and it's probably a good thing. I don't think he'd be as helpful as you think he'd be. I mean, if he remembers to focus on the enemy his roid rage may help but once he goes through withdrawal he's going to be an unholy terror."

"So he does take steroids."

"They all take steroids." Watts rolled his eyes. "Normal men don't look like that. Some of them even inject those *muscles* into their bodies. Totally fake."

"Fake muscles, fake boobs, not news in Hollywood," Justain cut in. "Those things out there are what we should be concerned with. Everyone is dressed and ready. Can we shut up now and get moving? I'd like to get to my yacht and out of these pants as soon as possible."

"Yeah, sorry." Mike situated everything in his backpack, zipped it back up and slid his arms through the straps. "Is everyone ready to move?"

"Just tell us what to do," Betty said.

Mike took another look at the security camera feeds on the laptops, noting the lobby was still clear. "Misty, take the controller and draw the infected all the way to the left end of the hall. We'll wait until we can see it's all clear to pack up the laptop and move. Everyone else, keep hold of your shit and move when I say move."

Misty slid her arms through her own backpack straps and picked up the controller. She watched the security footage while working the control, taking advantage of actually being able to see where she directed the toy car this time. It took her a few tries to figure it out, but the noise caused by her experimentation effectively drew the infected outside their room away. By the time they'd reached the area the car had been left she'd figured out what to do and mastered leading the group past the elevator, down the hall, and around the corner.

"This is so much better, actually seeing where I'm directing this thing."

"Yeah, you did great," Mike told her as he nodded

toward Watts who stood by to disconnect the laptop. "Now just keep your thumb down on the lever just like before. It'll keep making noise when it hits the wall and hopefully keep them entertained while we get on the elevator."

Watts disconnected the laptop and slid it into the suitcase he'd set on the bed. Once he was all zipped up, Mike looked around the room, quickly assured himself everyone had everything they were going to take with them, and moved toward the door.

"I go first, Misty and Emma are after me, then Betty and Watts. Justain, you're on rear duty again."

"Why am I bringing up the rear again?"

"You made the decision to wield the battle axe, now deal with the consequences."

"If I die, no one gets on my yacht so remember that if the shit hits the fan."

"Will do." Mike placed one hand over the Ka-Bar at his hip and opened the hotel door with his other. He took a quick peek out into the hall to assure himself they were safe and proceeded to move toward the elevator. "Keep that lever down."

"I know, I know," Misty's whispered response warmed the back of his neck, she was wedged so close to him.

They reached the elevator without incident and Mike punched the button with the arrow pointing down.

"Wait, don't you need to get a car to run down?" Misty asked.

"The lobby was clear on the feed," he answered as the elevator opened, the bell dinging loudly, "and we just rang that damn dinner bell so I'd rather not send a car down and have to wait. Everybody in the elevator, now!"

He stood aside and allowed everyone to enter before him so he would be the last one in and the first one out when the doors opened again on the lobby floor.

"Move it, move it," he ordered as he saw an infected man turn around the corner at the end of the hall. He studied the man a moment, noting how he looked normal except for the paleness, cloudy eyes, and awkward gait before he stepped into the elevator and pushed the button to close the doors.

"Are we sending a car out ahead of us?" Misty asked, tossing aside the no longer needed controller and reaching for a backpack zipper to retrieve another car.

"No. The layout of the lobby is different than the upper floors and we might actually draw infected into it so when the doors open we run for the big car we left and hit the street," Mike answered right before the elevator doors opened and the bell chimed. "I hate that damn bell. Let's go, people."

He stepped out of the elevator, scanning left to right as he beelined for the bigger remote controlled car they'd left there. Looking through the glass revolving doors, he saw infected people milling about. "Shit."

"Get the car in the door," Misty said, grabbing the controller they'd left with it.

"We're sending the car out first," Mike explained to the rest of the group as he placed it in the door between two glass sections. "We'll wait until we draw the infected away and then we'll hit the street and hopefully we can find a vehicle but we have to be quick before a new group finds us. Justain, cover us."

He stepped back, not confident Justain actually would be much protection, but he had the battle axe. The best Watts could do would be swing his pack at something, unless his cousin had taught him some moves which he doubted, and Misty was on controller duty again.

"Ready," she said and pushed the lever down. The car hit the glass and whirred loudly. Mike cringed, afraid the noise would draw the infected on that floor right to them, and pushed on the door, helping the car to get through. He breathed a sigh of relief as the car exited the revolving door and Misty thumbed the lever to the left, sending the toy away from the hotel with the infected following it.

Then he heard something clatter off the lobby.

"What was that?" Watts asked, clutching his suitcase to his chest as Emma whimpered and grabbed him around his waist, hiding behind him.

"Everyone, stay quiet," Mike whispered as he quickly pried Emma's hands from his middle and gently pushed her into Betty Meadow's arms so he could pull the Ka-Bar free. Everyone froze as instructed. He glanced at Misty to make sure she was still controlling the decoy car. A quick look showed her thumb remained pressed on the lever despite her hand shaking slightly. Her wide, glossy eyes stayed fixed on the street beyond the glass doors.

Another noise came from the hall, a whoosh followed by a clunk and the breaking of glass. Something scraped against something. He imagined a pale infected person shuffling down the hall, leaning against the wall, knocking off framed pictures and whatever other décor the hotel had used to make the place welcoming. He hoped it was just one.

"Maybe it's a cat," Watts suggested, voice low.

Even better, but Mike didn't hold out much hope for that scene. He wasn't positive, but he doubted a cat would make it alive through a room of infected people and he knew the hallway the noises came from was the hallway leading to the banquet rooms he'd seen on the monitor. "How are the streets looking?"

"Still some stragglers," Misty whispered, voice quivering. "I'm keeping the car at a slow speed so they stay interested but those in back don't seem that interested."

Something else crashed, closer to the mouth of the hallway and Mike heard the unmistakable groan of someone infected with the virus. "Watts, grab another car out of Misty's backpack and put it outside. We need to get those stragglers moving. Betty, don't let Emma see anything. Justain, get ready to swing that battle-axe."

"Are you fucking serious?" Justain asked.

"Swing the damn axe or kiss your ass goodbye," Mike

said as two pale men in Armani suits emerged from the hallway. Their milky white eyes seemed to lock on to Mike and his group the moment they stepped into the lobby. The dark-headed one in front let out a loud groan that almost sounded angry and it was quickly echoed by the blond man behind him. For a moment, Mike thought they might be alerting the rest of the infected on the floor to the fresh meat they'd found in the lobby and the thought of them communicating in such a way nearly sent a trickle of piss down his leg.

"Shit," Justain said as they approached. His eyes watered and his hands trembled. Behind them, Watts whimpered.

"Get the fucking car out there, Watts." Mike white-knuckled the handle of the Ka-bar and surged forward, pretty sure Justain was frozen solid in fear. Acting on instinct, he raised the Ka-bar as he leapt forward, grabbed the dark-headed infected man's left shoulder with his free hand and brought the Ka-bar down as the man turned to take a bite out of him. Before the man could get his mouth on Mike's arm, his blade was in the unfortunate soul's ear. Mike yanked up on the blade as he pushed the man's body down, effectively slicing up through the head until the blade stuck.

"Justain!" he yelled as he had to resort to placing his foot on the infected man's shoulder to give him the needed leverage to pull his Ka-bar free of the man's cranium. All the while, the second infected man moved forward, closing in for the kill. "Justain! Damn it!"

He heard a battle scream and looked up just in time to see a red-faced Betty Meadow swing the battle axe and connect the blade with the blond man's midsection before she fell to the floor in an awkward heap. "Chrissakes! How much does that thing weigh?" she asked as she rolled to her knees, narrowly avoiding getting covered in blood and other disgusting matter as the blond man's upper half folded in on itself.

Mike finally managed to yank his Ka-bar free just in time to see the blond's upper body crawl toward Betty, mouth opening and closing viciously. She let out a blood-curdling scream, echoed by Emma, as Mike reached the still moving half-man and sank his blade into its brain, going in through the ear again, and thankfully not getting stuck. He had no time to feel relief. The screams had drawn the attention of every infected person on the floor, judging by the sound of numerous shuffling feet and groans coming up the hall.

"Time to go." Mike reached down and yanked Betty up by her hand before turning and pushing a blinking, fish-mouthed Justain toward the revolving door. "How's it look?" he asked, not seeing anyone immediately outside through the glass doors.

"I think I got all the stragglers up far enough," Watts said, holding down the lever on a remote. Misty still held her thumb on the remote to the larger car with one hand while holding Emma tightly tucked under her other arm.

"We can't wait anymore. Betty, take Emma. Watts you go first, then Misty. Keep the cars moving. Betty, you and Emma after them, Justain, and then me. Go, go, go!"

Justain protested as Mike directed him forward. "My battle axe!"

"It's worthless if you're too chicken-shit to use it," Betty called back as she and Emma slid in between two revolving panes of glass, following Watts and Misty out.

"What she said." Mike shoved Justain into the door and dove into the section behind him as multiple infected people started to pour out of the hallway. He quickly pushed forward until they all stood outside the hotel.

"Now what?" Betty looked from left to right like the rest of them, scanning for threats, as she held Emma tight against her, the girl's face lost somewhere in her bosom.

"We find a car and see if Watts can hotwire it. Think you can manage finding an unlocked car?" Mike asked Justain as he moved forward and started pulling on door handles of cars left abandoned along the curb.

Justain blinked for a moment then shook his head as it reddened with indignation. "Of course I can. I'm not incompetent!"

Betty hmmphed and cast a worried glance toward the lobby. "I don't see a way to lock this door from the outside. Those beasts will be out here in no time."

Mike cursed as he pulled up on yet another locked door handle and looked back at the door. "You're right. We have to get some distance. Everyone run up ahead the way the infected went."

"The way the infected went?" Justain's eyes bulged. "Are you nuts?"

"Misty and Watts have been running the cars that way. The infected that way are following the cars. We don't know what the hell we'll run into in the other direction so yes, we're going in the direction of the ones following the cars. If you don't like the plan, you're free to stay here and deal with what's about to come through that revolving door."

Mike motioned for the others to move and they started forward at a jog, not a very quick one considering Betty wore borrowed sandals and could trip over the hem of her borrowed track pants at any time. After they moved up a block he threw a glance back to see Justain had decided to join them and was running as fast as he could in the too-tight pants. He resembled a living scissors. Mike might have laughed if he hadn't noticed the infected starting to pour out of the revolving door behind him.

"Start checking cars," he instructed the rest of the group who were maintaining his speed. They all started pulling up on door handles, even Emma, desperate to find transportation, preferably transportation they could get inside of and worry less about getting grabbed or bitten.

A loud shriek penetrated the air and Mike looked toward the noise to see Justain had grabbed the handle of a car with an alarm system. "Shit."

"That's going to draw back all the ones we led away from here!" Misty cried, throwing her hands up in the air.

Mike looked ahead of her, trying to estimate how far ahead the ones they'd led away were, and looked back at the group still pouring out of the hotel behind Justain, noticing more spilling out onto the street from alleys and side streets. Justain pumped his arms back and forth, his massive gut jiggling as he literally ran for his life. He might actually reach them but if they didn't find an escape car they'd all be dead soon after anyway. Mike balled up his fist and took a deep breath. He was going to have to bust his way into a car and hope Watts could get the damn thing running.

"I found one!" Watts yelled from down the block.

Mike froze, looked over and saw Watts slip inside the driver's side of a cab that had been abandoned in the street. Blood and innards painted the front of the cab, indicating there'd been an accident. Mike couldn't understand why anyone would get out of a vehicle in the middle of a zombie infested street unless the poor fool hadn't realized what was happening.

"Everyone in the cab now!" he instructed, waving the women toward it as he glanced back at Justain to find the man gaining ground but huffing and puffing like a heart attack could happen at any moment. "Come on, Justain! Move your ass or get it chewed off!"

He turned and ran for the cab. If he'd had a gun he would provide cover, but he didn't and there were too many infected people after Justain for him to even make a dent with a blade. The remote car trick wasn't going to work with a car alarm blaring away and fresh meat moving on the street. Emma and the women had reached the safety of the cab and dove into the backseat. Mike jumped into the passenger side and looked down at Watts, fooling around with wires under the dash. "Please tell me you got that shit figured out."

"I think so. Give me a moment."

Mike looked back up the street, Justain was almost to them but he was moving slow, his age, weight, and the likelihood he'd never ran a day in his life working against him. The infected horde was close on his ass. "Dude, we don't have a moment."

The car revved to life. Watts and the women sent up a collective scream of triumph as Watts pulled himself into the driver's seat and closed the door. "Tell me which way to go, man!"

"Make room for Justain," Mike told the women in the back. Watts, just be ready to floor the gas when he gets his ass in here. Don't even wait for the door to close, just burn rubber."

"Will do, bro." Watts put on his seatbelt, gripped the steering wheel and bit down into his bottom lip as they all watched Justain make a mad dash for the car.

Watts revved the engine and Justain's eyes widened with fear before narrowing with steel determination. He scrounged up an energy burst from somewhere and surged forward, diving into the backseat the second he got close enough.

"Go!" Mike ordered as Justain's hefty body landed halfway in the backseat, on top of the women's laps, and poor Emma, who'd been sitting on Betty's lap to make room. Watts floored the gas and sped off, Justain's feet still hanging out of the open door.

"Pull him in!" Mike instructed the women groaning under the man's weight, and turned around to help them.

"Get your fat ass off of us!" Betty snapped, shoving Justain away from them, onto the floor as Mike kept hold of the back of his shirt, afraid what his fingers might accidentally encounter if he tried to heft him from the waist of his pants.

"Where to?" Watts asked.

"Just keep going straight," Mike told him as he pulled up on Justain's shirt. "Pull your fucking legs in so we can shut the door!"

With a lot of grumbling and cursing, Justain managed to tuck his legs in under him and get to a kneeling position so Misty could reach over and pull the door shut. "Unbelievable," he muttered, pulling himself up until he could squeeze himself onto the seat. "When this shit is over none of you dumbasses will ever work in Hollywood again."

Mike turned and slid down into his seat. He put on his seatbelt and sighed, looking around him as Watts flew down the street. Once they'd made it past the group of infected people who'd come from the hotel, they only saw stragglers or smaller clusters here and there, but that was all they saw. Abandoned cars, dead bodies, and infected people. He looked up at buildings they passed and wondered if any of them held life or were they all infested like the hotel they'd just left.

"Justain, shut the hell up," he muttered. "When all this is over, I don't think there's going to be a Hollywood left."

"If we can't get on that yacht and out on the water I don't think there's going to be an us left," Betty added.

No one disagreed.

10

"Well, this is a beautiful sack of shit," Teague said, passing his binoculars back to Manny.

"Let me see!" Larry grabbed for the binoculars, but Manny's elbow connected with his head and knocked him onto his back.

"I wouldn't suggest getting back up," Manny said as he looked through the binoculars to get a closer look at the scene before them.

"You don't have to be so rude," Larry said, rubbing his head. "You're using my van, and I'm the one who suggested the yacht."

"We've already established that it's because of you and your van we had to evacuate Mimi's in a hurry," Ladeja said, straining to see what the men were looking at. They'd noticed a heavy guard up ahead as they'd neared the Santa Monica coastline and pulled over along the curb, shielded by the tree line. Had they continued forward, it was guaranteed they'd hit a military checkpoint. Without binoculars, all she saw was what looked like a wall of soldiers lining the marina. "Why won't they let people get on their boats and leave?"

"I think we're all under quarantine," Forrester said.

"The whole damn country."

"Makes sense," Manny said, passing the binoculars to O'Donnell. "Other countries have probably issued warnings against anyone leaving. It might start a damn war."

"Then why are we still sitting here?" Ladeja asked, jittery at the thought of being fired upon if they managed to get to a yacht. "We need to find someplace safe."

"I really don't think that exists on land anymore," Manny replied.

"Containment might not even be possible," Teague added. "I've seen some shit online about incidents in other countries, but nothing official. I think other governments are trying to keep a lid on it. It's bad enough Russia knows their plan worked with us and we're going to hell over here, but if they know they've started this shit elsewhere? They'll try to take over the whole damn world."

"Like you said, there hasn't been an official statement," Forrester told him. "We can't believe everything internet trolls post. All we know for sure is it's here and we are not safe anywhere there's people."

"We're not safe anywhere we're going to get shot at," Ladeja added. "That's a lot of armed men out there guarding those yachts. If we even manage to sneak past them and get on a yacht, they'll open fire on us the second we start to move out, if keeping us grounded is what their orders are."

"We need a diversion." Manny looked around. "I see absolutely nothing useful."

"We—"

"Nobody's interested in seeing your tits," Manny cut Cynda off before she could make the suggestion for the umpteenth time since they'd started the trek to the coastline. "You and your sister walk up to those men and try to seduce them, you're going to most likely be shot or arrested."

"Let them try then," Ladeja murmured, earning grins

from the men, except for Larry, who busied himself ogling Mimi's assets as she continued to sulk in the corner, annoyed to have lost her comfortable house.

"I wouldn't be smirking over there if I were you, O'Donnell. You still work for us," Cynda warned him.

"Yeah, I believe I told you earlier that I quit. If not… I quit. All settled." O'Donnell's eyes narrowed as he craned his head to see something in Teague's side mirror. Ladeja followed his line of sight and caught the image of a red sports car right before it sped past them. It sped by too fast to get a good look inside, but it appeared to be filled to capacity.

"Are they going to try to run through the security?" she asked.

"Hell if I know," Manny answered, "but it could be the diversion we need." He and the security guards checked their guns, gearing up.

"Can you get us closer?" O'Donnell asked.

"Not without risking our cover," Teague answered. "We're better off leaving the van here and footing it down the hill to the coastline. They're focused on the checkpoint that's up there, especially now that someone just went speeding right toward it."

"We're moving out now?" Ladeja looked around frantically. "Are you sure about this? This doesn't seem like the best idea."

"It's the only one we got right now," O'Donnell said, leaning forward to confer with the two guards sitting in front. Teague had the binoculars. "What's it looking like?"

"Shit," Teague said a second before gunfire erupted. "Guys… I think your girl is right about this being a bad idea. They're not just opening up major firepower on civilians. I'm pretty sure they just killed a fucking kid."

"Move!" Forrester yelled, pointing down the hill to where a group of armed soldiers emerged.

"Fuck!" Teague dropped the binoculars, put the van in Drive and floored the gas. Everyone in the back fell and tumbled as Teague sped them out of the danger zone.

Ladeja got to her hands and knees just as they sped past the security checkpoint, Teague going around and not through it. She caught a quick glance at the massacre that had just occurred through the van's back windows as they left the grisly scene behind. She didn't know who had opened fire first, but the group in the car had apparently not planned on taking a no for an answer when they'd tried to get through the blockade. They'd died trying, evidenced by the bullet-shredded bodies left behind.

Mateo curled into a ball against the back of Teague's seat and started crying. Manny eased over to the boy and clamped a comforting hand onto his skinny shoulder. He didn't say anything, just offered his presence for support. As the others in the back righted themselves, Mimi took a few shots at Larry's head and chest, cursing him for his failed rescue attempt. Teague, Forrester, and O'Donnell conferred with each other on what the hell to do next, and Ladeja reached out to her son.

Cory batted her hand away and pulled his knees to his chest. "My dad wouldn't have me out here running around in a van. My dad would have me safe with my own personal bodyguard who knew what he was doing."

"Cut your mom a break, kid," Manny said. "No one knows what the fuck we're dealing with here. This isn't normal shit."

"Manny—"

"No, Ladeja. The kid's been a disrespectful little shit since this started. I can't just sit here and let him—"

"Well, it's not your place, is it?" Ladeja snapped, her mama bear instincts kicking in. Yes, Cory was being horrible toward her, but he was hurting.

Manny's eyes widened, wounded, but only for a moment before his nostrils flared and he shook his head as if shaking her off and her kid too. Ladeja sighed. She felt something for Manny, but her kid came first and just because Thunda was dead didn't mean Manny, or any other man for that matter, could just step in and play father figure without her consent.

"Look out!" Forrester yelled as a yellow cab came speeding through the bend they'd been winding around.

"Hold tight!" Teague hollered as he jerked the steering wheel in the opposite direction, but clipped the cab anyway, sending it flipping through the air as they themselves went off the road.

Ladeja grabbed Cory and covered him with her body, not concerned with whether he liked it or not, as the rest of the women in the back screamed and clung to one another, Chelle momentarily forgetting the issues between her and her sisters. Manny wrapped one of his large hands around her arm and together they braced themselves for the impact they feared coming as they worked together to ensure the boys would be protected.

The van careened through dirt and bushes and narrowly squeezed between two trees before skidding to a stop. Everyone lurched forward, especially those in the back without seatbelts or actual seats.

"Everyone all right?" Teague asked, unbuckling himself before turning to check the occupants in back.

Ladeja ran her hands over the boys, checking for injuries. Cory again pushed her hands away, and she reflexively grabbed his wrists and squeezed them tight as she battled with herself not to lash out. Manny squeezed her shoulder and raised his eyebrow as she met his gaze. She nodded, answering his silent question. She was cool. Her temper had flared, but she was all right. She loosened her grip on Cory's wrists and rubbed his head. "Just making sure you're all right, baby. I know you're upset, but I love you. I always will and I'll never let anything happen to you."

Cory didn't say anything. She didn't expect him to, but it still hurt.

"Everyone seems fine back here," O'Donnell said, having quickly checked over the women, "but Larry might need a hospital soon."

Ladeja turned to see Mimi kicking the rotund man with her stilettoed foot. "We almost died just now and you're copping a feel?" she screeched. "Are you serious?"

"I was just making sure you weren't hurt, my angel!" Larry pleaded with her as he rolled into a ball and covered his head with his hands in an effort to protect himself. "You're going to stab a hole in me!"

"Damn right I am!"

O'Donnell reached out and grabbed Mimi's ankle before she could finish docking Larry like a pizza crust. "That's enough."

Forrester opened his door and started to step out.

"Where the hell you going?" Teague asked.

"Dude, we were just in an accident, and that cab was flipped. We have to check on them."

"The hell we do," Mimi said. "We need to find shelter somewhere."

"He's right," Ladeja said. "There could be kids. We can't leave without checking on them."

"You're not bringing them back here to share our vehicle," Cynda said.

"Wanna bet?" Forrester asked. "We got the keys, and we got guns. All you have is money that I don't think anyone here but you cares about right now and a set of boobs no one cares to see no matter how many times you offer. If there's people in that car in need of help, they're going to get it, and that includes a ride if we wrecked the shit out of theirs."

Forrester slammed the door closed behind him and Teague followed suit.

"I'll go with them," Manny said, moving toward the van's back doors.

"Right behind you," O'Donnell said.

"Wait!" Mimi grabbed O'Donnell's arm. "Who'll stay here and protect us if something happens while they're checking on the people in the cab?"

"I'll protect you," Larry offered, visibly hurt.

"Shut up, Larry," Mimi and the Camilleri Sisters said in unison.

"Stay here," Ladeja said, reading the indecision in O'Donnell's eyes. "They do need someone to protect them, especially the boys. I'll go in case there are kids or they just need an extra set of hands." She moved toward the back of the van where Manny stood just outside, waiting.

"You guys be quick," O'Donnell warned. "That wreck made a lot of noise and we don't know who or what we've got around here. Don't waste time if you can't save anyone."

Manny helped her out of the van and they both nodded at O'Donnell before jogging ahead to catch up to Teague and Forrester, who were moving at a quick clip toward the direction of the curve where they'd hit the cab.

"You know what he was getting at?" Manny asked.

"Yeah, we might find a car full of dead people," Ladeja answered, her stomach churning. She prayed no kids had been in the cab.

"Or people better off dead," Manny added. "We'll have to check for signs of infection before we bring them back with us. Any signs and we leave them. Understand?"

Ladeja nodded. "You won't get an argument out of me. Not after seeing the aftermath of not putting Mara out of Mimi's house."

"Yeah, but would you feel the same about a kid?"

She didn't answer. She didn't want to think about such a scenario and hoped she wouldn't have to.

"I wasn't trying to step on any toes with Cory or put my nose in where it doesn't belong—"

"I don't want to discuss this now," she cut him off as they neared Teague and Forrester. "I appreciate all the help you've given us, but Cory is my son and I will deal with him how I see fit. Right now we need to concentrate on finding that cab and helping those people if we can, so we can get back to the van and get out of here."

"I think we found it," Manny said as he nodded ahead, gesturing toward the rising smoke visible over the rock wall.

The three men picked up the pace, sprinting around the bend, and Ladeja followed suit. The cab had turned over on its roof and flames shot out of the engine as an Asian man and a young blonde woman appeared to be pulling others out of the vehicle, or attempting to. A young blonde girl sat next to the burning vehicle, her knees to her chest, looking on as tears poured down the sides of her face.

Teague and Forrester quickly moved the blonde woman aside, passing her back toward Ladeja as they took over her efforts to help whomever remained in the back of the cab while Manny helped the Asian man pull a frighteningly pale man from the front.

"Get away from the cab," Ladeja urged the blonde woman, pushing her away from the burning vehicle before bending to help the younger girl to her feet. "Let's get you a safe distance."

"You can't," the girl mumbled so low Ladeja just barely heard her, but even if she hadn't, her hopelessness was right there in her eyes.

"Well, I'm damn sure not going to give up," Ladeja replied, forcing down her own fear as she walked the girl toward the road, away from the wreckage. She waited until their feet were on asphalt to turn around and check out the progress on the people remaining in the cab. The driver had been pulled free of the car and laid out on the ground. Manny squatted next to him, two fingers at his neck, checking for a pulse. After a moment that seemed to drag on endlessly, he looked up at the Asian man and shook his head.

The blonde woman gasped and Ladeja turned to see tears spill from her eyes as the young girl erupted into deep, wracking sobs and wrapped her arms around her waist. Familiarity washed over Ladeja then. She'd seen the woman somewhere before, the Asian man too.

"No!" the man screamed as he turned away from the dead body and fell to his knees to pummel the earth with his fist. He looked up to the sky and let out a scream of pure anger and it hit Ladeja where she'd seen him. He was an actor, not a huge star, but he'd been in a few things. She safely guessed the woman was an actress too.

"Was he family?" she asked the woman.

"We just met him," the woman answered, "but he was a good guy. He saved our lives." She broke down into whole body-shaking sobs and buried her face in the younger girl's hair as they held on to each other and wept for their fallen party member.

"I got her free!" Forrester yelled as he dug his heels in and pulled. Ladeja saw the top half of an older woman start to slip out of the back as Manny went around the other side of the cab.

"I tried getting to him through that side, but the door won't open," Teague yelled to him as he grabbed the heavy woman under her arm and helped Forrester, who struggled to get the woman pulled free. "This thing's gonna blow! We need to save who we can and run!"

The Asian man… Mark or Matt or… Ladeja couldn't recall his name, rose to his feet and ran toward the cab.

"Leave him!" The blonde yelled, realizing he was rushing toward the vehicle to help Manny free the occupant on the far side. She pushed the young girl into Ladeja's arms and rushed forward herself. Ladeja quickly grabbed her, catching only her shirt at first, but that was enough to slow her down until she could get a good grip on her arm.

"Let me go!" the woman yelled, then lowered her voice as she pleaded with her eyes. "That man is not worth any of their lives. I can't let any of them die for him."

The older woman was now free of the vehicle and being dragged across the dirt as the two security guards didn't wait for her to get her footing. They looked back at the cab with terror in their eyes as Manny and the other man worked together to get the last occupant out. Now that the woman had been removed, they could get to the man inside, the man the blonde now screamed at them to leave behind.

"They have to save him if they can!" Ladeja told her, wrapping her arm around her neck as the woman drew from whatever energy reserves she had left in her body to make a desperate last attempt to get to the men and pull them back. She struggled to keep hold of the woman and as Teague and Forrester neared them, she stuck her knee into the back of the blonde's knee, causing the woman to go down into a kneeling position. She quickly followed her down and held her there as Manny and Mike pulled the last man free and helped him to his feet before turning to run.

"Fucking hell!" Teague yelled, dropping the older woman Ladeja now realized was Betty Meadow in a ridiculous outfit, clearly not her own, to grab and aim his gun at something in the distance. He'd started shooting before Ladeja could turn her head. Once she did, she saw a group of infected on the road, moving toward them.

The young girl screamed and Ladeja quickly grabbed her, shoving her behind her body as she backed away. She cut a glance toward Manny right as the car exploded. There'd been a second of silence full of dread as she'd sensed what was about to happen and then *BOOM*. Orange and yellow flames burst out of the windows as glass shattered and metal flew before turning into a living creature that swallowed the vehicle whole.

Ladeja instinctively shoved the girl to the ground and covered her with her body. She heard the air being sliced as something flew over her and the intense heat of the fiery wreckage licked at their bodies. The girl screamed and writhed beneath her, but the sound was muted as her ears rang from the blast. She waited as long as she dared to raise her head and look around, searching for Manny and the others.

She saw Teague and Forrester scrambling to their feet, guns in hand, looking toward the place the infected had been emerging from. The blonde woman and the Asian actor whose name hadn't come to her yet helped a bruised and bleeding Betty Meadow to her feet and cast a look her way. The man said something to her, but she couldn't hear him. A horribly loud whirring had accompanied the ringing in her ears. She shrugged, a reflex action to not knowing what he had said and assuming it had been a question.

The girl rose to her knees and turned toward her, still freaking out. Ladeja couldn't help her. She couldn't help anyone until she found Manny. She couldn't think until she saw him.

The ringing stopped and noise flooded her, the sudden deafening onslaught of it hit her like a physical blow, nearly knocking her back but she fought against it, clapped her hands over her ears and searched through the smoke for the man she suddenly realized she couldn't lose.

A hand clamped onto her shoulder and she spun, instinctively throwing a punch. Manny caught the punch effortlessly, grinning as he shook his head, but only for a second before he shoved her and the younger girl behind him and raised his gun in the direction the infected had been approaching from. As the smoke started clearing, the infected appeared, the blast seeming to have no negative effect on them.

"We're just going to waste bullets," Forrester yelled over to him. "We saved all but the driver. I think it's time to haul ass back to the others."

"Or they could haul ass to us," Teague said, laughing as he looked behind them. "Bastard must have hotwired it."

Ladeja turned to see the van approaching, O'Donnell at the wheel. He twisted the steering wheel to the right, turning the van completely around as he brought it to a screeching stop. The back doors immediately opened and

Chelle and Larry gestured for everyone to hurry and get in. Not needing to be asked a second time, the group piled in, the women and girl first, followed by the actor and the man in the too-tight clothes, Manny, and Forrester. Teague ran around the front and hopped into the passenger seat. "Thought you could use a ride," O'Donnell said as the back doors closed and he floored the gas. "We heard the blast and figured it would draw all the infected in the area, so we'd better grab you and get out of here. There's a ticking in the engine, but the van seems to be fine otherwise."

"You're Misty Waters," Larry said, ogling the blonde woman. He wiped his chin, Ladeja was pretty sure due to drooling, as Mimi looked at him incredulously, actually miffed her stalker dared lust for someone else. "And you're Mike Rha," he continued, moving on to the rest of the new members of the group as they sped away from the crash scene. "And Betty Meadow? Or are you an impersonator?" He leaned closer to the disheveled Grammy and Oscar award winning superstar. "Some of you drag queens are really amazing with the makeup."

The singing actress walloped him with an impressive backhand before sagging against the back of the driver's seat next to the boys. "I'm not a drag queen, you grotesquely misshapen fool."

"You're Emma Whitman," Mateo said, his voice soft and his cheeks pink as he eyed the young girl as best he could with his head bowed shyly.

The young girl nodded and scooted in close to Misty and Mike. The entire group seemed to keep their distance from the other man with them. Ladeja noticed the blonde deliver a lethal look his way and receive a withering glare accented by flaring nostrils in return.

"Uh, excuse me," Cynda said. "Have these people been checked for bites or scratches or whatever causes this infection to spread? It's nice you saved them or whatever, but do they have to be in the same vehicle with us?"

"We're not infected," Mike Rha said. "We were headed to Justain's yacht when your van clipped us, taking out our ride and killing our driver."

"I'd say we owe them," Ladeja said, holding Cynda's gaze with a look she intended to promise a repeat of the last punch she'd thrown her way.

"Harry Justain?" Cheyanne studied the large-bellied man in the tight black clothes. "Is this a new look, Juicy?"

"I was without clothes when my hotel room was invaded by people who wanted to eat me," the man answered with no hint of amusement before turning his attention to O'Donnell. "Driver, you're going the wrong way. We need to get to my yacht."

"You won't get on your yacht," Forrester advised as O'Donnell shot an annoyed look Justain's way via the rearview mirror. "We just came from there and had the same idea. Military is turning people away and if they don't go quickly and quietly they slaughter them with way more bullets than necessary. Women and kids too."

"You've got to be kidding," Misty said.

"No, we saw it happen," Ladeja assured her.

"We also saw a bunch of infected coming from that way," Manny added. "That blast had to draw infected from all over. I heard shots from that direction. If it isn't already, I imagine that spot will be swarming with infected soon. The sound of the explosion would draw them, but once they see all those military personnel, they'll go for that fresh meat."

"If the military is all killed off, we can get on the yacht," Justain said, not seeming the least bit concerned with the lives of the men guarding the border. If anything, he seemed to brighten at the thought of the armed men being wiped out, clearing the way for him to reach his yacht.

"Or we could get killed ourselves," O'Donnell advised him. "Maybe after a while we can try the coastline again. Right now, we need to find somewhere to hole up that's secure. If you've been watching the news, you know the roads to the camps set up for survivors have all been jammed up and the military is busy with hospitals and trying to contain areas hit hard."

"And this area doesn't qualify?" Betty asked.

"Apparently, not as bad as hospitals. We're on our own. Anyone know of a place we can take cover until the military can get to us? The gas in this van will only take us so far, and I'm in no rush to stop at a gas station." O'Donnell seemed to emphasize his point by swerving around a trio of infected people in the road.

"What about the megachurch?" Mateo asked. "It's huge and they have to take us."

The motley group of survivors looked at each other, considering.

"Is he talking about that enormous church with the pasty douchebag preacher with the creepy-ass smile that televises his sermons?" Teague asked.

"I think so," Ladeja answered. "Do you think anyone would be there?"

"That place is a fortress," Chelle replied. "It would be a great place to hide if we can get in. Jonathan Olsen has other properties though. I don't know if he'll be there."

"It's in Hollywood," Justain said. "We have me, Betty Meadow, Mimi Perry and the Camilleris in this van. It doesn't matter if he's there or if it's just the night watchmen. Whoever's there isn't going to turn away this much money and celebrity status."

Ladeja had no clue who the man was supposed to be, but assumed from his comment he was in the business somehow, or at least a very wealthy man. She started to point out that a church couldn't be bribed, but as he'd said, it was Hollywood. Something told her a Hollywood megachurch was a totally different animal than the little churches she grew up with in Oakland. "We go to the church then," she said, looking at her guys, smiling a little when she realized she'd included Mateo and Manny in that category.

"What?" Manny asked, looking down at her. Even while sitting side by side, he towered over her, a mighty, protecting source of comfort.

She shook her head, not ready to share her feelings, to tell him how scared she'd been when she'd thought he'd blown up with the cab and that she'd lost him before they could really begin whatever it was she felt starting between them. "I'm just glad we're all here together, safe and sound."

The van hit something and jostled everyone around.

"What was that?" Ladeja asked, turning toward the front in time to see a man hit the windshield before rolling over the roof of the van to fall on the road behind them as O'Donnell swerved to miss a woman and made a sharp left turn.

"Not much room to maneuver," Teague answered, O'Donnell far too focused to. "We're headed back to Hollywood to try the church. Everyone hold on. This could get real bumpy. I'm pretty sure that area is heavily populated and where there's lots of people, there's probably lots of infected."

"Yeah, we just escaped a hotel," Mike said. "There were floors of them and we heard a lot of them in the rooms too."

Ladeja shuddered. "I can imagine. How did you get out?"

"A little ingenuity and the help of some good people," he answered. Next to him, Misty wiped her eyes and took a deep breath. Ladeja offered her what she hoped was a consoling look, recognizing the action as an attempt not to break down and cry.

"I'm so sorry about the accident," Ladeja apologized. "The soldiers at the coastline had just killed women and children for trying to get past them to a boat and we were fleeing before they could do the same to us.

"It's not your fault," Mike said. "Watts actually

confessed to not having a license after we'd already taken off with him in the driver's seat. He was a smart guy, real tech savvy. It wasn't safe to stop and change seats and since he'd hotwired the damn thing, I figured he could drive it. You didn't have to come back for us. Thank you for doing that."

"Thank us if we actually save you," O'Donnell said, swerving around a wrecked car. "Not to scare everyone, but I'm seeing lots of white-eyed freaks."

"Hang on, everybody," Teague said. "Floor this bitch and plow through them, man. If we get stuck, we're dead."

O'Donnell followed the order and floored the gas, speeding toward the church as fast as he could while swerving left and right to avoid infected people shuffling aimlessly in the streets. Those he couldn't miss rolled up and over the van or bounced off the sides. The survivors in back clung to each other, desperately trying to stay upright as the thumps of infected bodies shook the van and knocked them around. Ladeja held a boy under each arm as Manny wrapped one of his around her, only needing one arm to provide solid support. Mike Rha held tight to Misty Waters and Emma Whitman. The older Camilleri sisters clung to each other as Justain held his own near the back of the van and Forrester sat sandwiched between Betty Meadow who clung to his right arm and Mimi, who tried to cling to his left while batting away Larry who just tried to cling onto any part of her his pudgy fingers could get to. Ladeja nudged Manny and nodded toward Chelle, who'd been abandoned by everyone. Manny reached out and pulled the young woman to them, using his free arm to bring her into their little huddle.

The older Camilleri sisters huffed and speared the younger sister with dagger eyes, seeing her protected under the arm of the sexy security guard. Ladeja nudged Chelle and gestured toward the pair, and they shared a look before losing themselves to a fit of chuckles.

"What in the hell can you be laughing about now?"

Manny asked, which only made them laugh harder. Until they ran over a small cluster of infected people and the back doors flew open.

Having been sitting right in front of them, Harry Justain fell backward, screaming as his hands flailed wildly for purchase. Mike Rha rushed forward as Forrester and Manny quickly tried to detach themselves from the women they protected to aid him.

"No!" Misty screamed as Mike took a leap and snagged Justain's forearm as his body tumbled from the van.

"Slow down!" Manny yelled as he and Forrester each grabbed one of Mike's legs and worked together to keep the man from falling out as he pulled Justain back in.

"We can't!" O'Donnell yelled. "Get those doors closed!"

"We can't with you speeding," Forrester yelled back, grunting as he helped Mike finally pull Justain all the way back in the van.

"Slow down a little," Manny hollered, moving closer to the back. "Just enough so we can get the—"

"Fuck!" O'Donnell tried to miss an abandoned car and hit a small group of infected at just the right angle to cause the van to go up on just its two right wheels as it rolled over them. The occupants in the back tumbled toward the right and Ladeja's heart seized as she saw the two boys fly over her and soar toward the wide open rear of the van.

She couldn't scream. She couldn't say a word. She couldn't even draw a breath. Her son's life flashed before her as his eyes opened wide in terror and in that moment he reached for her as he had when he was a toddler, when he loved her more than anyone. He reached out for her to save him and she watched the fear in his eyes turn into disbelief as she, too, reached out, but only managed to grab Mateo. The van dropped back down to all four wheels as Cory and Cheyanne tumbled out of the back.

"No!" Ladeja screamed, finally finding her voice as her son's body hit the road and rolled head over heels. She lunged forward, but a powerful band wrapped around her torso, holding her back as Manny leaped from the moving vehicle. The van had slowed down as it righted itself and the back doors slammed closed. Justain quickly took advantage of the opportunity to lock them as Cynda and Chelle went to the windows to see what had happened to their sister.

"Stop!" Ladeja screamed as she pushed at the arms wrapped around her midsection, identifying the band that had kept her from following her son out of the van as Forrester. "We have to stop for them! Let go of me!" She beat at Forrester's arms and when that didn't work, she threw her head back, connecting with his chin.

"If we stop now, we all die," Teague told her as Forrester grunted in pain.

"My son is out there!"

"I'm sorry," O'Donnell apologized. "I really am, but we can't all die."

"Manny went out after him," Forrester said, his speech a little impaired from pain. "He's a tough guy, and he's armed. He knows we're going to the church. He'll bring him back to you."

"What about Cheyanne?" Cynda asked, tears filling her eyes.

"I'm sure he'll protect them both," Forrester assured her as Ladeja struggled in his arms, writhing and now clawing at him, desperate for him to release her.

"Damn it, Ladeja, look out there! You can't save him!"

She looked out the windows and saw what looked like a sea of infected pouring out onto the stretch of road between them and where her son had fallen out. Forrester was right. She'd be dead in seconds if she stepped out of the van and if they tried to go back, they'd only get stuck. Her son was out there and she couldn't get to him. She'd had her moment to save him and she'd failed. Tears flooded down her cheeks as she dissolved into deep, body shuddering sobs which only grew stronger as they continued driving farther away from where she'd lost her son and the man she'd for a brief moment imagined a future with.

"I'm sorry," a small broken voice said from beside her. "It should have been me."

She caught her breath and looked over to see Mateo's pink, puffy, tear-soaked face full of pain. The fight went out of her and she went from kicking and clawing to melting into a puddle of helplessness against Forrester's chest. Sensing the shift, he loosened his grip on her, allowing her to crawl to the young boy and wrap her arms around him. Part of her was angry at the boy, angry for being the one she'd grabbed, but mostly she was angry with herself. She was Cory's mother. She was supposed to give her life for his and she'd failed to do that. She didn't tell Mateo this. She didn't tell him anything as she held him, wishing he'd fallen out of the van instead of her son.

"Almost there!" O'Donnell called back to them ten minutes later. They'd had to slow down as the route to the church had become congested with infected, abandoned vehicles, and other roadblocks. Ladeja hadn't stopped crying, but the tears fell silently. Cynda and Chelle both openly wept. The animosity that had been between them when they'd first entered the van evaporated as they shared the worry for their sister. The others just sat together in the back, looking whipped. No one knew what to say, and it was just as well. Ladeja didn't want to hear any platitudes. Nothing they could say would make her feel better.

The church loomed ahead of them. All the time she'd lived and worked in the area, Ladeja had never been so close to the church. It was massive, with windowless walls on the first floor and strong-looking doors. She estimated at least a thousand spaces in the parking lot surrounding the building, or buildings, she realized as they drew closer. It definitely put the mega in megachurch. Many of the parking spaces were taken, indicating they hadn't been the only ones to think of the church for shelter.

"It looks like others are here," Misty said. "This is a good sign." She looked back at the others with eyes full of hope, but the hope dimmed when she looked at Ladeja.

Ladeja couldn't drum up any happiness at finding the shelter, not when she had no clue if her son had found one. For all she knew, he was dead, and so was Manny.

O'Donnell ignored the parking spaces and got as close as he could to the building, parking the van right up next to the sidewalk leading to the front doors. "Everybody out," he ordered. "There are stragglers in the parking lot and we want to get in quick before they reach us."

Justain opened the back doors, and they exited, Ladeja moving slower than the others. Mateo stayed with her, holding her hand, and Chelle joined them, resting a hand on her shoulder. "Manny will keep Cory safe," she told her. "I know he'll protect that boy with his life. It's so obvious he loves you."

Ladeja didn't say anything. She didn't want to think about it or speak about it. She just wanted to find a numb place inside herself to hide away in until her son returned or she left the world to find him where she was afraid he'd went.

The megachurch perched on a hill so the walkway leading to the doors was uphill. Large flowering bushes also hedged it in the same yellow, pink, and purple scheme as the rest of the grounds. The flowers appeared to have not been cared for in days, nor the grass that needed a good mowing, but the bushes lining the walkway still maintained their blossoms. One of them began shaking and before Ladeja could register why, a man stepped out and promptly tackled Cynda, knocking her to the ground before taking a huge bite out of her ass.

Chelle screamed, but before the armed men with them could do anything, two infected women and a teenaged infected boy emerged from the hedge closer to the doors. Cynda screamed for help as the man who attacked her shook his head in her ass like a dog wringing the life out of caught prey, and rose to his knees, chomping on a silicone implant with an almost confused expression on his face. Chelle burst out laughing and quickly clapped her hand over her mouth before looking at Ladeja in complete horror. Ladeja understood. She might have laughed at the absurdity of the picture herself had she not went to some dead place inside her, completely numbed by her loss. She just nodded her head and patted Chelle's shoulder, unable to form words as Mateo clung to her waist. The other women huddled together behind Mike, and the security guards worked together to take out the immediate threat while Justain swiveled his head in all directions, looking out for more infected.

Teague, Forrester, and O'Donnell used blades to kill the infected that had surprised them on the walkway, except for the one who'd bitten Cynda. Teague had shot the man before he could figure out the implant wasn't meat and go in for another bite, firing a bullet that drew the attention of every infected person within hearing distance of it.

The infected close to them now taken care of, Chelle and Teague rushed toward Cynda as O'Donnell attempted to open the church doors and found them locked. He pounded on the heavy doors and yelled for help.

"There's a camera," Forrester said, pointing at the security camera over the door before walking directly in range of it to speak to whomever watched them from within the building. "We need shelter!"

"More are coming," Justain said, his voice full of fear as he looked past them into the parking lot. "We have to get inside now." He walked to the camera. "Do you know who we are? Harry Justain, Betty Meadow, Mimi Perry, the Camilleri family. I demand you let us in now!"

"We cannot allow entrance," a voice boomed out of the speaker to the right of the door.

"Maybe you didn't hear me," Justain said, "or maybe

you're ignorant. Do you know who you're talking to?"

"We have taken all we can," the voice said. "We pray you find shelter."

"You're a church!" Betty Meadow yelled, storming up to the camera. "You can't turn people away!"

"I'll tweet this out to the world when this is over," Justain yelled. "I'll ruin you!"

Mike joined them. "We have children! You have to take the children!"

O'Donnell and Forrester tried to pry open the doors while Teague and Chelle tended to a screaming and writhing Cynda. The others pleaded with the man denying entrance while Mateo stood with Ladeja, who couldn't bring herself to say or do a damn thing. It was as if her whole body had frozen over, the fire within her snuffed out with the loss of her child.

"We have to get in there," Mateo told her. "This is where Manny will bring Cory. We have to be here."

The ice broke. Ladeja looked around, turning toward the parking lot where infected stragglers steadily shuffled toward them, ready to end their lives. If her son had lived, if Manny had saved him, he'd be traveling across that parking lot soon. Mateo was right. They had to be there. She had to be there to make sure no one turned her son away if he'd made it. She'd failed him once and she could not fail him again.

She joined the others at the security camera. "My name is Ladeja Craig. I just lost my son. He might be alive and if he is, he's going to come here looking for me. We have another young boy and a young girl. She's a sweet, innocent kid and so is Mateo. He lost his mother. He heard her being eaten alive right outside his bedroom and when we ran into trouble, he suggested the church. He has been put through hell, we all have, but I think most of us quit believing we'd be saved. This young boy thought of the church when he was in need. He thought of *you*. If you turn us away, you're turning away a boy who had faith that the church would save him and telling him he was wrong. You say you pray we find shelter? We found it here. All you have to do is open the doors and save our lives, or you can deny us and you can send this young boy out into the world knowing that the church didn't care, that his faith meant nothing, but if you do that how can you call yourself a church? How can you call yourself a Christian?"

Static came out of the speaker for a moment, then it went silent as if the man behind it had something to say, but changed his mind.

"That was a damn good speech," O'Donnell said, "but I don't think it worked." He scanned the area. "There are windows on the second floor. If we can get up there, we can break in to one."

Mike joined him. "There's a flagpole. If we had rope, it might support us and we could climb up."

"I always keep rope and duct tape in my van," Larry offered. Mimi's face blanched to a deathly white, clearly creeped out by the thought of her stalker always carrying materials he could bind her with.

There was a series of clicks and the church doors opened. Four armed men in designer suits stepped out. "The woman who was bitten cannot enter. The rest of you can, but you need to get inside quickly. We don't want them piling up against our doors again," the sandy-haired man in front said as he nodded beyond them to the infected steadily approaching.

"You can't leave me!" Cynda cried. "I'll die out here."

"You were bitten," Teague told her. "You're going to turn."

"It got my implant! I'm fine! It just hurts."

"It hurts because that man bit through your skin and tore some out with the implant," Chelle said between sobs. "You're infected."

"You're just going to leave me? I'm your sister! You can't leave me out here to turn into one of those things or to let them eat more of me!"

"Everyone go inside," Teague said, looking at his gun. "I'll take care of Cynda and join you in there. I'll make sure she doesn't suffer."

"You bastard!" Cynda screeched at him.

"Get in now or you lose your chance," the church guard said, shooting down an infected woman who'd reached the walkway.

Justain rushed inside, not needing another invitation. The others followed suit, casting sad looks Chelle's way as she kneeled next to her sister. Ladeja passed Mateo off to Misty and hung behind, wanting to help Chelle inside in case the teen couldn't bring herself to leave her sister's side. "Chelle, let Teague take care of Cynda for you. You shouldn't see this."

"You bitch!" Cynda yelled at her, tears streaming down her flushed face. "Why don't you pull the trigger? You know this is what you've wanted since Thunda left your fat ass for me!"

Ladeja opened her mouth to tell Cynda if her ass hadn't been so fattened up with implants, the infected man might have missed her, but caught herself before she could let the petty remark slip. "Come on, Chelle. It's time."

"You can't leave me, Chelle!"

Chelle sniffed, all her earlier anger at her sisters' betrayal gone as she watched Cynda beg to not be left alone. "I'm so sorry, Cynda. It has to be this way. There's no way to save you."

Cynda's eyes hardened for a moment, but she took a deep breath and nodded her head as she sat up and opened her arms wide. "Goodbye, sis. I love you."

"I love you," Chelle said back, hugging her sister.

The moment Chelle's arms wrapped around Cynda, the older sister viciously bit the teen's neck. Chelle cried out in pain and pulled back, revealing a bloody gash. "Now you'll die with me, you bitch!" Cynda spat, blood dripping down her chin. "You don't get to let someone shoot me and live!"

"You fucking demon-bitch from hell!" Ladeja screamed, lunging forward to punch Cynda in the face, but she felt herself pulled away before her fist could connect. "Let me at her!" she screamed, kicking her feet out as one of the church guards flung her over his shoulder and took her away. She pummeled his back, screaming to be let down so she could beat Cynda to a pulp and give her the death she truly deserved but he carried her inside and delivered her to O'Donnell before shutting the doors and standing guard before them with two of the other guards.

A gunshot rang out and Ladeja hoped Cynda had felt pain. A moment passed, and another shot came from outside. This one made her cringe and weep in silence because she knew it had been for a good-hearted girl who'd deserved a better ending than the one she'd gotten. More shots rang out. She counted ten before there was silence, then the security guard's voice came from beyond the door. "Let us in."

The doors opened, and the sandy-haired guard stepped inside with Teague. Ladeja stared straight into his eyes, not wanting to see any bodies that might lie beyond the door.

"Chelle didn't suffer," Teague said, and she fell to the floor, sobbing.

"Do you think they made it?"

Manny looked at the young boy and nodded. "Your mother is strong and O'Donnell is tough. So are Teague and Forrester. They made it. Hell, if we could make it through all those infected on the road when we fell out of the van, they definitely made it."

"You didn't fall out," Cory told him as they shared the box of dry cereal they'd found in the breakroom of the small memorabilia shop Manny had broken into. "You jumped. Why?"

"Why wouldn't I?"

"You think saving my life will help you get my mom," Cory said, setting the cereal box aside. "You risked your life for nothing. Mateo and I were both falling out of the van, and she grabbed him. She watched me fall, and she grabbed him."

Manny opened his mouth to explain what had happened when movement out the side of his eye caught his attention. He looked out the window and sighed. "There she is. Damn. I can't let her stay like that. I'll be right back in a flash, all right?"

Cory nodded, looking away from the floor-to-ceiling glass windows that made up the front of the shop. Manny didn't think any less of him for it. The kid might have an attitude problem, but he was still too damn young to see what he'd had to see over the past few days.

Manny scanned the street before slipping out of the glass door to approach the woman walking drunkenly in the street. He shook his head, disgusted, as her milky white eyes locked onto him and she changed direction to approach him.

"I'm sorry, Cheyanne. I'm sorry I couldn't save both of you. I had to choose the boy. I'm sorry they didn't finish you off once they started in," he added. "I'm sorry you turned into this."

She opened her mouth and snarled at him just before he plunged his blade into her head, saving her the only way he had left to. "I truly am sorry," he repeated as her body fell to the ground and he left her in the middle of the road, shaking his head, marveling at the odds of her actually shuffling along right in front of the little shop he'd chosen to hide out in until they were rested up and ready to continue their journey to the church where he knew Ladeja would be waiting. Maybe it was his punishment. He'd chosen to save the boy, so he had to see the fate of his choice.

He noticed a group of infected up the street headed his way and quickened his step, but when he reached the shop, the door wouldn't open. He pushed again, looking through the glass at the boy standing behind it. "Cory, open this damn door right now."

The boy shook his head. "You're only trying to save me to get with my mom. She let me fall. She saved someone else's son and let me fall."

"Damn it, boy. That is not what happened. Now you open this damn door!"

Cory shook his head and walked away.

"Cory!"

Ladeja's son disappeared into the back of the shop, leaving Manny locked outside as the infected drew closer.

***

Zombiewood is a spin-off of the One Nation Under Zombies series and the story will continue in Zombiewood 2.

ABOUT THE AUTHOR

Raymond Lee is a horror/thriller author who lives in the south and prefers animals to people. Zombiewood is a spin-off of the One Nation Under Zombies series, available now.

IF YOU ENJOYED THE BOOK PLEASE LEAVE A REVIEW!

Printed in Great Britain
by Amazon

18113737R00150